ALWAYS WILL

ALWAYS SERIES BOOK 2

CLAIRE KINGSLEY

Always Have LLC

Published by Always Have, LLC

Edited by Larks and Katydids

Cover by Passion Creations by Mary Ruth

ISBN: 9781542809849

www.clairekingsleybooks.com

❀ Created with Vellum

ABOUT THIS BOOK

Selene Taylor is the first to admit her dating life is a disaster. She has a weakness for the wrong men—bad boys with bodies to drool over and attitudes like they're God's gift to women.

But her professional life? It's right where she wants it.

Until her company is bought out by a man from her past, and she finds herself with a sexy new boss.

Ronan Maddox doesn't just play the game. He wins. He's an adrenaline junkie who lives for the thrill of the chase. But he flirts with more than danger when he discovers one of his new employees is the one woman who still haunts his dreams.

Another bad boy is the last thing Selene needs, and Ronan's reputation is well-earned. But as soon as he sees her, he knows what he wants, and he'll stop at nothing until she's his.

Selene is a risk, but risks are what Ronan lives for.

1

SELENE

*A*idan, my date, is talking about his day. I wrap my hand around my wine glass and cross my legs, trying very hard to act interested.

I should really be fair and call Aidan my boyfriend. We've been seeing each other long enough that this isn't just a date. We've been on a lot of dates, and although we haven't talked about it I know he expects we're exclusive.

On paper, Aidan is perfect. He's handsome, and tall—which, considering I'm five-eleven, is an absolute must. He's smart, and has a stable career in finance. He's a far cry from the bad boys I usually date.

And that's precisely why I've been seeing him.

After two crappy relationships last year—one who was cheating on me when he went out of town on business with what my best friend Kylie called his *trip whores*, and one who tried to break up with me via text shortly after we got back from a trip to Mexico—I decided enough is enough. I always date the same kind of men: hot as hell, with a body to drool over and an attitude like they're God's gift to women. Why I find that sort of arrogance attractive, I don't know, but clearly my radar is broken.

So I took a break from men while I focused on helping with Kylie's wedding. She married my twin brother, Braxton, a couple months ago. If you had told me a year ago that Braxton would be married to anyone, let alone our best friend, I would have thought you were crazy. I didn't think he had it in him to commit to someone. The three of us have been close since we were kids, and I always felt like I needed to protect Kylie from Brax. My brother is a great guy, but he was such a man-whore. The last thing I wanted was for Kylie to get hurt.

Little did I know that Braxton was crazy in love with her. I was almost responsible for ruining things for them, and I still feel horrible about it. In my defense, Brax lied to me about them being together, so what was I supposed to think? I always knew he had a thing for Kylie, but I figured he just wanted to bang her.

I'm really, really glad I was wrong. Watching them get married was probably the best moment of my entire life. There's so much comfort in knowing they have each other.

After the wedding, I made Kylie a deal: she has to approve of all my dates. I have no idea what criteria she's using, and the fact that the love of her life is my brother makes me question her judgment a little. But I needed someone else to weigh in. Clearly I'm not having any luck on my own.

She heartily approved of Aidan. I met him at my gym, which indicates he cares about his health. It took a while before he talked to me, even though we saw each other almost every day, which Kylie counted as a point in his favor. He asked me to go out for coffee, and I agreed so I could find out more about him. After that, I turned him over to Ky. She stalked him on social media and didn't find anything alarming. His Facebook feed didn't feature a bunch of women, or selfies showing off his abs. He seemed ... normal. Just an attractive man, living and working, and possibly looking for love.

What's not to like?

Aidan laughs, and I take another sip of my wine to hide the fact that I missed what was so funny. He's wearing a pale blue button-down shirt, the top button undone. I love that look on a man. Usually it would make me want to slowly unbutton the shirt, revealing the muscular body underneath. I'm pretty sure Aidan has a nice set of abs. The guy works out enough, and he's tall and lean, so he should. But looking at him, I'm not particularly tempted. We've been seeing each other for over a month, and we haven't slept together—which Kylie keeps assuring me is a good thing—but the problem is, I'm not sure if I want to.

"I'm sorry, Selene," he says. "I've been going on and on about me. What about you? How was your day?"

I know he actually cares about my day, and really, it's quite sweet. I need to cling to that when I start feeling bored.

"Stressful, to be honest," I say. "It's been a long week. Brad, the owner of my company, has been in all these closed door conference calls, and he went out of town last week and no one knows why. I work closely with him, and he isn't telling me anything, which makes me nervous."

He reaches across the table and touches my hand. "Uncertainty at work is the worst. I'm sorry you're going through that."

I smile at him. He really is nice. So why am I tempted to excuse myself to the restroom and come back, pretending I got an important call and have to leave?

Our waitress appears. "Can I interest either of you in dessert?"

Aidan raises his eyebrows at me. "Anything for you? Dessert or maybe coffee?"

"No thanks, I'm fine."

He looks at the waitress. "No, we're finished."

"No problem." She hands him the bill.

He pulls out a credit card and hands it over. He always at least tries to pay, but he doesn't get macho about it when I insist on picking up the bill. He's so damn agreeable. And there's never any expectation from him that I'll go back to his place. Come to think of it, he's never asked. We have dinner once or twice a week, and he always takes me home, walking me to my front door like a perfect gentleman. Maybe he's waiting for me to suggest we take things to the next level.

At first, I thought it was a good sign. He wasn't just trying to get laid. See? Nice guy. But at this point, I'm starting to feel like maybe I could use a man who put in a little more effort into getting me undressed. This slow and sweet thing was refreshing at first, but I wonder if he'll ever turn up the heat.

Can Aidan turn up the heat?

The waitress returns, and he signs the receipt. "Ready?" he asks.

"Sure."

He walks me out to his car and takes me home. Like always, he kisses me at my front door. The kiss is ... nice. Just like everything about Aidan. It's sweet, without any pressure to do more. He steps away while I open my front door, like he's fine with not coming inside, and says goodbye.

I sigh as I close the door behind me.

Kylie is on my couch, watching TV. She shuts it off when I come in.

"Hey, Ky."

"Hi, babe," she says. "How was your date?"

"It was fine," I say, without much enthusiasm. "Where's Brax?"

"Upstairs, asleep."

I roll my eyes. "Please tell me you weren't having sex in my kitchen again. I had to bleach my eyeballs after I walked in on you guys last week."

She laughs. "That was *not* our fault. You never come home

for lunch. Besides, you're the one who asked Brax to come over and unclog your sink again."

"I didn't think plumbing was such an aphrodisiac."

"Um, do you know your brother? He can make a sex game out of anything," she says. "But no, we weren't. He has a sinus infection, and he refuses to take a day off to get better. I forced him to lie down, and he fell asleep after about ten seconds. Then I got bored, so I came down here."

"He's such a guy."

"He really is," she says. "I hope it's okay we're here tonight. I guess I should have texted you first, in case Aidan was coming in. But I kind of figured he wasn't, so I thought you and I could hang out."

"You figured right." I slip off my heels and sit on the couch next to Kylie. "And it's always fine. You know that."

"So ... things still the same with him?"

"Pretty much," I say. "He's really very nice. He's polite. We have a nice time."

"But nice isn't doing it for you."

I put my feet up on the coffee table and sigh. "I guess I keep waiting for him to ... I don't know. Make another move. We're in this holding pattern, and I don't know why. He walks me up to my door every time he takes me out, and not once has he suggested he'd like to come in. Nor has he asked if I'd like to come to his place. Yet we keep seeing each other. If he wasn't into me, he'd break it off, right?"

"You'd think," she says. "You're just not used to dating a nice guy. He's taking his time. He wants to develop a good foundation first. I bet after a few more dates, he'll show you a whole new side of himself. He'll unleash the beast and fuck your brains out, and it will be totally worth the wait. You'll have it all: a nice guy who treats you well, respects you enough to get to know you first, *and* can make your toes curl."

"I don't think that man exists."

"Maybe it's Aidan," she says.

"I know. You're right. And it's not like I don't enjoy being with him. I do."

"Honestly, I don't know what your hang-up is," she says. "Everything you've told me about him is good. Your only complaint is that he's not trying to get you into bed. You realize that, right?"

I laugh and smack Kylie's arm. "It's not that. I mean, yeah, it's been a while and I'm getting a little antsy. But I'm just not sure if there are any sparks. I'd like to feel something. As it is, I'm kind of indifferent." I lean down and put my head on her shoulder. "Is it too late to take up your offer to be lesbians?"

She holds up her left hand, where her wedding ring sparkles. "Afraid so. You had your chance."

"Shit," I say. "Figures."

Braxton comes down the stairs, looking bleary-eyed, his dark hair a mess.

"Baby," Kylie says as he comes around the couch. "What are you doing up?"

He lies down and puts his head in her lap. "You were gone."

She laughs and runs her fingers through his hair. "You're sick. You should be in bed."

"I like being where you are." He drapes an arm over her legs and closes his eyes.

I bite my lip and look away to hide the tears that spring to my eyes. They're so cute it's ridiculous, and there's nothing better than seeing my brother so happy. It makes me love Kylie even more.

"Well, it's not even ten, and it looks like this is our Friday night," Ky says, glancing down at Brax, already asleep in her lap. "Want to watch a movie?"

"With wine?"

"Obviously."

"You guys sleeping here tonight?" I ask. Kylie and Braxton have their own place, and I still live in the house where Braxton and I grew up. Our parents died in a car accident when we were ten, and we stayed here with our aunt. After she died, we inherited the house, but Braxton insisted I be the one to keep it. He bought a condo that's walking distance from here, and I live in this big old place by myself. The three of us all lived here when we were in college, so Brax and Ky still have their own rooms, and crash here pretty regularly. Of course, Kylie sleeps with Braxton now, instead of her old room downstairs. But it still works. I like it when they're here. I get lonely living here all alone.

"Most likely," she says. "You mind?"

"Never."

"Thanks, babe."

I get up from the couch. "I'll change into comfies and get us wine so you don't have to move him."

"Thanks," she says with a laugh, and leans down to kiss Braxton's forehead.

I head upstairs to my room. I don't use the master bedroom. To be honest, I haven't been in that room in years. It must be horribly dusty. But the house is big, with six bedrooms and four bathrooms, so there's more than enough space. I've updated and remodeled a lot of it, but my parents' old room is the one area I won't touch.

I change from my work clothes into yoga pants and a tank top, and grab a fluffy blanket from the foot of my bed. My pants don't quite make it to my ankles, so I guess I'll say they're capris and pretend it's not because I'm so fucking tall. Kylie always says she's jealous of my legs, but she has no idea how hard it is to find clothes.

I head downstairs and pour two glasses of wine. I snuggle up next to Ky and we find something to watch. Drinking a bottle of wine and watching a movie with my best friend is certainly not the worst way to spend a Friday night. But I can't help but wonder if I'm wasting my time with Aidan. If maybe there's someone else out there.

Someone with a little heat.

2

RONAN

The plane takes off, and my adrenaline starts pumping. I went through my preflight safety check on the ground. My gear is perfect. I glance over at the jump coordinator and he gives me a nod.

The noise of the engine roars in my ears and I watch the ground fall away as we ascend. The sky over Lake Elsinore is completely clear. It's the perfect day for a jump. Two other guys are suited up next to me. I don't know them, but the calm looks on their faces tells me everything I need to know: They're pros. We'll have a solid jump today.

My blood pumps harder, and the weight that always sits on my shoulders lightens as we gain altitude. My head clears. I know the rush is coming, and my whole body lights up with anticipation. I start to feel alive again.

My brother Damon calls me an adrenaline junkie, and makes sure to relay our parents' distaste for my hobbies whenever we talk. I suppose I can't blame them for their concern. My folks are decent people, but they've never understood me—especially not the man I've become.

I'm a risk taker. I always have been. I was the kid who

thought that if I tried hard enough, I could fly like Superman. And I definitely tried. I had fear in those days, but I fed off it. Fear drove me to go bigger, higher, faster. The crashes were learning experiences. I still felt afraid, but I pushed through it and did crazy shit anyway.

I lost the fear later.

Now the only times I really feel alive are moments like this.

Wind rushes past the plane; the engine roars. The pilot takes us to eighteen-thousand feet, high above the world. My heart races. Everything stands out—my vision is sharp, my thoughts completely focused. My lungs expand, taking in oxygen, clear and clean. Every muscle is coiled and ready.

It's like the moment before orgasm. The tension mounts, pressure and heat building. You know it's coming—the explosion that's going to rock through your whole body and take you down.

I live for that shit.

The jump coordinator opens the door, and the change in pressure sucks the air from my lungs. The pilot holds, cruising in a steady line along the flight path. The first guy gets in position. He's given the all-clear and he lets go, disappearing from my sight. The second guy has his turn. He moves out to the jump position, waits for the signal, and he's gone.

I move to the open door and ease myself outside the plane. The air rushing by tries to rip me out and hurl me to the ground. That's when the euphoria starts to creep in, seeping its way into my head. My mouth turns up in a smile. I'm on the verge, in that place before the climax. Soaring above the world, death chasing me, nipping at my heels.

I get the nod and let go.

I fall away from the plane so fast the noise of the engine is instantly gone, replaced by the deafening blast of the wind. I spread my arms and legs wide, loosening the flaps of my wingsuit, and catch the air. It lifts me up, jerking me higher, and I tip to the side before I correct and get my balance.

I'm fucking flying.

I holler into the air, my voice fleeing behind me. The wing-suit keeps me gliding, more than falling, as I cut through the air. The world is so far away it's meaningless. I'm in the sky, riding the motherfucking wind. Elation barrels into me, crashing through my mind, leaving nothing in its wake. I'm as clear as the sparkling water of the lake below me, higher than any drug has ever gotten me.

The ground gets closer and I lean to the left, staying on target with the landing zone. I've done this jump dozens of times —enough that I'm starting to crave more. I want to go higher. Faster.

I started out skydiving, and after hundreds of jumps I wanted something else. I went on a bungee-jumping kick one summer, but those jumps are over too fast. I started BASE jumping off buildings and bridges. Even the near-miss I took off a cliff in Nevada didn't faze me.

When I met a guy who did wingsuit diving, I knew I had to try it. I was addicted from the first jump. It's like skydiving on steroids. The suit catches the wind, and you ride it like a fucking bird.

I don't have much time before I have to pull my chute. I spread my arms wider to catch more of the wind, and it lifts me a little higher. I'm saturated with adrenaline, falling so fast I'd never survive the crash if I hit the ground. The landing site comes into view and I hesitate, my hand on the cord. I need to pull it, but I'm not quite ready. It's too fucking good; I don't want it to stop. I'm flying and falling all at once, the rush through my mind and body so much I almost can't breathe.

I'm completely alive.

Three seconds. That's all I have left.

Two.

One.

I pull the cord and my chute billows out behind me, jerking me upward as it catches the air. The harness tightens around my chest.

I float toward the ground, steering as I go. The ground crew is waiting. The other two jumpers are already on their feet, repacking their chutes. I pull on the steering lines, keeping my approach steady. The ground surges toward me and I'm hit with another kick of adrenaline. Landing is another rush, a moment of danger, the time when things often go bad.

But death won't take me yet.

I nail the landing, running as my feet touch the ground, my chute falling behind me. My breath comes fast and the euphoria holds.

I'll be high for hours after that jump. It was perfect.

We pack up our gear, and a truck takes us back to the hangar. This will be my last jump at Lake Elsinore for a while, but they have such a good crew I'm going to have to get down here again soon. I'm moving back to Seattle in the morning—whether permanently or just for a few months I haven't decided yet. I'll have to see how things go with the company I'm buying.

I get another little hit at that thought. I'm taking a big risk, both professionally and financially. But that's why I can't resist. If this gamble pays off, I'm not only going to make a shit ton of money, I'm going to make a huge impact in the markets I'm targeting. No one ever got anywhere without putting themselves out there and taking chances. Those chances are what I live for. I go from one to the next, always craving another. Always craving more.

I've had a great run in San Francisco these last five years. I've achieved everything I set out to do, and more. Now I wonder, what sort of rush does Seattle have in store for me?

3

SELENE

a meeting request pops up on my screen and I feel a sense of dread. It's for this afternoon, which is so last-minute, and as I look down the list of attendees, I see the entire senior staff and management team. I have a feeling this might be where Brad breaks it to us that something big is going down.

I hope I don't lose my job. It isn't that I couldn't find another one—but I love working at Vital Information. It's literally the one part of my life I can truly say is going perfectly. I was hired about four years ago, and I feel like I finally found my niche. I'm the Brand Manager, and I've worked side by side with Brad for the last few years. We have an excellent team, with people who actually pull their weight, and we've done a lot of great things with this company. We have patents pending on several devices that track health and nutrition information, and we've gone so far beyond what we thought possible just a few years ago.

But the signs that something is changing have been there for a while. I suspect we're about to hear the word "downsizing."

After lunch, I join my colleagues in the large conference room. I'm one of the first to arrive, so I take a seat on the far side of the table and answer some emails while I wait. It gets stuffy as the room fills, and I pick my hair up off my neck, wishing I wore it up today.

I check the time on my phone. Brad's late. I stop myself from rolling my eyes. It figures he'd get everyone in here and make us sit around.

Finally, Brad walks in, dressed in a button-down shirt and tie, his graying hair cut short.

"Sorry to make everyone wait," he says as he walks to stand in front of the whiteboard. "It's been a busy day. Busy few weeks, really."

He pauses, and the tension in the room thickens.

"I apologize for the radio silence these last few weeks," Brad says. "I realize it hasn't escaped anyone's notice that something is going on, but for a variety of reasons I haven't been able to talk publicly about it. Until today."

Another pause. I shift a little and cross my legs.

"As of about twenty minutes ago, the company has been sold."

The room erupts with questions and sharp inhalations of breath. I don't say anything, just stare at Brad in disbelief. Sold? How could he keep this from me? I've been busting my ass trying to keep us afloat, pulling Brad's weight every time he went on one of his many vacations. The least he could have done is told me privately.

I lean back in my chair, already mentally updating my resume. I know what happens when a company is sold. The buyers always have their own people. I might have a few months, but I should start getting my name out there immediately, because there's no question in my mind that my time here is short.

Damn. It's so disappointing.

"Listen." Brad puts his hands up, trying to get control of the meeting. "I realize this is a surprise—but believe me, this means big things for VI. There was no way I was going to turn over my company to just anyone, and I can assure you, the new owner doesn't plan to gut our staff. He bought this company because of all of you."

Right. I've been through a buyout before, at my last company. They always say that, but as soon as the new owner is in the building the layoff notices start flying.

"I'm sure you all have a lot of questions, and I'd like to take some time to answer them now," Brad says. "I already have a companywide memo set to go out after our meeting, so you're welcome to tell your teams the news. This is all out in the open now. But I want to emphasize that no one needs to be worried about their job."

Brad's eyes sweep the group, coming to rest for half a second on each of our faces. Despite my frustrations, he's been a decent guy to work for. He trusts me to do my job and gives me a lot of autonomy. But he spent the last two years growing the company at such a rapid pace, it was obvious it was going to crash and burn. I'm not surprised in the least he had to bail out.

People start asking questions and his answers seem genuine, if vague. Despite his claim that we don't need to be concerned about losing our jobs, he can't give any specifics as to the new owner's plans. In fact, he hasn't mentioned who the new owner *is*. There are several contenders, as far as I know—competitors who I suspect would love to get their hands on our tech.

Finally, I raise my hand.

"Selene," he says.

"Who exactly bought us out?"

"That's a good question." He opens his mouth but the conference room door opens and he stops.

A man walks in. He's wearing sunglasses, as if he just came in from outside, and a crisp white shirt with the top button undone. His dark hair is slightly unruly, in a way that makes him look confident rather than messy. He flashes Brad a smile as he slips the sunglasses from his face.

My breath freezes in my lungs. Oh shit, it can't be.

Ronan Maddox.

I try very hard to hide my surprise as Ronan shakes hands with Brad. I can feel my face flushing, and I desperately hope I'm sporting enough of a tan to hide it. I haven't seen Ronan in five years. Not since his last night at Tech Solutions, our former company. A bunch of us from the office went out for drinks—a little going-away party celebrating Ronan's last day. The night ended with Ronan and me sleeping together in his hotel room.

And I never heard from him again.

Fuck. This is bad. This is so, so bad.

I have a very staunch *no dating coworkers* rule. My dating life might be a disaster, but that's one choice I'm sure of. Dating people at work never turns out well. I made a very ill-considered exception for Ronan that night, both because he was leaving— so technically we didn't work together anymore—and because he was extraordinarily convincing. Looking at him now, I remember why, and my heart beats a little faster.

He's … gorgeous. Tall and lean, with high cheekbones and a chiseled jaw. He looks every bit as incredible as he did five years ago. More, in fact.

"Everyone, this is Ronan Maddox," Brad says. "He's been running Edge Gear for the last several years, and took them from a small firm with less than a million in sales annually, to a powerhouse with one hundred million in annual sales last year, and on track to double that this year. I assure you, VI is in excellent hands with Ronan."

Ronan nods, tucking his sunglasses into his shirt pocket. I want to crawl under the table and hide. I flip my hair forward a little and look down at the table, hoping he doesn't notice me, knowing that's incredibly unlikely.

"Thanks for the introduction," Ronan says, and his voice sends a shiver up my spine. Damn him, he even *sounds* better than I remember. "I'm sure this is a surprise to everyone, but let me assure you, nothing is going to change at this point. I'll be meeting with you individually over the coming weeks to get a better feel for your departments and your roles here, but I have no plans to make sweeping changes right out of the gate. VI isn't going to be absorbed by Edge. I see this as a distinct set of brands, and you are all my experts. I need you to bring me up to speed and help keep things running smoothly while we make this transition."

I lift my eyes just enough so I can see him. Perhaps his little speech should reassure me that I won't be laid off this week, but hearing his voice is doing nothing but make my heart race. That night was...

I really need to stop thinking about that night. It was years ago, and if Ronan has held to his reputation I'm sure there's been a long line of women who came after me. In fact, I doubt he even remembers me. We didn't know each other well when we worked together. The most we ever spoke was at that cocktail party. He hit on me at work, but I always shut him down. I suppose he thought he might get lucky that night, since he was on the way out, and had a way around my rule.

Of course, he was right.

He keeps talking, answering a few questions. He doesn't seem to notice me. I stay quiet, my eyes on the table, so I don't attract his attention. I'm so glad I sat at the far end of the large conference table. Maybe I can get through this meeting without him realizing I'm here. I'm torn between hoping he doesn't remember me, and feeling prematurely offended that he could have forgotten.

"Excellent," he says when the questions die down. "Thanks, everyone, for coming."

I look up, hoping everyone will stand and I can keep a few people between myself and Ronan while I sneak out the door. He opens his mouth as if he's going to say something else, and his eyes meet mine.

I see almost nothing on his face, save a slightly lifted eyebrow. People get up and he turns to greet someone approaching him.

I breathe out a slow breath, trying to calm my thundering heart. If he recognized me, it's obviously not fazing him in the slightest. I'm both relieved and mildly insulted. I slept with the man. It would be nice to think that was enough to make me stick in his memory.

And I clearly did not forget him.

We all file out of the conference room. Ronan is in the far corner, talking to several other people, as I leave. I get back to my office and sit down, wondering what the hell just happened.

It had to be Ronan Maddox. Of all the people in the world who could buy out the company I work for, it had to be a man I spent a night with.

A stupid, reckless night.

A hot, sweaty, *unforgettable* night.

But I am *not* dwelling on that. I am a professional. This doesn't change anything.

I will do my job, and that's the end of it.

4

RONAN

*P*eople leave the conference room and some guy whose name I've already forgotten corners me. I say the right things and give him the right smile, but my attention just walked out of the room on a pair of mile-long legs.

Selene fucking Taylor.

I barely kept the surprise from my face when I realized she was sitting at the back of the conference room. I meant to spend more time familiarizing myself with the company roster before this meeting, but I don't know if I would have believed it even if I saw her name. There could be more than one Selene Taylor in Seattle, couldn't there? It's not a common first name, but she can't be the only one. There's no fucking way I bought the company *she* works for.

But there she was—sleek brown hair, soft bronzed skin, dark eyes, full mouth. Holy shit, I still remember what it felt like to kiss that fantastic mouth.

I don't know why she stands out the way she does. We only spent one night together. Maybe it's because finally getting her into bed felt like conquering Mount Everest. Many men try, few succeed, and she made it almost impossible for me. She was clear from the moment we met that she did not date men she worked with. And she wasn't kidding.

A lot of women say that, but if you pursue them hard enough, they relent. Not Selene Taylor. She kept me at a distance—a huge fucking distance—the entire time we worked together. I didn't think she had a single weakness. I knew she dated. She just stuck to her one rule like it was iron clad, and there was no way I could get past it.

Until my last night at Tech Solutions.

A big group of us went out for drinks, and I found Selene standing alone at the bar, sipping a dirty martini. I love a challenge, and the fact that Selene had been inaccessible to me for so long made her completely irresistible. I spent time talking with her, and the more we chatted the more I realized she wasn't just a stacked piece of ass with a face to match.

She was smart, and funny. She had a quick comeback for every one of my lines, never missing a beat. A woman like that could keep a man like me on my toes. That's a rare thing.

I was a predator, circling my prey, and it wasn't long before that rule of hers didn't seem to matter so much anymore. After all, technically we no longer worked together. Our chemistry was off the charts—I think we'd both agree on that. I took her back to the hotel I'd rented for my last couple of nights in Seattle, and we lit that room up.

She was every bit as delicious as I imagined she would be. Tight, toned body. Legs for days. A set of tits that would make a swimsuit model jealous. She felt better than she looked, if that's even possible. I strummed her like a fucking harp, making her pant and writhe. I watched her come the first time, pinned beneath me, and the orgasm she gave me was nothing short of epic. We were drenched and spent, sprawled out across the sheets, trying to catch our breath. Then I teased her, tasted her, got her hot again. The second time went from soft and slow to blazing hot and rough in the space of about two seconds.

Fuck, I can't believe I remember it so well. It was five years ago, and it's not like there haven't been women since—quite a few, as a matter of fact. But that is one night I'll never forget.

And now she works for me.

I shake hands with what's-his-name, and manage to extricate myself from the conference room. I know everyone has a lot of questions. I just bought out their company and the entire staff must be waiting for the news that I'm bringing in my own people to replace them. But the truth is, I probably won't.

A few will have to go—that's inevitable. But it was the owner who was making a mess of this place. There's a lot going right in this building, and with me at the helm we're going to fucking *own* this market. I'll only shake things up if I have to; for now, I'm content to let this ride and make big staffing decisions later.

I head to my new office. Brad cleared out late last night, so no one would realize. That was his call, not mine. The guy wants out of this place something fierce. He assured me he'll be available if I have questions, but I know he's full of shit. He's taking his cut and running—probably somewhere tropical. I get the feeling Brad hasn't been completely honest with the federal government on his personal tax returns.

I did my due diligence; my lawyers assure me the company itself is squeaky clean. Brad, though? I know the type. He probably has money stashed somewhere overseas. It doesn't make a bit of difference to me. I'm all for risk taking—it's one hell of a rush—but there are boundaries even I won't cross. Tax evasion happens to be one of them.

There are a few boxes of my things already sitting on the large mahogany desk. Behind it, huge windows overlook downtown. I didn't think I would, but I missed Seattle. San Francisco was a great place to live, and it was definitely the right move for my career. But it's good to be back.

I sit down and open my laptop, but I'm distracted. Instead, I lean back in my seat and put a hand to my chin. The presence of Selene in my new company presents me with an interesting dilemma. There's no doubt that woman was off the charts. And I'd be kidding myself if I tried to believe she didn't leave her mark on me. So few women do.

None have, in fact. Not for a very long time.

I know that's why I never called her. It's easy to blame the move. I was literally on the road to California the next morning. My stuff was on its way, my new condo purchased, new job waiting for me.

And that one night made me question it all.

I woke up in the morning to her dark hair spilling across the pillow, the soft curve of her body beneath the sheets, and I wasn't so sure I wanted to go. One night with a woman—no matter who she was—should not have made me question my life choices.

So I did the asshole thing and left, brushing her off like our night together didn't mean anything. Like it was just a good time after some drinks, and I was happy to be on my way. After that, I doubt I'm on her list of men she cares to see again.

What is she thinking now? At the meeting, I didn't see her long enough to read her expression. I wish I'd noticed her when I first walked in. She had the advantage there—she got to watch me for a while before I realized she was in the room. What did she think when I came in? Was she pissed? Interested? Disgusted?

Did her panties get a little wet?

There are a lot of reasons I should steer clear of Selene. She works for me now. I assume she maintains her rule about not dating coworkers. And there's something about her—something that makes me nervous in a way I haven't felt in years. It makes me wonder if I should stay far away from that magnetic woman.

Selene is a risk. A big one.

But risks are like crack to me. I can't resist.

5

SELENE

*a*idan pulls out my chair and I take a seat. We're out for dinner. Again. Though the restaurant is new, so I suppose he gets points for that. His hand caresses my shoulder as he moves around the table to sit down. That's some extra touching from him. Interesting.

I give him a nice smile and pick up my menu.

I haven't seen Ronan since the meeting yesterday. I'm not sure if he was in the office today—I didn't see any sign of him, and I avoided the hallway that leads to his office like the plague. The anticipation of having to speak to him face to face is getting worse. I wish I got it over with yesterday. I could have stopped by his office to say hello. It's not like I don't have a reason. I worked closely with Brad, and I have a lot of valuable information that Ronan is going to need. But mostly I want to get that first conversation over with so we can move on.

Instead, I'm sitting with my boyfriend (he *is* my boyfriend, right?), completely distracted by thoughts of another man. That's really not good.

"So," I say, trying to stay in the moment. "How are you?"

Aidan smiles over his menu. "Not bad. You?"

"Lots going on at work," I say. "Our company was bought out."

He winces. "That's not good. Are you worried about your job?"

"Well, the message we're getting is that no one is going anywhere, but I'm not sure how much I trust it." After all, that line came from Ronan—and I don't trust that man any farther than I could throw him.

"Are you going to start looking for a new job?"

"Definitely."

As I peruse the menu, the back of my neck prickles. I have the distinct feeling that someone is watching me. I shift in my seat, telling myself I'm being paranoid. We're in a busy restaurant. A lot of people could be looking in my direction.

The feeling doesn't go away. I glance over my shoulder and almost drop my menu. Ronan is sitting across the restaurant, his hand resting on his chin. Our eyes meet, and he makes no attempt to hide that he's staring at me.

I quickly turn back to Aidan.

"Are you okay?" he asks. "You look like you just saw a ghost."

I do my best to smooth out my expression. "Yeah, I'm fine. What are you going to order?"

Aidan opens his mouth to answer, then looks up in surprise.

Ronan's smooth voice almost makes me jump out of my seat. "Selene."

Oh, for fuck's sake. Of course he would come over here and interrupt my date.

I decide to play it off like Ronan isn't the only man here who has seen me naked. "Ronan," I say. "What a surprise."

"Excuse me for interrupting." His eyes flick to Aidan, and immediately back to me. "I saw you sitting here and had to come say hello."

"Aidan, this is Ronan Maddox," I say, gesturing between them. "Ronan and I used to work together."

Aidan and Ronan shake hands, but Ronan hardly looks at him.

"And it appears we work together again," Ronan says.

"Do you?" Aidan asks.

"I'm sorry I haven't been by your office yet," Ronan says, keeping his eyes on me, as if Aidan didn't speak. "I had meetings with my lawyers all day."

"There's no need to apologize," I say. "I wasn't expecting you."

"No?" He grabs a chair, slides it up to our table, and sits down. "I certainly didn't intend to go this long without saying hello. We have a lot to catch up on."

"Which I'm sure we can do another time," I say.

"So how have you been?" Ronan asks. "It's been what, five years?"

"Only five?" I ask. "It seems like it's been much longer."

One corner of his mouth curls up. "I remember it like it was yesterday."

My heart skips a beat, and it's all I can do to keep my breath from catching. His gray eyes hold onto mine.

The waitress comes back to our table. "Do you need a menu?" she asks Ronan.

"He's not staying," I say.

Ronan's eyes move from me to the waitress, like he's trying to decide his next move. "Of course not." He stands. "Pardon the interruption. I'll see you in the office, Selene."

The waitress looks at me expectantly as Ronan walks away. I pick up my menu and order one of the first things I see. I hate that I'm so flustered. She takes Aidan's order, and the pause gives me a second to collect myself.

"I am so sorry about that," I say after the waitress leaves. "That was so rude of him."

"It's all right," Aidan says. "Did he recently join your company? That's odd that they'd be hiring in the midst of a sale."

"No, he's the one who bought us out," I say.

Aidan's eyebrows lift. "And he's someone you know?"

In some ways, not at all. In other ways, intimately. "We worked together about five years ago. I didn't know him very well."

"He seemed to think he knew you quite well," Aidan says.

Aidan isn't stupid. I know he could see what was in Ronan's eyes when he looked at me. But my past isn't any of Aidan's business, and I have no desire to share what happened between Ronan and me.

"I think he's just like that," I say with a shrug. "That's why I steered clear of him when we used to work together."

Aidan seems to accept my explanation. I make it through dinner, although I'm very much ready for this date to be over. I feel like I need to get my head on straight, and I can't do it while I'm trying to make conversation with Aidan.

I decline dessert and we go back to Aidan's car. He gets in the driver's seat and hesitates. He glances at me and I can tell exactly what he's thinking.

It's finally happening. He's going to make a move.

Damn, why did it have to be tonight? Is this what I want? Is Aidan what I want? Ronan left me so flustered, and I'm still trying to get my thoughts in order.

Memories keep flashing through my mind. The sound of Ronan's voice was enough to send me back in time, to that crazy night we spent together. It was electric. As hard as I've tried to forget, it's stayed with me, and seeing him again is leaving me off balance.

"So, Selene," Aidan says. "I was thinking."

I raise my eyebrows and try to keep my face relaxed.

"Instead of going out, maybe Friday we can do a night in," he says. "I'd love to cook you dinner at my place."

I let out the breath I didn't realize I was holding. Thank God he doesn't mean tonight. I can agree to this, can't I? Even dinner at his place won't necessarily mean he expects me to sleep with him. It makes it more likely, but he's clearly not the type to lay on the pressure. I'll be able to make a decision then.

"That sounds nice," I say with a smile.

"Great," he says. "And hey, what about tonight? Are you up for a drink?"

"You know, I have to be at work early tomorrow," I say. "We have so much going on, I feel like I should get home and get a good night sleep."

Aidan smiles at me. It's a pleasant smile. He pulls out of the parking spot and flips on the radio, tuning it to another station.

I hate this station.

I look out the window as we drive through the city, heading toward my place. I need to figure out whether I want to continue with this relationship, and I need to do it fast. I don't want to take things to the next level with him if I'm still feeling so uncertain.

The trouble is, it's so disappointing. I really thought I was doing things right this time. Aidan is all the things I told myself I needed: responsible, sweet, mature.

But his taste in music is genuinely awful.

No. He's a good guy, and I despise the thought that I'm one of those women who gives truth to the phrase *nice guys finish last*.

Then again, the nice guy thing is proving to be pretty dull.

Am I searching for reasons to walk away? Am I craving the rush of a hot hookup so much that the slow build of a real relationship just doesn't do it for me?

But Aidan also wears deodorant that clashes with his cologne.

I caught a whiff of Ronan when he sat at our table. He smelled sort of woodsy and clean.

I need to stop thinking about Ronan, especially while I'm trying to work out how I feel about Aidan. Because my relationship with Aidan—whatever it is, and wherever it's going—has nothing to do with Ronan. I can't let it have anything to do with Ronan. Regardless of whether I keep seeing Aidan, Ronan is the absolute worst kind of man for me. He's everything I'm trying to stay away from: rich, arrogant ... and yes, excruciatingly handsome.

But he also slept with me and blew me off, so I don't even have to wonder what sort of man he really is. There's no telling myself he might be a good guy under that confident and aggressive exterior. I've been to the show, and seen behind the curtain.

He's just another bad boy, and that is the last thing I need.

6

RONAN

I head into the office early. Yesterday's meetings took up more of my time than I anticipated, and I have a lot to catch up on. There's a coffee shop in the lobby of the building, so I veer in that direction before going upstairs. Even at seven in the morning, there's a line.

When I get closer, I spot her. Selene. Dressed in a white blouse and blue skirt, she's hard to miss. Her back is to me and I take a moment to appreciate her. Fuck, those legs. I love that she still wears heels, even though she's so tall. There's an *I don't give a fuck* quality about a tall woman in heels, like she's daring the men of the world to judge her for being able to look them in the eye. Or look down on them, as the case may be.

I'm tall enough that she won't look down on me, even in those hot shoes. Unless she's straddling me, in which case I welcome the angle.

It's no particular surprise to run into her in the lobby of our building, but I *was* surprised to see her at the restaurant last night. She was obviously with a date, but there was no way I could leave without talking to her. Catching her off guard was perfect. I saw the surprise on her face when I approached her table, but she still had plenty of sharp comebacks.

The guy doesn't concern me. I watched them for a while before she saw me, and it looked a lot like an awkward first, possibly second, date. Even if it's not, he doesn't mean anything to Selene. That much was clear. I won't have any trouble getting past that little hurdle.

There are other reasons Selene is going to be a challenge— but fuck, I love a challenge. That must be why I can't get her out of my head.

She gets to the front of the line and orders, then stands to the side to wait for her coffee. Another woman waiting strikes up a conversation with her. Selene's caught up chatting and doesn't appear to notice me. It gives me a chance to watch her. Her clothes are tasteful, but anything would look sexy as fuck on that body. Her hair is up, showing the soft curve of her neck. She smiles at the other woman, nodding as she replies. She really is exceptional. It's hard to believe that, five years later, she's still single. I would have thought some asshole would have managed to get a ring on her finger by now.

Luckily for me, no one has.

I place my order and walk over to stand next to her.

"Morning," I say.

She looks at me, her eyes a little wide. I startled her. Good. I like keeping her off balance.

"Good morning." She glances back at the woman she was talking to, but I seem to have stopped their conversation in its tracks. "Do you need something?" she asks.

"Other than you, alone in my office?" I ask.

Her lips part and her eyes flick to the other woman. "Ronan."

"What?" I ask. "Did you think I was hitting on you with that comment?"

The barista calls a name and the woman stares at me with an open mouth for a second before she goes to get her coffee.

Selene says goodbye and turns back to me. "Yes, the thought did occur to me."

"Good," I say. "Because I was definitely hitting on you."

She raises an eyebrow.

"I just want to make sure I'm being clear," I say.

"Is that what you're doing?"

"Would you prefer I play games with you?" I ask.

"I'd prefer it if you keep things professional," she says.

The barista calls her name and she grabs her coffee. I think about abandoning my order and riding up the elevator with her, but I decide not to push her quite that hard. Yet.

I spend the rest of the day getting caught up and putting things away in my office. I don't like clutter where I work. It's too distracting.

I kept on Brad's old assistant, Scott, but I'm pretty sure I'm going to have to bring my assistant Sarah up from San Francisco. Sarah kicks all kinds of ass and she's quick enough to keep up with me. I'll make do with Scott for now, but I can already tell he and I aren't a good match. He seems fairly smart, but he doesn't have that go-getter attitude I like to surround myself with.

Scott comes in and I glance at the clock on my laptop screen. It's nearing five-thirty.

"I found the profit/loss spreadsheets you wanted and emailed them to you," Scott says.

I nod. "Good, thanks."

"If you don't need anything else today, I think I'll head out," he says.

"You can tackle this in the morning, but I need to find a current market analysis," I say. "Did Brad have something like that?"

"You should ask Selene Taylor," he says. "That sounds like something she'd have."

"All right, I'll do that. See you in the morning."

Scott nods and leaves, closing my door behind him.

Interesting. That's not the first time today someone told me to talk to Selene Taylor in response to a question I had. A clearer picture of this company is starting to form. I'm realizing there are a few specific reasons Brad didn't run this company into the ground, and Selene appears to be one of them.

I haven't bothered her all day, so I decide to swing by her office and see if she's still here. She might have gone home for the day—she was in early, so she'd be justified in doing so. As I round the corner, I realize that I really hope she hasn't left. I'm starting to crave her, and my blood pumps harder as I walk. I feel the leading edge of a rush, like the first hit of adrenaline when I'm going up for a wingsuit dive.

Fuck, this woman is going to get me in trouble.

I get to her open door and catch a glimpse of her. She's sitting at her desk, and some guy in a cheap polo and black Converse is talking to her.

"So when are you going to let me take you out?" the guy says. By his tone, he's trying to make it sound like he's kidding, but leaving it open in case she actually bites.

"Never, Justin," she says, without looking up from her laptop.

"Come on, Selene," he says. "What if I get Seahawks tickets?"

"My brother gets me tickets all the time," she says. "I'm good."

I step through her doorway. "I haven't been to a Hawks game in years."

They both look up at me, and Justin's eyes widen.

A flash of emotion moves across Selene's face, but it's gone in half a second and she's all business. "Ronan," she says. "Do you need something?"

"I need a lot of things, but most of them would be better without an audience."

She raises an eyebrow at me—she has that expression down —but I feel a hit of satisfaction at the slight flush of her cheeks. Justin's mouth drops open.

I walk in and take a seat in a chair facing her desk. "Mind if I sit?"

"Apparently not." She looks up at Justin. "Are you heading home for the night?"

"Yeah." His eyes flick toward me, then back to her.

"Sounds good," she says. "See you tomorrow."

Her voice is friendly, but I can hear the boundary she sets, like it's a fence this Justin guy is going to have to be content to look over. I can tell he hears it, too—and by my guess, he's used to it.

Interesting that he still tries. I suppose I'm not the only one who finds Selene hard to resist.

The difference is, this guy doesn't have a prayer.

"See you," he says, then turns to me. "Um, goodbye, Mr. Maddox."

I give him a pleasant smile and nod.

"What do you want, Ronan?" she asks.

I decide the only approach with her is the direct one. Targeted strike, going straight for the kill. "Dinner with you, tonight, and you in my bed afterward."

She rolls her eyes and crosses her legs. "Honestly, Ronan, I don't know what you think you're doing."

"I don't think I'm doing anything," I say.

"No? What was with that comment while Justin was here?"

"What comment?" I ask, feigning ignorance.

She lets out a sigh. "Look, I realize that you and I have a certain ... past. But I'm determined not to let that influence our working relationship. Whatever happened between us was a long time ago. Now you own the company I work for. You're my boss. I think we can both be adults about the situation and move past whatever history we have."

"Of course we can," I say. "Quite honestly, I'm looking forward to working closely with you."

She raises her eyebrow again.

"I'm being serious," I say. "I keep hearing your name come up from the rest of the management team. I have a feeling Brad was relying on you pretty heavily to keep things from completely crashing and burning around here."

Her face softens a little, and I see a hint of satisfaction in her eyes.

"Thank you," she says. "The last year has been ... trying. Brad seemed to think he could run his company by making sweeping changes and spending too much money, and then running off on vacation for a month, leaving the rest of us to deal with his bullshit."

"That's definitely my impression," I say. "I've been meeting with Brad for the last eighteen months, and half the time he was calling me from beaches or ski resorts. It's interesting, because the guy honestly had no idea how he'd gotten his company into so much trouble. Over the last six months, he seemed to start to get it, but I think he just wanted out."

"I think he didn't want to work," she says. "He had this idea that he'd build up the company enough that it would somehow run itself."

"Good thing he's gone," I say.

Since we started talking about the company, her posture has completely changed. She's no longer standoffish, no longer leaning away from me with her arms crossed. She's much more open, and although she's talking about her frustrations, her tone of voice is relaxed.

I'm so fucking turned on by this *competent businesswoman* thing she has going on.

"I suppose," she says.

"But you aren't so sure about me," I say.

Her lips part like she's going to say something, but she hesitates.

"You can be honest with me," I say. "I walked in here a couple of days ago like I own the place. Of course, I do own the place, but that's beside the point. What are your concerns? Other than the fact that you want me to bend you over your desk right now and fuck you senseless."

"Goddamnit, Ronan."

I laugh. I know I went too far with that comment, but I can't help it. "I'm sorry. Really, serious question. What are your concerns?"

She puts her hand to her mouth and tilts her face, looking at me almost from the corner of her eye. "My concern," she says, "is that you're going to fundamentally change the direction of our products—that you wanted this company so you could take what we're doing and integrate it with your gear and apparel lines. But what we do here is so much more than that. Our products are changing how people take charge of their health. The research team is on the brink of making our devices much more portable, and the tech is state-of-the-art. People will be able to provide incredible amounts of data to their doctors, nutritionists, and trainers. We're not just counting the number of steps people take or tracking the calories they consume. We're talking about devices that collect an enormous amount of data about a person's body, nutrition, and activity level, and put it into a usable form. This is going to help people make better decisions about their health, with real data to back it up. So my concern is that you're going to turn it into a toy. A gadget for rich kids who want to have the latest cool piece of hardware to show off to their friends."

"A toy? Why would you think I see it as a toy?"

"Because that's what you do, Ronan," she says. "Your company makes fancy toys."

My first instinct is to be pissed, but I didn't get where I am today by only listening to people who agree with me. At Edge, it's always been the people who pushed back that led to our best breakthroughs.

"How is it my products are toys, and yours aren't?" I ask.

"Edge is all about high-end apparel and gear," she says. "Technical apparel, sure—and I'm not belittling that. You create quality products, and you have excellent brand recognition. That isn't easy in that market, and I respect what you've done. But we aren't designing products for wealthy weekend warriors who want to look legit while they go rock climbing. We're designing products for the average person who wants to take charge of their health and live a better life."

I lean back in my chair. "You think I'm a snob."

"That's not what I said."

"No, but that's what you're thinking," I say. "Mr. Rich Man only cares about selling toys to the wealthy. You look at me and all you see is a guy dripping with privilege."

"I didn't say that, either."

"You didn't have to," I say. "Where did you go to college?"

"Excuse me?"

"College. Where did you go?"

"University of Washington," she says.

"I went to Stanford."

"And your point is what?" she asks. "That you went to a prestigious and expensive school?"

"My point is scholarships," I say.

"I'm not following you."

"I went to Stanford entirely on scholarships," I say. "My parents could never have afforded to send me to an Ivy League school. Hell, my parents couldn't have afforded to send me to the local community college, so it was all down to me. In case you were assuming that I come from money and had everything handed to me on a silver platter."

"I told you, that isn't what I meant."

"That's okay," I say. "You can make it up to me by coming to dinner with me tonight."

"No."

I hold her gaze, and my mouth turns up in a slight smile. "Do you have other plans?"

"That's none of your business," she says.

"You don't have plans, but I'll take a rain check anyway." I stand up and straighten the cuffs of my sleeves. "I have a lot of work to do, so I'll chat with you later."

I don't really want to walk away, but I know it's the right move. She and I are in the midst of a fencing bout, and although she scored a few points on me, I think I'm in the lead.

Barely.

I need to take a breather before we go in for another round.

7

SELENE

*I*nstead of pushing myself to make a decision about Aidan, I postpone our date.

Is it the adult thing to do? Hardly. But the fact that I'm agonizing over it is telling me something. If it felt like the right thing to do, I wouldn't hesitate. It's not like I jump into bed with every man who buys me dinner, but I've never been shy about sex. I love sex. I love good, hard, passionate sex. But a man I sleep with is always a man I really, really *want* to sleep with. By the time we hit the sheets, I'm aching to see what he can do to me.

With Aidan, there's no ache.

So I tell him I can't make it on Friday, and spend the evening alone. I pick up dinner on my way home from work, and don't answer the text I get from my brother until it's too late for me to go out. A boring Friday night is my penance for lying to Aidan.

Working with Ronan remains ... awkward. At least, it's awkward for me, although I try to hide behind a mask of professionalism. He seems completely at ease, even when he's looking at me like he's imagining me naked—which the asshole probably is. Every time we're in the same room together, he finds a way to make a comment that leaves me on edge. And he clearly doesn't care who hears him. Nothing he says is genuinely inappropriate, but he's obviously flirting with me. I'm sure everyone else can tell.

And when he catches me alone, he holds nothing back. I try to make sure that happens as little as possible.

But I can't avoid him. There's been a constant stream of meetings to get Ronan up to speed. I do have to admit that it's refreshing to work for someone who wants to be involved. Brad would rant about the state of the company, dump a huge set of projects on everyone, and then take off. Ronan is in many ways Brad's opposite. In meetings, he listens more than he talks, sitting back in his seat, his eyes intense. He has a way of making people feel at ease, even though we're all still getting to know him and everyone is nervous about their jobs. So far he seems content to let us continue to do our jobs while he eases himself into his new role.

I'm surprised. And maybe a tiny bit impressed.

Thursday morning, I get an email from Ronan. *Team meeting. Noon. Capital Grill. Lunch is on me.*

I've been putting in a lot of hours lately, and lunch out actually sounds like a nice change—even if it is a working lunch. I send a quick reply. *Thanks. See you then.*

It's a short walk to the restaurant, so I grab my purse at about ten to noon and head down the elevator. I don't see anyone else from the office going in the same direction, so I check my email again from my phone, worried I got the time wrong. I hope I'm not late. But his message says noon. Maybe I'm the only one who will be on time.

I walk into the restaurant and find Ronan waiting up front.

He pockets his phone and smiles. "Thanks for coming."

"Sure," I say.

The hostess grabs two menus. "Your table is right this way."

She leads us to a small table near the back. I glance around, looking for a larger one. Ronan sits and the hostess gives me an expectant look, so I take the seat across from him. She hands us our menus and walks away.

"I thought we were having a team lunch," I say. "This is a table for two."

"There are some things I need to go over with you," Ronan says.

"Just me?" I ask.

"Just you."

"Ronan—"

"It's work-related," he says.

I put the cloth napkin in my lap and pick up the menu. The waiter comes by and I order a grilled chicken Caesar. Ronan orders the salmon.

"You can get more than a salad," Ronan says after the waiter leaves. "I won't even expect you to put out."

"God, Ronan, you're an HR nightmare."

His mouth turns up in a grin. It's downright predatory.

I really need to get some control over this situation.

"Okay." I fold my hands and put them on the table. "I'm actually glad you pulled this supposed *team meeting* on me. If we are going to make this work, we need to set some ground rules."

"For what?" he asks.

"For working together."

He looks so relaxed, leaning back in his seat, with one wrist resting on the table. "What sort of ground rules?"

"For starters, I am not going to date you," I say.

"Define dating."

"You're really going to be difficult, aren't you?" I ask.

He just smiles.

"Dating means ... going out as a couple, just the two of us," I say.

"But sharing a meal as colleagues doesn't count?" he asks.

"I guess not."

"Deal. What else?"

"I'm *not* sleeping with you," I say, my voice firm.

"Yet," he says.

"Ronan."

"Fine, we'll come back to that later. What else?" he asks.

"We won't come back to it later. And no ... shenanigans in the office."

He laughs. "Shenanigans? You're going to have to be more specific."

"You need to stop hard-core flirting with me in front of my coworkers."

"No flirting in front of coworkers," he says. "Fine. What else?"

"No closed door meetings in your office just the two of us," I say.

"That I can't promise," he says. "There are a lot of reasons I might need to have a closed door meeting with you."

I sigh. "Fine, closed door meetings with legitimate reasons only."

"Is wanting to fuck you on top of my desk a legitimate reason?" he asks.

"Ronan!"

"All right, all right," he says, his one dimple puckering. "Anything else?"

"Just ... keep it professional," I say.

"Always," he says. "My turn."

"Your turn?"

"If you get to make demands, I think it's only fair that I do, too," he says. "Every business negotiation has a bit of give and take."

I raise my eyebrow. "What do you have in mind?"

"Neither of us date other people," he says.

"What?" He cannot be serious.

"I don't want you dating anyone else. And I won't either."

"You have got to be kidding me," I say.

"Not in the least."

I tilt my head to the side. "I'm already dating someone. Are you actually suggesting I break up with him?"

"Dating someone? Who?"

I roll my eyes. "Aidan. You interrupted our date the other night."

"Him?" he asks. "That had to have been a first date."

"Not even close."

"Second?"

"No, I've been seeing Aidan for a while.".

He waves his hand. "Regardless, it doesn't count."

"Why doesn't it count?"

Ronan's eyes never leave mine. "It won't last."

"How would you know?"

That wolf smile creeps across his face again. "You haven't even slept with him yet."

My mouth drops open, and I snap it closed as fast as I can. "You don't know that."

"Yes, I do," he says. "You definitely haven't slept with him. And you aren't going to."

"Is that a demand?"

"No, it's an observation," he says. "I don't have to demand anything, because you already know you're going to break up with him soon. After that, my rule applies. No dating anyone else."

"And how long does this rule apply?" I ask.

"As long as yours do."

I laugh and shake my head. "So, your rule is that we can't date other people, but I can date Aidan, because you think I'm going to break up with him anyway."

"Exactly."

"And unless I change my mind about my rules, I can't date anyone else?" I ask.

"Right."

"But you can't date anyone either," I say.

"Absolutely."

I narrow my eyes at him. "If I agree, that means no one-night-stands. No getting around it by bringing women home without taking them on a date."

He leans forward, resting his forearms on the table. "No dates. No sex."

"Why would you do that?" I ask.

He smiles again, but doesn't answer.

I stare right back at him. What he's asking is ridiculous. If Aidan is an exception, I can keep dating him as long as I'd like. Maybe I *will* sleep with him. I can go on, happily seeing Aidan, while Ronan has to spend his nights alone.

Of course, the thought of staying with Aidan just to piss off Ronan makes me a little queasy. I absolutely hate to admit it, but Ronan is probably right. He's a self-absorbed asshole, but he's perceptive. And if I don't stay with Aidan, do I really want to abide by Ronan's terms? Not date anyone else?

I'm sure he'll be the one to cave, and then our little agreement will be over. I don't think a man like Ronan goes very long without a woman in his bed. How long can he hold out? A week? A month? Maybe I *should* agree to this, just to watch him squirm. I can walk by his office every day, knowing he's not getting laid. That might be worth a no-dating spell, just to see it play out.

"Fine," I say. "No dating other people. But if you cave, that part of the deal is off."

"I won't," he says. "And if you do, no more ground rules."

"All right." I reach out a hand and he takes it. "Agreed."

He sits back in his seat, his eyes never leaving mine. I'm clearly getting the better end of this deal, but somehow I can't shake the feeling that he has the upper hand.

8

RONAN

I'm late to the meeting, so I slip in quietly and take a seat along the wall behind the full conference table. Selene glances over and briefly meets my gaze. I have a hard time reading her. She could be hiding any number of things behind those dark eyes. Is she annoyed I came in late? Glad to see me? I rest my elbow on the arm of the chair and put a hand to my chin as I watch her. The guys from the development team are well into their presentation, and she listens to them intently.

I love being able to look at the soft lines of her face. She has amazing bone structure. I listen to the guy talking—I'm actually pretty impressed with the development team here; these guys know their stuff—but I don't take my eyes off Selene.

The little ground rules she set last week gave me the perfect opportunity. I love knowing she's available, even if she continues to keep me at a distance. I get the feeling she thinks the *no dating other people* rule will be a struggle for me. She doesn't realize I wouldn't be dating anyone else regardless of our agreement. I don't want to. It's an odd feeling, to be so attracted to this woman that I can honestly say I'm not interested in anyone else. I knew it from the moment I saw her sitting in the conference room. I'm not entirely comfortable with it, but it isn't something I can deny. I want Selene, and I'm willing to wait until I can have her.

The engineer from the dev team continues his talk, and people ask a few questions. Selene was right, these guys are doing some pretty amazing shit. They're still testing some new features, but the way the new device collects data is rather remarkable. Brad literally had no idea what he was sitting on. I think part of his problem was that his company surpassed him. He got things off the ground, and brought in the right people—which is why this company has done as well as it has—but he didn't have enough vision. He was too pedestrian, not able to see the true potential of the team he built.

I get a little buzzed as I listen, thinking about the possibilities.

Before they're quite finished, I decide to duck out. This group is a well-oiled machine, and my gut tells me I need to give them space so they'll keep producing.

I stop by Scott's desk on the way to my office. "Can you order in some dinner and have it delivered around five-thirty?"

"Sure," Scott says. "Anything in particular you want?"

"Not really." I need to find out what Selene likes to eat, but since I'm flying blind I'll let Scott order something. "Just no sushi. I like to pick that out myself. And make it for two."

Scott's brow furrows, like he's confused, but he just nods. "Okay."

I have a couple long conference calls that take up my afternoon. I get off the phone and glance at the time. Five-fifteen. I send Selene an instant message. *I need to see you in my office.*

It takes almost a full minute for her to reply. She can't have left yet, can she? I don't think she usually leaves until well after six, at the earliest.

Sure. I'll be there in a minute.

I drum my fingers against my desk while I wait for her. My

door is open, but she knocks a couple times as she stands in the doorway.

"You needed to see me?"

"Have a seat." I gesture to the chair across my desk. "But leave the door open."

She gives me a wry smile and sits down, crossing her legs. She looks beautiful in a black-and-gray wrap dress and dark red heels.

"How was your day?" I ask.

"Fine," she says, her voice hesitant. "Yours?"

"Full," I say, leaning back in my seat. "Brad disappeared off the map, and my lawyers needed a few more signatures from him. So that's going to be interesting. I liked what the dev team had to say earlier, though."

"Yeah, they've made progress faster than we were anticipating," she says. "They're hitting a few snags with the new device, but it sounds like they'll be ready for more in depth testing soon. That's great news."

"That is great," I say.

Scott pokes his head in, holding a takeout bag. "Your dinner."

"Perfect," I say. "I'll take it. You can head home if you're done for the day."

Selene starts to stand up. "I guess I'll leave you to your dinner."

"No," I say as I take the bags. "It's for both of us. Thanks, Scott. I'll see you in the morning."

Scott leaves, closing the door behind him, and Selene stares at me.

"Will you get the door?" I ask. "I believe we agreed it's supposed to remain open."

She narrows her eyes at me, and gets up to open the door—

but only a few inches. "What are you doing?" she asks as she sits back down.

I move my laptop to the side and take out the boxes. Two orders of some sort of stir fry chicken and vegetable dish, and it smells fantastic.

"I'm getting out our dinner," I say. "I admit, I'm not sure what this is. Scott ordered, but it smells good. What do you think?"

"I think you are not going to trick me into dating you," she says.

"Who said anything about a trick?" I ask. "This isn't a date. This is two colleagues sharing a meal together, which we agreed is acceptable." I push one of the boxes toward her and hold out a plastic fork.

She takes it and scoots the box to her side of the desk. "You're pushing it, Ronan."

"I'd like to push all this shit off the desk and lay you down on top of it," I say.

"We said no more flirting," she says, pointing the fork at me.

"We said no more flirting *in front of your coworkers*," I say. "We're alone."

She rolls her eyes. "A technicality. Besides, who flirts like that? You have no appreciation for subtlety."

"I understand subtlety very well. I'm just choosing not to use it," I say. "Tell me how I *should* flirt with you."

"You shouldn't."

"That's not fair," I say. "You won't go out with me. The least you can do is let me tease you a little."

"Is that what this is?" she asks. "Teasing?"

"This is whatever you want it to be, Selene," I say. "You're in the driver's seat. What do you think about that?"

"I think that I'm in a relationship with someone else, and you're my boss."

"You haven't broken up with Aaron yet?" I ask.

"Aidan."

"Whatever."

She takes a bite, and I wonder if she's avoiding my question. "No. As a matter of fact, I'm seeing him tomorrow."

"I hope you have a good time."

"No, you don't," she says.

I shrug. "Why not? I have no problem with you having a pleasant evening."

"He's cooking me dinner at his place." She meets my eyes and there's a distinct note of challenge in her voice.

The thought of her being in that guy's house pisses me the hell off, but that fire in her eyes is such a turn on. It's making me hard as fuck. "You're threatening me," I say.

"How is that a threat?"

"You want to make me jealous. So you're dangling the possibility that you'll be sleeping with someone other than me tomorrow night."

"I do not want to make you jealous," she says. "That's ridiculous."

"It's only ridiculous because you're still lying to yourself."

She puts down her fork. "And what lie is that?"

"That you don't want me as much as I want you."

"Did you bring me in here to push boundaries, or do we have a legitimate reason to be having dinner together in your office?"

"Both."

She shakes her head, but she doesn't get up.

Dinner is good. I grab us a couple bottled waters from my mini-fridge and steer the conversation back to work topics. Selene relaxes, and we discuss some of the issues the sales team has been having. She has a lot of good ideas, and I'm impressed with how much she knows about the other departments.

We talk for a long time after we finish eating. I'm not sure what time it is, but I don't want to call attention to the fact that it's late by checking. Selene vents about how difficult it was to work with Brad over the last year, and I talk about my decision making process in buying VI. She asks a lot of questions, and I can tell she's trying to figure me out—understand my motivations.

Her passion for her work shows. It's clear to me that Brad was underutilizing her talents. She knows this business intimately, and she cares about what she's doing. That's a rare thing in an employee.

As much as I want to fuck Selene until she screams my name, I also know I'm walking a very fine line with her. She's not just a random piece of ass. She's so much more, and as I talk to her I feel a twinge of something I haven't felt in many years: Fear. It's such an unfamiliar sensation, but the novelty makes it intriguing. I've jumped out of airplanes hundreds of times and never once have I been afraid. It isn't that I don't understand the risks. It's that risks don't scare me. If it's my time to go, there's nothing I can do to stop it, so I might as well live hard while I'm here. I realize I'm not normal in that respect—and I wasn't always this way—but I have my reasons.

Why do I feel this foreign emotion when I look at this woman? What is it about her that scares me? I'm insanely attracted to her—more than I've felt for anyone in a very long time. Is that all it is? The fact that I'm willing to swear off other women just so I'm available for her, and so she stays available to me?

I'm not sure. I'm putting on a good front, like I have her all figured out, but the truth is, she's bringing something out in me I thought I buried a long time ago. And I'm not sure how I feel about that.

Selene picks up her phone and her eyebrows lift. "It's after eight."

"Is it really?" I grab my phone and check the time. She's right. We've been talking for almost three hours. I knew time was passing, but I had no idea it was that long.

"Sorry," she says. "You probably had things to do tonight, and here I am talking your ear off."

"Not at all," I say. "This is why I invited you in here."

She smiles as she gets up. "And I thought you were just trying to get past my rules."

I stand and walk toward the door with her. "Oh, I am. And I will. You can be sure of that."

She stops at the door, her hand on the knob. I love how she's tall enough to look me right in the eyes.

"No, you won't, Ronan. I won't make that mistake again."

A flash of anger runs through me. Mistake? The words *Fuck you, then* are on the tip of my tongue, but I stop. I know in an instant that if I lash out at her now, we won't recover. Ever.

I step closer, invading her personal space. She stands her ground, holding my gaze. The hit of anger makes me want to be aggressive. I reach out and put my hand in her hair, running my fingers through the dark silky strands. I grab it at the base of her neck, just hard enough that I have her in my control.

"It won't be a mistake the second time."

Her eyes widen and her lips part. I'm so close to kissing her. If she so much as touches her tongue to her lips, I won't be able to resist.

But now isn't the time. I let go of her hair and brush it back behind her shoulder.

"Thanks for joining me for dinner," I say and step away.

She takes a deep breath, and her breasts strain against her dress. "Goodnight, Ronan." She leaves and shuts the door behind her.

I rub my hands up and down my face. Fuck, I'm so hard my dick aches. I wanted to drag her across my office by her hair and bend her over the side of my desk. She has no idea how much self-control it took to let her walk away.

I head straight for the private bathroom, glad it has a shower. I need to get off, now, or I'm going to go nuts. Jacking off isn't going to do much more than take the edge off, but right now the edge is fucking sharp. My Selene fantasies are going to have to do, until I can get my hands on the real thing.

9

9

SELENE

I walk away from Ronan's office, my heart racing. That bastard made my pussy so wet, I was literally clenching my thighs. I should have told him not to touch me, but holy shit, that was a turn-on. I can barely think straight.

I'm so grateful it's late and no one else is in the office. My face must be beet red. I head back to my office to grab my things. I need to get out of here. Now.

I walk over to the other side of our floor to take a different elevator. He could be leaving too, and I cannot risk being in an enclosed space with him right now. I was half a second away from biting his lower lip. God, his mouth is perfect, and it isn't helping that I've tasted it before. He was so close I could feel his body heat, and he stared at me with such an intense look in his eyes.

The elevator takes forever, and I look over my shoulder a few times, wondering if he's going to follow me. I hate that there's a part of me—a bigger part than I would like to admit—that wants him to. I'm still breathing too hard. I glance behind me again and get a whiff of him. Why the hell do I still smell him? I grab a section of my hair and bring it up to my nose. That's where it's coming from. It's faint, but distinctly Ronan.

Damn him, he should not smell so good.

I take the elevator down, and head out to my car. I know exactly what my problem is. I'm horny as fuck—and I hate that word. It sounds so juvenile, but damn it, I want to get laid. It's been a very long time and that is the *only* reason Ronan had that effect on me.

It is *not* because he's the sexiest motherfucking man I have ever met, and it is *definitely* not because I loved it when he got aggressive with me.

There's no traffic, so I get home in about fifteen minutes. I go inside and change out of my work clothes, putting on my too-short yoga pants and a t-shirt. And new panties, because yes, my thong is no longer wearable. Downstairs, I pour myself a glass of wine and sit down on the couch. My heart rate returned to normal on the drive home, but I still have an uncomfortable pressure between my legs. I take a sip of the Cabernet. Hopefully the wine will help me calm down.

I grab my phone and bring up Kylie's number. I really need to talk to her.

"What's up?" she says when she answers.

"I don't even know where to begin."

"Uh oh," she says. "Do you need me to come over?"

"You don't have to," I say. "But do you have a few minutes to talk?"

"Yeah, of course," she says. "What's going on? Did something happen with Aidan?"

I hear my brother say something in the background, and I hope I didn't interrupt them. I know they're still newlyweds and everything, but *ew*.

"No, it's not about Aidan. Not really." I take a deep breath.

"You know how I told you my company has a new owner and things are weird at work?"

"Yeah."

"Well, there's something else I didn't tell you. My new boss is a guy named Ronan Maddox. I worked with him about five years ago, but he moved to San Francisco."

"Okay..."

I put my hand on my forehead. "So I kind of slept with him on his last night here, before he moved."

"Wait," Kylie says. "You hooked up with this Ronan guy five years ago, and now he owns your company?"

"Yes."

"Fuck, Selene, that's awkward," she says. "Is it weird?"

"Kind of?" I say. "He fluctuates between being completely professional, and hard-core hitting on me."

"Your boss is hitting on you?" she asks. "That's not good."

I sink back against the couch cushions. "I know."

"Selene," she says, her voice serious. "You aren't actually thinking about letting something happen with him, are you?"

"No, I..." I let out a breath. Damn it, that's exactly what I'm thinking. I called Kylie because I know she'll talk me out of it, but now I'm not so sure I want her to. "I've been very clear with him that there is no way. I even set out ground rules and he agreed to them."

"Good for you," she says. "You have to set boundaries with this guy, especially if he's asshole enough to hit on you at work."

"I know," I say. That is bad, isn't it? "Ky, the man literally told me he wants to fuck me on top of his desk. Can you imagine?"

"Holy shit," she says with a laugh. "You need to steer clear of him, do you hear me? A man like that is everything you do not need in your life. You need a good guy, not another bad boy, remember?"

"You're right." I take another deep breath. "And besides, I'm seeing Aidan on Friday at his place. He's going to cook me dinner."

"See? There you go," Kylie says. "Aidan to the rescue."

"Yeah, I guess."

"Stop it, Selene," she says.

"Stop what? What am I doing?"

"You're trying to find a reason that something might work with Ronan," she says. "I can hear it in your voice."

I hear Braxton in the background. "Tell her to stay the fuck away from him, and if he messes with her I'll break his face."

I laugh. If you look up the word *overprotective* in the dictionary, there's a picture of my brother.

"I'm not trying to find a reason," I say. *Keep telling yourself that, Selene, and maybe it will start to be true.* "He's just throwing me off."

Kylie lowers her voice, like she doesn't want Braxton to hear. "He was that good, huh?"

"God, Ky, the sex was off the charts," I say. "There's a reason I remember it so well."

"What happened after you slept with him?"

I wince. "He blew me off."

"Fuck him, then," Kylie says, emphatic. "No, not literally. Don't fuck him. God, Selene—you're dating someone else, and Ronan is your boss. Those are two very good reasons to get him out of your head. Add in the fact that you've been there, done that, got the shitty t-shirt. I don't care how magical his cock is. That is not what you need."

"I know," I say. "You're right. You're completely right."

"Is your vibrator broken or something?" she asks. "It sounds like you need to use it."

"That's rich, coming from you, Miss Squeamish about getting herself off," I say with a laugh.

"Don't mess with me, babe, or I'll start telling you why I

haven't needed a vibrator since ... oh I don't know, since your brother started fucking me last year."

Braxton laughs in the background.

"Somehow, I'm going to make you pay for that remark," I say. "Hanging up now."

I hit *End* and toss my phone on the couch next to me, then take another big drink of wine. I need the rest of the bottle to get the image of Kylie and my brother out of my head.

ON THE DRIVE TO Aidan's house Friday after work, I'm so tense my neck hurts. I shouldn't be this nervous for a date, especially since it's a guy I've been seeing for a while. It's not the good kind of nervous, either—the kind where you're so excited to see him, you have butterflies. My stomach is in knots, and I'm filled with a sense of dread.

Ronan was all business today, as if nothing happened last night. Although, technically, nothing did happen. Other than he made me question every boundary I've ever set at work. I was relieved that he didn't try to touch me or get in my personal space again. As stressed as I am about this date with Aidan, I don't think I could have handled it.

I park outside Aidan's building and he buzzes me in. His condo is on the fourth floor in a nice, modern building a bit north of downtown. He meets me at the door and gives me a quick kiss on the cheek.

"It's good to see you," he says. "I feel like I haven't seen much of you lately."

I tuck my hair behind my ear. I changed out of my work clothes, but decided not to dress up or dress sexy. I put on a light blue sweater and jeans, with wedge-heel sandals. Aidan is dressed casually—for him, anyway. He could have gone to work in the shirt and slacks he's wearing.

He goes back into the kitchen and pours me a glass of wine.

"Thanks," I say when he hands it to me.

"Dinner will be a few more minutes," he says. "I can get out some cheese if you'd like."

"No, thanks." I hold up my glass. "I'm good with wine for now."

He smiles as he stirs something on the stove. "Great. Make yourself at home."

I wander out to his living room. He has music playing in the background—some sort of soft jazz that sounds like elevator music. He doesn't have any personal photos displayed, just a few pieces of art on the walls. Landscapes. Boring ones.

God, Selene, quit judging him.

I take a seat on his dark gray couch and set my purse next to me.

"How are things at work?" he asks.

"Fine," I say. "Just busy, mostly."

"Is everyone adjusting to the new boss?"

I think about Ronan and my heart skips a little. "Yeah, everyone seems to be."

"That's good," he says. "Any luck on the job search?"

I take a sip of wine. When I heard the company had been sold, my first thought was to get my resume out there. But I haven't even updated it yet. "Not really. I haven't been looking that hard."

"You should, don't you think?" he asks. "At least see what opportunities are out there."

His comment shouldn't irk me. I'm the one who said I was going to look for a new job. But I find myself biting back a sharp reply.

"Yeah, I will. I've just been busy." I take another drink.

A timer dings.

"I think everything is just about ready," he says. "Go ahead and have a seat at the table and I'll bring it out."

I sit at the round glass table, and he brings out two plates of chicken Parmesan. It does smell good. He sits down and offers me more wine, but I decline. My glass is still partially full, and I don't want to drink much tonight.

We chat while we eat. He tells me a little about his day. He always talks about work. I wonder if he has any actual hobbies. There's nothing in his condo that would indicate he does anything other than go to work and take me out to eat once in a while. No photos on the wall, or coffee table books that might show his interests. He has a thing for bad music, I know that much. At least he can cook, I suppose.

"Thank you," I say when I finish. "This was really good. You're a great cook."

He smiles. "Thanks. I don't do enough of it, to be honest." He picks up his wine and takes a sip, his eyes never leaving mine.

He wants to have sex. I can see it. He's looking at me differently. His posture is relaxed, one elbow resting on the table, but there's tension in his face. He's thinking about it right now, wondering how he's going to bring it up. I see confidence in his eyes. He's sure I'm going to say yes.

I sip my wine, and look down at my plate. I don't want to sleep with him. For so long, I've been telling myself that I need to give Aidan a chance, that maybe if we take our relationship up a notch or three physically, I'll feel more of a connection to him. But sitting here with him now, I know I won't. I've tried to give Aidan a fair shot—he's supposed to be the nice guy I need —but this relationship isn't going anywhere.

I don't want to think about the fact that this means Ronan was right.

"Dessert?" he asks.

I never have dessert with him. It isn't that I don't like dessert. I love sweet things. But by the time we finish dinner, I'm always ready to go. I feel the same way now—like I need an excuse to leave.

I open my mouth to reply, when my phone dings.

"I'm sorry." My purse is still next to the couch, so I get up. "I thought I turned the sound off. Let me just check my messages really quick."

"Of course," he says.

I sit down on the edge of the couch and pull out my phone. I have a text from Ronan. *Need an excuse to get out of your date yet?*

I have to stop myself from smiling. I should be annoyed, but fuck if his timing isn't perfect.

"Sorry, Aidan," I say. "I just need to answer this really quick."

My date is going fine, thank you very much. We had a lovely dinner.

"No problem," Aidan says. "I'll just clean this up." He takes our plates to the kitchen and turns on the sink.

Bullshit. You're a caged animal, trying to find a way to open the locked door.

Just as I start to type, he sends another text.

I have the key.

I stifle a laugh and glance up at Aidan. He's doing the dishes.

Hardly. I can leave anytime I want.

His response is quick. *Good. Meet me at that wine bar by the office in fifteen minutes.*

No dating, Ronan.

Not a date. Same as two colleagues sharing a meal, but it's wine.

I sigh. *We need to add a no drinking together rule.*

Sorry, terms have been set. Should have brought that to the original negotiation.

I decide to fuck with Ronan a little. *Regardless, the terms of our*

agreement permit my date, including any other activities I choose to
engage in with said date. I'll see you Monday.

I look over at Aidan again. He smiles at me from the sink. I
do need to leave, and I need to be honest with Aidan about why.
But I'm not meeting Ronan tonight.

I put my phone away and walk into the kitchen. My stomach
does another tumble, like it did on the drive over. There's no
easy way to do this, but I need to get it over with.

He turns off the water and raises his eyebrows, his face
pleasant.

"Aidan, this dinner was really nice," I say, "and you're a very
nice guy."

His smile fades. "But?"

"But, I don't think this is right for me," I say. "Honestly, I wish
it was. You have so much going for you, and when you meet the
right woman I know you're going to make her very happy."

"Oh," he says. "I guess I thought we were really hitting it off."

"It's not that you aren't a nice guy."

"You said that already," he says. "I just don't understand. I've
been doing everything right, following the list."

"What list?" I ask.

He glances away. "It's nothing."

"You have a list? What does that mean?"

"I follow a very well-respected author, and he provides a
variety of helpful tools on his website."

"Author of what?"

"He's a self-help guru," Aidan says. "He writes for a male
audience, giving relationship advice."

"So this whole time, everything you've done has been an
item on a checklist? Are you kidding me?"

"No, I'm not kidding," he says. "It's a valid technique."

"Valid technique? For what? What is this, some sort of list of
steps to get a woman in bed?"

"Not exactly. Sex is just one part of the overall process." He shakes his head. "Honestly, I'm baffled. You fit all the criteria from his quiz. I followed the checklist to the letter, and it was working perfectly."

No wonder everything has felt so forced and clinical. He wasn't trying to establish a solid base to build a lasting relationship. He was following a fucking checklist.

"Sorry to burst your bubble, but it was not working perfectly." I grab my purse and head for the front door.

"Selene, wait."

"No," I say. "Some online quiz is not going to magically produce the woman of your dreams. You can take your self-help moron and creepy checklist, and find someone who will fall for that bullshit. I'm sure she's out there, but she sure as hell isn't me."

He says something else, but I'm out the door too quickly. He better not follow me. A quiz? Is he fucking kidding? Unbelievable.

I hurry out to my car and drive away. I have to circle around the block to get on a street that will take me home, and just the sight of his building sends a chill down my spine. God, to think I was actually trying to talk myself into sleeping with that guy. Is this what happens when you try to date a nice man? You wind up with a guy who can't think for himself?

I get home and pull into my garage, remembering my phone dinged with another text before I left Aidan's. It's from Ronan.

If your lack of sex tonight leaves you restless, call me. I'll be happy to provide relief.

I roll my eyes. I'm sure he would. *Our agreement stipulates we don't sleep together.*

His reply comes as I walk in the door. *Consider it a freebie.*

That's very generous of you. /sarcasm

I'm a very generous man.

I set my phone down on the counter. I'd be lying to myself if I say I'm not tempted. But sleeping with Ronan would be an absolute disaster, no matter what he says about it being a "freebie." There's no such thing.

Good night, Ronan.

Good night, Selene. See you Monday.

10

RONAN

Scott leaves my office after a meeting with me and Janine, the HR Director. He's a good kid, but I talked Sarah into coming up here for at least the next six months. She should arrive any time. Janine and I found another position for Scott, so I didn't have to let him go. I think he was actually relieved—I'm not an easy guy to work for.

I swing my chair around to look at the view through the big windows while I return a few calls. The sky is clear, the sun glinting off the glass windows of the buildings across the street. I feel a familiar twitch: the desire to fly. It's been too long since I've had a good hit of adrenaline. I'm starting to get edgy.

There's a knock at my door, and I glance over my shoulder. Sarah stands in the doorway, dressed in a dark blue dress with a slim gold belt, a pair of sunglasses on her face. Her blond hair is pulled up and she has a black bag hanging from her shoulder.

"Great," I say. "Email it to me, and we'll talk more next week." I hang up the phone, look at Sarah. "About time."

She pulls the sunglasses off and makes a show of rolling her eyes at me as she takes a seat on the other side of the desk. "You're giving me a raise."

"Am I?"

"Yes," she says, meeting my eyes. "Or I'm going back to San Francisco."

I crack a small smile. I already had her raise processed through HR, but I like fucking with her. "Guess you better go back to the airport, because you're nuts if you think I'm paying you more than I already do."

She pulls her laptop out of her bag and sets it on my desk. "I'm nuts for working for you."

"This is the best job you've ever had," I say, leaning back in my seat.

"Right," she says, with another eye roll. "You're still giving me that raise."

I look up at the knock on my half-open door, to find Selene looking in. Her hair is down, which is definitely my favorite look on her. She's wearing a fitted white shirt with a wide collar and a pair of dark slacks that remind me of how long her legs are. Fuck, she's spectacular.

"Sorry to bother you," she says. "Do you have a second?"

"Absolutely," I say. "Come on in. Sarah, this is Selene Taylor. Selene, Sarah Reynolds. Sarah works for me at Edge, and she's transferring here."

Selene smiles and shakes hands with Sarah. "Nice to meet you."

"You too," Sarah says.

"Again, sorry for interrupting, but Marketing wants to move the meeting this afternoon to noon instead of three," Selene says. "I want to be sure you can still make it before I respond."

I look at Sarah.

"Don't look at me," she says. "I just got here and I don't have your calendar synced yet."

"Noon is fine," I say. "Thanks."

"Great, see you then," Selene says and walks out the door, closing it behind her.

Sarah looks at me with her eyebrows raised.

"What?" I ask.

"What was that?"

"What was what?" I ask.

Sarah nods toward the door. "That. Is there something going on with her?"

"I have no idea what you're talking about."

Sarah gives me her *I know you're lying through your teeth* look. She's worked for me for about four years, but we've been friends since college. I can't get much past her. "I saw the way you looked at her. Please tell me you aren't sleeping with an employee."

"Not yet."

"Ronan," she says, her voice stern, "you realize that's a terrible idea, right?"

I rest my hand on my chin. "No, it's a risk. There's a difference."

"Ah," she says. "I see what's happening."

"I don't think you do."

"No?" she asks. "Let me guess and you can tell me if I'm right."

I arch an eyebrow at her. "Fine."

"She turned you down, probably because she's as smart as she is gorgeous and she knows sleeping with her boss has the potential to ruin her career," Sarah says.

Ruin her career. I do not like hearing that. I shift in my seat, but don't say anything.

"Now, you see her as a challenge," she continues. "She's the next jump spot you need to conquer."

Ordinarily, Sarah would be right. Most of the women I've

dated have a similar story. They present a challenge in one way or another, and fuck if I don't love the chase. It's a rush.

I need the rush.

It would be easy to agree with Sarah, to say that I'm attracted to Selene because she's hard to get and I want to be the man who gets past her defenses again. It wouldn't be a lie. But it wouldn't be the whole truth either, and I don't think I want to try explaining it to Sarah.

I can't explain it to myself.

"Not quite," I say.

"What does that mean?" she asks.

"It means you don't quite have it right," I say.

She narrows her eyes at me. "What's going on with you?"

"We're done talking about this," I say, and the casualness is gone from my tone. I'm not kidding. I pick up my phone to glance at the time. "We have some time before the marketing meeting. Your desk is right out there, if you want to get settled first, but I have some things I need to go over with you."

"All right, back to business," Sarah says. "I have some things to review from Edge, but there's nothing that can't wait. Where are we with the contract?"

"I'm close to setting up a meeting," I say. "But I need to get the team here on board first."

"You haven't told them?" Sarah asks.

"Not yet," I say. "Everyone here is still reeling from the sale. That jackass Brad didn't give them any warning, so they had no idea it was coming. I need to gain their trust before I spring this on them. It represents a pretty big change in direction."

"It does, but at the end of the day, we all need to do our jobs," she says.

"True," I say. "But I could also lose half the dev team and then we'd be fucked."

"You need an ally," Sarah says. "Someone who holds a lot of sway here who can champion this for you."

My mouth turns up in a smile. "I know the perfect person."

Sarah crosses her arms. "Let me guess? The smoking hot brunette you were thinking about shagging on this desk?"

"How do you know I was thinking about shagging her on my desk?"

"Because I know you," she says. "Are you sure she's the right choice, or are you just looking for an excuse to spend time with her?"

"Both."

"At least you're honest," Sarah says. "Just make sure you're thinking with your head, and not your dick."

"Classy."

"It's why you love working with me."

"This is still strictly confidential," I say. "I want to have a few more things solidified before I bring anyone else in on this, even Selene."

"That's fine," she says and starts gathering up her things. "Just keep me posted. If we're done here, I have a desk to set up and an apartment to find. I don't want to live in a hotel forever."

"Fair enough. Marketing meeting is in the conference room at noon."

She stands and shoulders her bag. "Sounds good." She pauses at the door and looks back at me over her shoulder. "Put my raise through, or I swear to God, I'll quit."

"Don't threaten me," I say. "And your raise already went through."

She gives me a satisfied smile and closes the door behind her.

11

SELENE

I get into the office early and set my coffee down on my desk. I like the quiet before everyone else starts to arrive. Things are starting to settle down since the disruption that is Ronan. Despite the fact that he's a more active owner than Brad was, I still have a never-ending list of things to do. I boot up my laptop and answer a few emails while I sip my coffee.

There's a report from the sales team, and as I scan the numbers I realize there are a few discrepancies. I should go over this with Ronan. I glance at the time. It's not quite eight, but he's usually in the office early. I decide to pop in and see if he's here.

Sarah isn't at her desk yet, so I go straight to his office. His door is open a crack, and I push it open wider.

"Ronan?"

He's standing next to his desk, his hair wet, wearing nothing but a towel around his waist. He puts his phone down and smiles at me.

"Oh, shit," I say. "I'm sorry."

"No, it's fine," he says. "Come on in."

"I can come back later." I try to stop myself from staring.

Holy hell, he's gorgeous. His broad chest is still a little wet, and his rippling abs glisten. Why does his body have to be so perfect? He turns toward me, and I almost choke. I don't remember that tattoo on his chest, but fuck it's hot.

One corner of his mouth turns up. "Sorry, I went for a run and decided to shower here."

"Really, I'll come back." Why aren't my legs moving? My hand feels like it's glued to the doorknob and I can't turn around.

"Should I get dressed, or close the blinds?" he asks.

I should not be thinking about the fact that we're probably alone, because the office is essentially empty, and if he did close the blinds... That's a very good reason for me to turn my ass around and come back when I'm sure he's dressed.

But god, he looks good.

"Clothes," I manage to say. I need to get myself together so he doesn't see how flustered I am.

Though it's probably too late for that.

His dimple puckers with his smile. "I'll be right back."

He goes into the bathroom, but leaves the door open a crack. Of course he doesn't shut the door all the way. As if I'd be tempted to peek while he's getting his clothes on.

Fine, I'm tempted.

To keep my eyes away from the bathroom door, I look at the photos on the wall. There are several of him skydiving, taken from various angles—some in the air, and one just as he's landing. Another shows him rock climbing. He's clinging to a smooth face of red rock, shirtless, his muscles taut.

Looking at his pictures isn't really helping.

He comes out of the bathroom, mostly dressed. He's wearing dark gray slacks, but his shirt is open and his hair is still damp. Why does he have to be so fucking sexy? I want to grab him by the waist of those slacks and run my tongue down his abs.

"Is this better?" he asks, raising an eyebrow.

I blink, making sure to focus on his face. "Mostly."

He smiles. He knows exactly what he's doing. He's such a showoff, but god, he does it so well. This should not be working for me, but I'm getting hotter by the second.

"Do you need something, or did you just miss me?" he asks as he starts buttoning his shirt.

"No, I was wondering if you saw the email with the sales reports." I resist the urge to fan myself. I'm a little warm. "It looks like there are some discrepancies and I thought we should go over the numbers."

"How about over dinner?"

"Ronan."

"It's well within the rules," Ronan says.

"Colleagues sharing a meal?"

"Precisely."

"How about now?" I ask.

"Actually, I have a phone conference in about ten minutes," he says. "And I have meetings all day. I don't think I'm free until at least five thirty. We can order in, or go out. Up to you."

I sigh, but he just gives me one of his infuriating smiles.

"Just order in."

"Great," he says. "I'll see you tonight. Unless you'd like to stay and help me with the rest of these buttons?"

"Goodbye, Ronan." I spin around and head out the door before I lose all reason and take him up on that offer.

KYLIE TEXTS me shortly after my dinner meeting with Ronan, asking if I want to meet her and Brax at Brody's for drinks. I have just enough time to go home and change. I throw on a light gray t-shirt with a cute little martini glass on it, and a pair of jeans.

Brody's is walking distance from my house, and it's a mild night, so I grab a light jacket and head out.

I find them at a table near the back.

"Hey, you guys, sorry I'm late," I say as I slide into the booth across from them. "Work has been crazy."

Kylie pushes a full shot glass toward me. "You need to catch up."

I laugh. "How many have you guys had?"

"Two for me, three for Brax," she says.

"Just two?" I say.

"I'm half his size," Kylie says.

I toss back the shot. It burns something fierce and I can't help but wince. "What the fuck was that?"

Braxton laughs. "It's called *kick in the balls*. Lives up to its name, doesn't it?"

"I'll say." I take a sip of ice water to wash it down.

"So what's up with you?" Kylie asks.

"Work is busy," I say. "My attempt at dating a so-called nice guy was a spectacular failure. So, yeah, basically the usual."

Kylie makes a face. "I sort of feel responsible for that."

"Don't," I say. "You couldn't have known how weird he was. I should have trusted my instincts earlier."

"So, speaking of dates..." Kylie says.

A waitress comes by with a basket of homemade potato chips. I pop one in my mouth.

"What?"

"Don't say no until you hear me out," she says. "I had a meeting with one of my design clients, and he is seriously the nicest guy."

"No," I say.

"You haven't heard me out," Kylie says. "He's tall, good-looking, and he's one of the owners. I've met with him a few times, and he's so chill. I think you'd really like him. Look, I found his Facebook profile."

She holds up her phone showing his profile picture. I have to admit, the guy is attractive.

"All right, he's cute," I say. "But you can't be serious. You're trying to set me up with one of your clients?"

"Sure," she says. "I already know he's single."

"How do you know that?" I ask.

"Well, he kind of hit on me a little bit," Kylie says.

I glance at Braxton and raise an eyebrow.

Braxton scowls and puts an arm around her. "I'm getting her a backup ring."

Kylie laughs. "A prong on my ring broke and it was at the jewelers getting fixed, so he didn't know I was married. *Hit on me* is the wrong phrase. He asked if I was seeing anyone, and if not, maybe I'd like to have coffee. He was super nice about it. When I told him I couldn't, he apologized and said he's just trying to put himself out there more. I think he's been burned a few times too."

Ordinarily, I might consider taking Kylie up on this. Goodness knows I set her up all the time before she got together with my brother—though, of course, that never worked out very well. But now that I'm no longer with Aidan, my no-dating pact with Ronan is in full effect. I take another sip of water to give myself a second to think. I don't want to admit I agreed to not date anyone else. They're going to think I'm crazy.

"That's okay, Ky," I say. "He seems nice, but I'll pass."

"Oh, come on," Kylie says. "At least give him a chance. Let me set up a coffee date. Super casual, no big deal. If you don't like him, you don't have to see him again. No pressure."

"Really, I'd rather not," I say.

"What are you hiding?" Braxton says, narrowing his eyes at me.

Fuck. I can't keep anything from Brax. He can read me too well. "I'm not hiding anything."

"Liar," Braxton says.

"I'm not lying," I say. "I just don't want to go out with the guy. What's the big deal?"

Braxton raises an eyebrow. "It's not a big deal. But I know you're hiding something."

I sigh. "Fine. I might have agreed to not date anyone for a while."

"What?" Kylie asks. "Agreed with who?"

"Ronan."

"What are you talking about?" Kylie asks.

"It's one of our rules," I say. "I said we need rules for working together. He agreed to all of mine, as long as I agree to not date anyone else."

Kylie stares at me with her mouth open. Braxton looks pissed.

"I know that sounds crazy, but he can't date anyone, either," I say. "And I was with Aidan at the time, and we agreed I could keep dating him, so it seemed like I was getting the better deal. But now that I'm not with Aidan, neither of us are dating other people."

"Why the fuck would you agree to that?" Kylie asks.

"Because that's how I got him to agree to my rules," I say. "And because I know he'll be the one to give in first. He can't date either, and that includes no sex. I figured I could forego dating for a while just to see him squirm. Plus it keeps him on good behavior at work."

"So what are these other rules?" Kylie asks.

"No sleeping together," I say, ticking them off on my fingers. "He can't hit on me in front of my coworkers, and he can't have me alone in his office with the door closed unless he has a work-related reason. Also, no dating. We can share meals as colleagues, but no dates."

"How often does that happen?" Kylie asks. "The sharing meals thing."

"I don't know," I say. "We have lunch together pretty regularly, I guess, but that's always for work. And sometimes he orders in dinner for us in his office."

"So, neither of you are dating other people," Kylie says.

"Right."

"But you have lunch and dinner with Ronan regularly."

"I suppose."

"Which means you're kind of dating Ronan," Kylie says. "By default."

"No," I say, holding up a finger. "I'm not dating Ronan. That's in the rules."

"You thought of everything, didn't you?" Kylie says.

I take another chip and smile. "More or less."

"Except you're basically dating him," she says.

"I am not."

"What did you do for dinner tonight?" she asks.

I open my mouth, then snap it closed again. Shit. "I had dinner at work."

"With Ronan?" she asks.

"Yes, but only because we had sales reports to review, and he was busy all day," I say. "It was six, and we were both hungry."

"So, you were sitting in his office, innocently reviewing sales reports," Kylie says, her tone amused. "Then you looked at the clock and realized it was late, so you grabbed some food and finished your little meeting?"

"Something like that," I say.

"Or did he order dinner and invite you to his office to eat with him?" she asks.

"Why are you picking this apart?" I ask.

"Because it matters," she says. "He's luring you in and you

don't even realize it. Or you want him to, and you're trying to play innocent because you know I'll tell you that you're being insane."

"I'm not being insane, and he's not luring me," I say. "God, he's not some creeper hiding candy under his coat. I saw him this morning and asked him to go over the sales reports with me. He didn't have time until later, so I agreed to meet with him over dinner."

"So it was a date," she says.

I glance at Braxton, but he just looks amused. "Thanks for not being any help."

"What?" he asks. "I'm not getting involved. You never want my opinion anyway."

"I'm not dating him," I say.

"You're so dating him," Kylie says. "This is like, office dating. He has you right where he wants you."

I'm about to say he doesn't want me at all, but there's no way I can say that with a straight face. Not with as many times as he's told me he wants to fuck me on top of his desk. "I'm in control of this situation."

"Sure, you are," Kylie says.

I lean back in my seat and cross my legs. I don't care what Kylie says, I *am* in control. Ronan might not agree, but I have him right where I want him.

Don't I?

12

SELENE

The wheels on my rolling luggage keep getting stuck as I walk into the airport. I'm already flustered, and my stupid suitcase isn't helping. I completely forgot I was scheduled to go to a conference in Denver this week. I got a reminder email to check in for my flight last night and had to scramble to pack. How I managed to miss putting a three-day out-of-town conference on my calendar, I have no idea, but I've been frazzled ever since I realized I forgot.

I try to get my boarding pass, but of course the kiosk isn't working. It tells me to see a ticketing agent. I stand in line for a while, hoping this isn't going to make me late for my flight. I wonder if anyone else from work is on the same flight with me. I think several other people from the office should be going. I would have chatted with them about it yesterday, if I'd had any idea this was coming up today. I wonder why no one else mentioned it.

The ticketing agent gets my boarding pass sorted. I glance at it before I head toward security. That's odd—why am I in first class? Brad's assistant Scott booked the travel arrangements before Ronan bought VI. I can't imagine Brad would have asked him to book me a first class ticket. I must have been upgraded.

There's a long holdup in security. The line literally stops moving. I glance at the time. I'm getting dangerously close to being late for my flight. I thought I left the house with plenty of time this morning, but Seattle traffic is absurd.

Since I'm just standing in one place, I give my brother a quick call.

"Morning," he says when he answers. It sounds like I woke him.

"Hi, Brax," I say. "Sorry to call so early. Listen, I just wanted to let you know I have to go out of town for a few days. I have a conference and I completely forgot about it until last night. I'm at the airport now."

"You should have told me," he says. "I'd have driven you."

"It's okay, I used Uber," I say. "Tell Kylie I'll talk to her when I get back."

"Sure," he says. "We should get together for drinks."

"Definitely," I say. "I'll be home Saturday, but I think my flight is pretty late."

"Cool," he says. "Text me when you land, and let me know if you need a ride home."

I smile. Braxton isn't nearly as big of a jerk as he thinks he is. "I will."

Security finally starts moving, and by the time I get to the gate the plane is already boarding. I breathe a sigh of relief. At least I made it.

I board the plane and look at my seat assignment again. It's definitely first class—row two, seat A. I stop in my tracks, staring at the man seated in seat B. It's Ronan.

He stands and takes my suitcase.

"I can get that," I say.

"I know," he says, but he puts it in the overhead bin anyway.

His seat is on the aisle, so he moves aside so I can get by him, then takes his seat next to me.

"Morning," he says with a grin, his dimple puckering.

I put my purse under the seat in front of me. "Morning. I didn't realize you were going on this trip."

"And I only realized the other day that we both were," he says.

I look at him. "Did you upgrade my seat?"

He just smiles.

I shake my head. "That's not fair to everyone else who's coming."

"No one else is coming," he says. "It's just the two of us."

"What?" I ask. "That's not right, I know there were others." He didn't cancel their trips so he could be alone with me, did he? He wouldn't go that far. Would he?

"Mary in Sales called me yesterday," Ronan says. "Both her kids have the flu, so she had to cancel. And there was one other person scheduled to come, but he quit when Brad left. I already had plans to attend, even before the VI sale went through. So yes, it's just you and me."

Three days in Denver with Ronan. Alone. Well, not really alone. We'll be at a conference with thousands of people.

I sit back in my seat. "Well, this should be interesting."

"It will, won't it?" He reaches over and plucks a piece of lint off my sweater, right at the neckline. "So tell me, do your rules apply if we're out of town, and there are no coworkers present?"

"Yes," I say, my voice firm. "They apply even more."

Ronan grins at me again and settles back into his seat. He's surprisingly subdued for the rest of the flight. We chat about work, but he stops making any advances on me. I wonder if he's trying to lull me into a false sense of security, or if he's actually backing off.

We go our separate ways at the convention center, checking

into our rooms at the adjacent hotel. Conference sessions begin
that afternoon, and after perusing the program, I decide on a
few that look interesting. I glance at my phone as I walk to my
first session, wondering if I should text Ronan and see where he
is. In the end, I don't. If we run into each other, that's one thing,
but I shouldn't encourage him.

The convention is sizable, with an attendance in the thousands. I've gone the past several years, and I always find it a
good use of my time. My first session is one of the large
meeting rooms and I find a seat off to one side. I glance back at
the door a few times. What am I looking for? Do I really think
Ronan is going to coincidentally choose the same session
as me?

I don't see Ronan for the rest of the afternoon. There's a
buffet dinner for conference attendees, and I grab a bite,
although I'm not very hungry. I listen to the final speaker of the
day in the huge ballroom. Ronan is probably here somewhere,
but I don't see him in the crowd.

Afterward, everyone files out. I'm about to go back to my
room when I feel a hand on my elbow. Ronan smiles at me and
leads me out of the press of people.

"How was your afternoon?" he asks.

"Good," I say. "Not a bad start. My second session was an
absolute snore-fest, but the others were interesting."

"Yeah, I walked out of my first session. The rest weren't bad."
He looks down at his hand, as if he just realized he's still
touching my arm. "How about we get a drink over at the hotel?"

I take half a step back. "I don't think that's a good idea."

He puts his hands up. "Honestly, I'm not playing games. It's
been a long day. I'm tired and I'd like to get a drink. It would be
nice to not be alone."

I almost hate to admit it, but I feel the same way. My feet are
killing me, but it's not even eight o'clock. The thought of

spending the rest of my night alone in my hotel room isn't very appealing. "All right."

"Besides, it's not like I can pick up women while I'm here," he says with a grin. "I can't violate the rules."

I smile and shake my head.

He keeps his hand on the small of my back as we walk to our hotel. I know I should tell him to keep his hands to himself, but I like the way it feels. My mind starts to drift to what it would feel like to have his hands on my skin. We *are* fifteen hundred miles away from any of my coworkers...

We get to the bar and find a small table. I take a deep breath. I need to stop indulging in those kinds of thoughts.

The waitress brings our drinks, setting them on little white napkins. We talk for a while about the conference—interesting things we learned, people we met. After we finish our drinks, the waitress brings more.

"So, did you grow up in Seattle?" he asks.

"I did. I actually still live in the house I grew up in. What about you?"

"Stockton, California," he says. "My folks still live there. You have a brother, is that right?"

I look at him for a second, narrowing my eyes. I can't tell if he's trying to pull something, or just interested in learning more about me. "I do. Braxton. We're twins."

His eyebrows lift. "Twins? That's interesting. What's he like?"

How do I explain my brother? "Braxton is ... well, he owns his own business, training college and pro athletes. He's kind of a showoff, but he's fun to be around. And he's extremely over-protective."

"Are you two close?" he asks.

"Very," I say. "We always have been. He lives right around the corner from me, so we see each other a lot."

"Is he married?"

"Amazingly," I say with a laugh.

"Why is that amazing?" Ronan asks.

"I didn't think Brax was the marriage type," I say. "But he married our best friend Kylie a few months ago. It's weird, because we've known Kylie since we were kids. We were always a little trio of trouble."

"And now they're a pair and you're on the outside," Ronan says.

"Sometimes," I say. "Although that doesn't bother me. He couldn't have married anyone better. Kylie's always been like a sister to me, so having her actually be my sister is fantastic. And I don't have to worry about not liking my sister-in-law."

"But?"

I take another sip. "I guess I'm still trying to process the fact that he got married before me. Braxton was a total man-whore before Kylie. I didn't think he'd ever get married."

"Is that what you're looking for?" he asks. "Marriage?"

I search his face for the innuendo in his question, but it seems like he's just curious. "Eventually, yes. I'd like that."

He nods and takes a drink.

"What about you?" I ask. "Siblings?"

"I have a brother," Ronan says. "Damon's a psychiatrist. He lives in Sacramento."

"Are you close?"

"We used to be," he says. "I don't think he understands me now."

"Did something change?" I ask. "Or did you grow apart as you got older?"

"No, something changed," he says. "I was in an accident in college. Things were different afterward."

"I'm sorry."

He looks away and I can tell he doesn't want to talk about it.

"It's all right. I survived. So how did you wind up living in the house you grew up in?"

I know he's just trying to change the subject, but I doubt my story is any better than the one he's trying to avoid telling. I'm never sure how to answer when the subject of my parents comes up. It tends to make people uncomfortable.

"It's not a happy story," I say. "My parents were killed in a car accident when Brax and I were ten."

"Oh, Selene," he says, leaning forward. "I didn't know. I'm sorry."

His sympathy is so disarming that I find myself continuing. "Thanks. I know what you mean about things being different afterward. In a lot of ways, it was the defining event of my life."

"Who raised you after that?" he asks.

"Our aunt," I say. "She came to live with us. She was older than our father, and she passed when we were eighteen. Braxton and I inherited the house, and we both lived there until we were done with college. After that, he insisted I keep it."

"Is it hard to live there?" he asks.

"Sometimes," I say. "I've redecorated a lot of it over the years, but I still have things that remind me of them. It really is a great house, although it's too big for just one person."

He pauses, his eyes never leaving my face. When he speaks again, his voice is softer. "I'm sure you won't be living there alone forever."

My heart flutters, and I take a sip of my drink to give me a second to recover. "I don't know. Sometimes it feels like I will be."

"Why?"

"That's a complicated question." Part of me wonders why I'm having this conversation with him. But he's so relaxed, his eyes intent on me like he's genuinely interested. He makes it easy to keep talking. "I guess I feel like I live two different lives. From a professional standpoint, I'm exactly where I want to be. I love my job, and I get a lot of satisfaction working for VI. But my personal life is kind of a mess. I tend to date the wrong men."

"Like Ashton?"

"It was Aidan," I say, my tone wry. "But no, Aidan was supposed to be different. He was supposed to be a step in the right direction."

A slight smile crosses his lips. "What direction is that?"

I shake my head and look away. "I don't know. A serious direction? I'd like to meet someone who doesn't look at me like a trophy, and ditch me when the next hot piece of ass comes along."

Ronan watches me with a hand to his chin. He's so sexy when he does that. He has this air about him, like he doesn't have a care in the world. It makes me want to crawl across the table and—

"You deserve that," he says.

I suddenly feel like I shared more than I meant to, and I'd like to get him talking. "Are you like me? You're a successful business owner. You just bought a new company. But you aren't married. Is your professional life on track, but your personal life is a mess?"

He hesitates, his tongue darting across his lips. "I guess that depends on who you ask."

"I'm asking you."

"I don't know," he says. "I think my criteria might be changing."

"Well, I hope you figure it out," I say.

He tosses back the last of his whiskey. "I have a confession. I lied to you about something."

"What?"

"I told you on the plane that I already planned to attend this conference before the sale of VI went through."

"That isn't true?"

"No," he says. "I found out that you were going a few days ago, and I switched the former employee's pass into my name. Then I changed your flight so we could fly here together."

I can't decide if I should be angry or not. "Seems like you went to a lot of trouble for nothing."

"Why *nothing*?" he asks, his brow furrowed.

"It's not like being out of town is going to give you a better chance of getting me into bed."

"I didn't drop everything to come to Denver with you for three days because I thought I'd get laid," he says. "I couldn't stand the thought of being away from you for that long. Believe me, I don't know what to do with that any more than you do."

I have no idea how to respond to that, and I touch my glass with my fingertips, wishing it wasn't empty.

"Don't get me wrong," he says, a hint of mischief in his tone. "If you invited me upstairs with you, I'd be there in a heartbeat. But I didn't come here expecting that."

"Good." I can't quite meet his eyes.

"What is it that's holding you back?" he asks. "Is it what happened before I left for San Francisco?"

"That's part of it," I say. "That and the fact that you're my boss. If something happened between us, everyone in the office would look at me differently. And when it's over, what am I supposed to do? I love my job, Ronan. I told you, it's the one part of my life that I'm proud of. I can't risk that."

"When," he says. It's not a question.

"Excuse me?"

"You said *when it's over*," he says.

"Ronan, we slept together once and I never heard from you again," I say. "Yes, I realize you were moving to California, literally that day. But would it have killed you to call? Send me a text? You didn't even say goodbye. Am I supposed to assume that five years later, you're not still that guy?"

He puts his hand to his chin and looks away. "I guess I deserve that."

"Yes, you do."

He pauses for a moment, then stands and meets my eyes. "Good night, Selene."

He walks away before I can reply.

13

RONAN

I'm up early on the second day of the conference. I'd like to pretend Selene didn't get to me last night, but that would be a lie. She did. It isn't that she doesn't trust me after I blew her off five years ago. She's right—I did blow her off, and she doesn't have any reason to believe I wouldn't do it again. I've had a lot of casual flings, and I'm not an idiot. I know when a woman wants more, and that's when I bail. It means I have a lot of women in my past who probably hate me, but I've never had it in me to give them what they want. I'm great at swooping in, showing a woman a good time, and blowing her mind in bed. Anything more than that? It isn't my area. That gets into territory I don't want to explore, and I've never been particularly tempted.

Until Selene.

I think that's why hearing her say *when it's over* was a kick to the nuts. She can see something happening between the two of us, but she can see the end as clearly as the beginning.

Why does that bother me?

I haven't contemplated a relationship with a future in a very long time. Women come in and out of my life, and I never worry about where it's going. We enjoy each other for a time, and move on. I've been content with that, happy to focus on my career and building my business.

But Selene's assumption that she and I would be temporary ... it hurt. That's so fucked up I didn't even know how to respond to her. I should have been able to smile and make a joke about being so good I'm unforgettable. But I couldn't. It was all I could do to look her in the eyes and say goodnight.

I feel dead inside. It's not unfamiliar. I feel this way a lot. It creeps up on me, and I realize I need to do something to jump start my heart again, like it's gone cold in my chest.

There's no way I can sit through a bunch of bullshit sessions today. I shouldn't blow this off—there are valuable opportunities for networking at this conference—but it isn't going to happen. I turn on my laptop, and after a quick search I find what I'm looking for. I need to get out of here—out of the hotel, out of the city. I need to do something to clear my head and flip my switch back to *On*. Otherwise, I'm going to find myself in a darker place than I want to be.

Forty-five minutes later, I'm driving out of Denver in a rental car to meet a climbing guide. He brought gear for two, since I don't have mine, and we hike out to the climbing spot.

Perched on a rock face, high above the ground, my adrenaline kicks in. I haul myself upward, pushing my speed, aching to get higher. The deadness melts away, replaced by the rush of danger. A wingsuit jump would have been better, but rock climbing was the best I could do on short notice. I take a deep breath of the fresh, clean air, and feel my lungs expand.

I look down at the ground, so far beneath me. I'm high enough that I'd smash against the rocks if I fell. Euphoria takes me, holds me in its grasp. My muscles burn as I climb, sweat dripping down my back. My heart pumps hard, and the deadness is gone.

The guide and I spend half the day climbing. He's a perfect match for me—experienced, with knowledge of the area and no need to make small talk. By the time I head back in to Denver, my head is clear. I feel awake again. Alive. A good climb was just what I needed.

It's late afternoon, and I take a much-needed shower in my room. I had a text from Selene, asking about lunch, and told her I'd meet her for dinner. I have some time, so I meet up with a few contacts in the hotel bar.

Selene walks in, and with my head still buzzing from my climb, she's almost irresistible. I'm overcome with the desire to grab her and claim that delicious mouth with mine. I don't give a fuck about her rules, or who's watching.

The hesitance in her eyes stops me. I take a deep breath and get my shit under control. I could probably talk her into spending the night with me. She'd be reluctant, but I can be very convincing.

The crazy thing is, I don't want her like that. I want something more from Selene than just another hookup. We had that once, and as incredible as it was, it wouldn't be enough. She needs to want me as much as I want her. She needs to let me in.

This is uncharted territory for me, but fuck if it isn't extending my climbing high.

"Where have you been all day?" she asks as she takes a seat at the bar next to me.

"I went rock climbing."

"Are you serious?"

"Of course," I say. "What did I miss?"

Selene fills me in her day. She made some good contacts and the keynote speech sounds like it was worth the time to hear.

"What made you decide to go rock climbing?" she asks. "Was that part of your plan, or did you just take off this morning?"

"I took off," I say. "I needed to clear my head."

"I can understand that," she says.

The bartender brings the dirty martini I already ordered for her.

"Thanks," she says and takes a sip.

I wasn't planning on talking to her about this yet, but my gut tells me it's time. "Selene, I need to bring you in on something."

She lifts her eyebrows. "What?"

"There's more to my purchase of VI," I say. "It wasn't just a good business opportunity. I'm going after something a lot bigger."

She leans back in her seat and crosses her legs. I can see the skepticism in her eyes.

"Hear me out," I say. "Edge Gear was always a tongue-in-cheek name, but we're working on things that are downright revolutionary. I bought VI because I want to integrate your technology with what we're doing at Edge. I plan to integrate the dev teams. I'm going after a contract worth tens of millions, possibly more, and I think we have a solid shot at it."

Her eyes widen. "Tens of millions? Contract with who?"

"It's a government contract," I say. "Military."

"Military?" she asks. "You don't want to weaponize VI's technology somehow, do you?"

"No," I say, putting up a hand. "The opposite, actually. We're developing state of the art protection gear—body armor, without the armor. I'm having some of the latest samples sent up and, honestly, it's going to blow your mind. If we integrate that with VI's data capture technology..." My mind swirls with the possibilities, and I get a jolt of adrenaline running through my veins. "Think of what that could do for soldiers in the field. State-of-the art protective gear with data about their physical state being constantly fed to a central location. This is sci-fi shit we're talking about here."

She keeps her eyes on me as she sips her drink. I can tell

she's not sure—but she's not arguing with me, either. I'll take that as a win.

"This isn't about toys," I say. "It's not about athletic gear. This is a new direction for both companies, but you have to see the potential. Edge and VI are a perfect match for each other. And this contract..." I take a sip of my drink before the adrenaline overtakes me and I start talking too fast. "This contract could be the first of many. There are applications in all branches of the military, not to mention law enforcement and private security. This is going to be huge, Selene."

"If you're taking all our resources away from our current projects—"

"No, this would represent an expansion. We'll still move forward with the next VI product, although of course the time-line to market might have to change."

"So why are you telling me?" Selene asks.

"Because I need your support," I say, meeting her eyes. "I need someone from VI on my side. I know the dev team is going to balk, but they respect you. They'll listen to you."

"I'm going to need more details before you can expect me to get on board with this," she says.

"Absolutely," I say. "When we get back to the office we can go over everything. I'm an open book when it comes to this. I'll be totally transparent."

"That's refreshing," she says.

I smile. I really do like working with Selene, and not just because I enjoy fantasizing about her. Granted, I do that all the time—all the fucking time, because god, it's a special kind of torture to spend so much time with this woman and have no access to her in the way I really want. But I feel like I can rely on her, and the list of people I can say that about is very short.

14

SELENE

*T*hings are quiet for a while after the conference in Denver. I'm busy acting as go-between for the marketing department and the sales managers, as well as keeping the dev team on track. I fall into a routine of meeting with Ronan over dinner more nights than not. Unless I have a time-sensitive issue, it's easier to wait and go over everything at once. I try not to think about what Kylie said about *office dating*. We've simply found an efficient way to work together, and if that means we enjoy each other's company while we eat several nights a week, there's no harm in that.

Friday night, we finish up our meeting, and some very good Italian food. I'm anxious to get home. Sunday is my birthday, so tonight Braxton, Kylie, and I are meeting up with a bunch of friends for drinks.

I close my laptop and grab my phone. "Thanks for dinner. Again. I'm going to head out."

"Do you have plans tonight?" Ronan asks.

I pause, suddenly wondering if I should invite him. "I do. It's my birthday on Sunday, so I'm meeting some friends for drinks tonight. It's just a casual thing, and the place is a little bit of a dive. But ... you could meet us there, if you want."

He lifts an eyebrow and his dimple puckers. "You want me to come out for drinks with you tonight?"

"It's a group thing," I say.

"Sounds kinky, but I'd like to keep you to myself," he says with a wink.

I roll my eyes and stand. "Well, if you want to come, we'll be at the Phinney Tavern around nine."

"Is it really your birthday?" he asks. "How did I not know that?"

"Why would you know my birth date?" I ask. "And yes, it really is. On Sunday, anyway."

He smiles, sending tingles down my spine. "I'll be there."

I KEEP GLANCING toward the front door, wondering if Ronan is really coming. The bar is busy, and most of our group is a few drinks in and feeling no pain. Originally I wanted to throw us a big party at my place—I love throwing parties—but our birthday kind of sneaked up on me this year. In the end, I decided it would be simpler just to go out, rather than try to plan something last minute.

Braxton has Kylie in a booth near the back, and I wonder how long they'll end up staying. He's always touchy with her, but tonight he hasn't kept his hands off her. His mouth, either. He leans in close, and it looks like they're talking, then he touches his fingers to her chin and kisses her. I'd be grossed out—he is my brother—but I'm kind of awestruck when I see them like this.

He loves her so much it makes my breath catch. He was never this way with any of the women he dated in the past. I wonder what it must have been like for him, being friends with Kylie for so long, watching her date other men. It must have been awful. Granted, he wasn't exactly sleeping alone all those years. But seeing them now, I'm both incredibly happy for them, and wishing I was lucky enough to find both a best friend and a lover in the same person.

A hand on the small of my back startles me and I turn to find Ronan smiling at me. He's dressed in a dark jacket over his button-down and slacks, and his hair has that slightly unruly look that makes him so intriguing. From the corner of my eye, I notice quite a few other women watching him. I'm hit with a little spark of jealousy, and a very strange sense of satisfaction at our *no dating other people* pact.

"Happy birthday," he says.

He's standing so close I feel like I can't quite breathe.

"Thanks."

He looks around, like he's taking in the scene. "This is a nice place. When you said it was kind of a dive, I had a different image in mind."

"Dive isn't really the word," I say. "It's mostly just casual."

"You didn't think I'd like casual," he says. "You still think I'm a snob."

"No, I don't think you're a snob," I say. "I just wasn't sure if this is your kind of place."

He laughs a little. "That's kind of the same thing. But it's your birthday, so I'll forgive you." He reaches into his pocket and pulls out a small box tied with a gold ribbon. "Here, I got you something."

"You didn't have to do that."

"I know. It's just a small thing." He holds it out to me.

I take the box and untie the ribbon. I lift the lid and find a thin silver chain with an infinity symbol in the center. "This is beautiful."

He steps a little closer and lowers his voice. "You told me you lost your parents. But they're never truly gone. They'll always be a part of you. Forever."

I touch the necklace with two fingers, not sure if I can speak. I lick my lips and swallow hard. "Ronan, this is ... I don't even know what to say."

"I know what it's like to lose someone," he says. "I saw this recently and thought of you. I know it isn't the sort of thing a boss gets an employee, but I figured maybe we're a little more than that now? Friends, at least?"

I meet his eyes, my heart in my throat. "Thank you. This is so thoughtful."

He smiles, and I'm frozen in place. The buzz of conversation hangs around us, but I'm transfixed. It's so strange to be with him here, surrounded by my friends. We only see each other when we're working. But here we are, standing in a bar on a Friday night. It feels so casual, like he could be a man I know from somewhere else. A man who isn't my boss.

Right now, I really wish he wasn't.

"Can I buy you another drink?" he asks.

My eyes flick to my glass, sitting on the cocktail table next to me. It's almost empty. "Sure. I'm just going to run to the ladies' room."

"Meet you back here," he says.

I tuck the box into my small handbag and head toward the back of the bar. My heart is beating too fast. I need to get myself together.

I step into the bathroom and take a deep breath. Was that Ronan who just gave me an incredibly sweet and thoughtful gift? And he did it with no innuendo, no jokes about wanting to get me naked in his office. I'm so used to verbally sparring with him all the time, I wasn't sure what to say. I need to get my wits back so I can thank him properly.

I reapply lipstick and take a few more deep breaths. I don't want to think about how close I was to kissing him. Goddamn, that man knows how to keep me off balance. I need to slow down on the drinks, or I'm going to do something I'll regret.

I open the door and almost run into a guy coming from the bar.

"Sorry." I try to step out of the way.

"That's okay," he says. He doesn't move, taking up all the space in the small hallway.

I try again to go around him, but he moves in front of me.

"Excuse me," I say.

"Look at those legs," he says, his voice slurring a little. He gets closer, looking me up and down.

I don't know who this guy is, but he's making me very uncomfortable. I take a step backward and put my hands up. "Can you let me past? I'm just trying to get back to my friends."

"Come back here with me first," he says.

He steps in and grabs my arm, his grip like a vice. I suck in a breath to scream at him to let go, but he clamps his other hand over my mouth and presses me back into the wall.

I struggle, trying to kick at him, but he's so much stronger than me. He lets go of my mouth and wraps his arms around me, crushing my chest. He shoves me further into the hallway. I scream, but unless there's someone in the men's room, I'm sure no one can hear me. The crowd and the music in the bar are too loud.

He pushes me against a door and opens it. We both stumble into the alley behind the bar. Fuck, I can't let him get me out here alone. I grab the door jamb, clutching at it with my fingers, but he manhandles me outside, and the door bangs shut.

I get in a good kick to his shins, then stomp on his foot. He grunts, but his grip on me doesn't loosen.

"Get the fuck off me," I say.

He makes a growling noise in his throat and pushes me up against the side of the building. I try to knee him in the balls, but he turns just in time.

"Struggle harder," he says into my ear. "I like it."

"Fuck you!"

I thrust up with my knee again but he wedges my leg against the wall with his, and puts his hand over my mouth again. His body pins me. I can barely move. My eyes widen as his hand reaches beneath my shirt and he squeezes my breast through my bra.

Oh fuck. This can't be happening.

Fear swirls through me and my heart thunders. I keep struggling, but no matter what I try I can't squirm out of his grip. He runs his tongue along my neck and shoves his hand into my jeans.

He shifts enough that I get my leg free and try to knee him again. He slams me back into the wall, knocking the breath from my lungs. I gasp, trying to breathe with his hand smashed against my face. His breath is hot on my neck, putrid with the stench of beer.

His hand slips and I get my teeth into the flesh of one of his fingers. I bite down as hard as I can. He lets go, but before I can move, he hits me across the face.

Pain explodes across my jaw, up the side of my head. I stagger to the side.

"Stupid bitch," he yells.

Instantly, his hands are on me again, and I'm up against the cold wall. My mouth is on fire and I think I hit my head against the wall, but I'm too disoriented to know for sure. My vision swims, and I hear the sound of fabric ripping.

His hand clamps over my mouth again and he stops, pressing me up against the wall. I hear a squeak, like hinges, and I realize someone is opening the door a crack.

I yell through his hand, but it's muffled. My shirt is ripped wide open, and I can taste blood. I struggle harder, willing whoever is at the door to open it all the way.

Please. Hear me out here. Please.

"Selene, are you out here?"

I scream again and drive my elbow up, into the underside of his jaw. I don't hit him hard, but it's enough to make him loosen his grip on my mouth.

"Help!"

The door flies open and Ronan steps out. His eyes widen and he lunges, throwing a punch that knocks the guy's head to the side.

The guy recovers almost instantly, answering back with a punch of his own. Ronan ducks out of the way, but another swing connects. Ronan takes the hit across the jaw and barrels into the other guy, landing another punch to his face.

Ronan's eyes are wild. "I'll fucking kill you."

The guy steps back, like he's not sure he wants to finish this fight. Ronan darts in and the guy blocks. He's drunk, but he seems to know what he's doing. Ronan doesn't let up, coming at him again despite the blood dripping down his chin. He lands a punch to the guy's gut, then another. The guy grunts and staggers to the side.

Ronan swings again and clocks him alongside the head. The guy seems to hover in the air for half a second, before his legs buckle and he collapses to the ground in a heap.

I take a shuddering breath while Ronan stands over him, breathing hard, fists opening and closing. He turns to me, his eyes still wide.

I grab the tattered shreds of my shirt with shaking hands and try to hold them together. Tears stream down my face; I can't stop them.

Ronan rushes over to me, taking off his coat. Gently, he puts it around me and holds it closed while I slip my arms into the sleeves.

"Come here," he says and wraps me in his arms. "Did he hurt you?"

I nod against his chest and he pulls away. I take a trembling breath. "Get me out of here. Please."

Ronan puts an arm around my shoulders and leads me through the alley toward the street. I spare half a thought for the guy lying unconscious behind us, but I'm so terrified I just want to get away from him.

"I'm parked up here," Ronan says. He holds me tight while we walk up the street, and my hands clutch the lapels of his coat, keeping it closed around me.

He pulls out a key and lights blink on a dark Mercedes sedan. He opens the passenger door and ushers me in, then goes around and gets in the driver's side.

"Where's your house?" he asks. His hands grip the steering wheel and his voice is thick with tension.

I give him directions and he pulls out into the street, taking me home.

15

SELENE

*R*onan is quiet on the drive to my place. I don't remember either of us picking up my purse, but somehow it's in my lap. I clutch it in my hands while I stare at the lights passing by.

We park outside my house. I'm still shaking as we go inside. Without a word, I go upstairs to my bedroom. I have to get out of these clothes. I can smell the stench of beer, feel his hand plunging into my jeans. I pull off my ripped shirt and change into a pair of leggings and an oversize blue sweater. I want a shower, but I don't want to leave Ronan sitting downstairs alone for too long.

I come out of my room and hear him talking. He says my name and gives my address. I wonder if he's talking to the police. We probably should have called them from the bar instead of leaving, but I couldn't think about anything other than getting away.

I'm still so shaken up that my hands are trembling, but I go downstairs and get my phone. Kylie and Braxton will notice I'm gone. I don't want them to worry, so I send them a quick text, saying I went home. I don't tell them what happened. I don't want to deal with Braxton freaking out, and he might kill the guy if he finds him. Literally.

Ronan puts his phone down. "I called the police and told them what I know."

I nod. "Thank you."

"Come here," he says and gently takes my wrists. He pulls me against him and wraps his arms around me. "It's over. He won't touch you again."

I let Ronan hold me. I don't care that he's my boss, or that he feels so good I don't want him to let go. Right now, I need him. I need him to keep his arms around me. I need to feel his breath against my hair, his strong hands on my back. I relax into him, closing my eyes.

After long moments, he pulls back and touches the side of my face with a gentle hand. "Did he hurt you?"

I nod and touch my jaw. "He hit me here."

Ronan's eyes flash with anger and his nostrils flare.

"Anywhere else?" he asks.

"I'll probably have bruises where he grabbed me, but I don't think it's serious." I brush his chin with my fingers. "You're bleeding a little."

He licks his lips and moves his jaw around. "I'm okay."

My body is still pressed against him, my face close to his. He leans his forehead against mine and wraps his hand around the back of my neck. I tilt my head so my mouth moves closer to his. Despite the way my jaw aches, I want him to kiss me. I want to feel his lips against mine. My heart beats faster, and I slide my hands around his waist.

His phone rings and I gasp. I step back, and he grabs it off the counter.

"Yeah. Yes, it is." He listens for a long moment. "Okay, thanks for letting us know." He hangs up and puts his phone down.

"That was the police. They're sending someone over to the bar. They'll call tomorrow if they need you to give a statement."

"Okay," I say.

He touches my face again. "You should put some ice on that."

"So should you. There's a bathroom over there if you want to clean up."

Ronan goes to the bathroom and I get a couple ice packs out of the freezer. I wrap one in a paper towel and press it to the side of my jaw. Now that I'm calming down, pain blooms across my face. My cheek throbs; my lip feels swollen. My stomach turns, and I'm dangerously close to losing it. I close my eyes, leaning against the counter to steady myself, and take slow breaths. I felt better with Ronan close, and I hope he hurries back out here.

I'm okay. It's over. I'm okay.

The front door opens. I hear footsteps coming toward the kitchen.

"Selene?" Braxton says. "Are you here?"

Ronan comes out of the bathroom holding a washcloth to his lip just as Braxton and Kylie walk in.

Braxton looks from me to Ronan, then back to me again. His eyes widen. Anger rips across his features and his body tenses up, his arms flexing.

"What the fuck?" Braxton asks and starts moving toward Ronan.

"Wait," I say, holding up a hand, and Braxton stops. "Don't, Brax. He didn't do this."

Kylie runs forward and puts her hand on Braxton's arm. Ronan looks between Braxton and me, like he's ready to get in his second fight of the night.

"What happened?" Kylie asks.

"Some psycho at the bar," I say. "Ronan stopped him."

Braxton glances at Ronan again, then rushes into the

kitchen. "Are you all right?" He tips my head to the side and looks at my face. "Did someone fucking hit you? Who was it?"

"I don't know who it was," I say. "Some guy grabbed me when I came out of the bathroom. He shoved me outside. I..." I look away. I don't want to tell them. I'll have to see it again if I talk about it.

Braxton's anger is so strong it makes my heart race faster. It's a twin thing; I feel his emotions sometimes.

"Did you call the police?" Kylie asks.

"Ronan did," I say. "They're sending someone to the bar."

"We realized we hadn't seen you in a while," Kylie says. "We were already on our way over when we got your text."

"I'm sorry, I just wanted to get out of there."

Braxton brings me in for a gentle hug, and rests his chin on the top of my head. I can hear his heart beating fast. "Holy shit, Selene."

Ronan walks over and stands on the other side of the island. I pull away from my brother and hand Ronan an ice pack. Braxton looks back and forth between us a few times.

"Thank you," Brax says to Ronan.

Ronan nods. "I'm just pissed it happened at all."

"I'm glad you were there," Braxton says. "Fuck, I want to kill that guy."

"Okay, Brax," I say, putting a hand on his arm. He is not helping me calm down. "Why don't you and Ky go home. I just need this day to be over at this point."

"Fuck that, we're not going anywhere," he says.

"Braxton." I meet his eyes. "I'm serious."

"I'll stay," Ronan says.

I look at Ronan. "You don't have to do that."

"Do you have a spare bedroom, or am I sleeping on the couch?" Ronan asks.

"Really—"

"Let me make this very clear," Ronan says. "If you ask me to leave, I'm going to sit on your front porch all night. So what's it going to be? Couch? Spare bedroom? Or am I sitting on the steps outside?"

I open my mouth to tell him he doesn't need to stay, that Brax and Ky will stay over if I need someone here. But as crazy— and probably foolish—as it is, I don't want Ronan to go.

"There's a bedroom right over there," I say, pointing to Kylie's old room. I look over at Braxton. "Brax, you guys can go home. I'm really okay. I just need to go to bed."

Braxton eyes move to Ronan, then back to me. "Are you sure?"

"Yes, I'm sure," I say.

Kylie meets my eyes. If I needed her, I'd be able to tell her with a look. I nod, assuring her I'm fine.

"We'll call you in the morning, okay?" she says.

I nod. "Sure."

Kylie tugs on Braxton's arm and speaks quietly to him. "You know she means it. She's okay."

"Lock the doors," Braxton says.

"I will."

He takes Kylie's hand and they walk toward the front door. I can feel his reluctance to leave, and he looks back at Ronan one last time before they disappear into the entryway.

The front door opens and closes, and I let out a long breath. "I'm sorry. Braxton can be ... intense."

"It's fine," he says. "I don't blame him. I'm surprised he was willing to leave."

"I am, too."

"I guess you don't need two of us standing guard over you tonight," he says.

I laugh, although smiling hurts. "I guess not."

Ronan comes around the counter and runs his hands up and

down my arms. "Why don't you get some rest? I'll be here if you need anything."

"Thank you," I say, and meet his eyes. "Really, Ronan. That would have been so much worse if you hadn't been there."

"But I was," he says. "I did what any man would do."

I don't think just any man would, but I smile. "Still, thank you."

"Get some sleep," he says.

A part of me wants to invite him upstairs. I'm exhausted, but I don't really want to be alone. I don't even have to wonder whether he'd accept. I know he wants me; he's made that perfectly clear. But my logical side speaks up, reminding me that I'm hurt and vulnerable. It would be easy to take solace in Ronan's arms, but what would happen next? What would we do when the adrenaline wears off and we have to face life again— the life where he's my boss and I have to keep him at a distance?

"I'll see you in the morning," I say, and go upstairs to bed.

"Selene."

A voice jolts me awake and I clutch at the sheets. My heart is racing, and I'm so disoriented I have no idea where I am.

"It's okay." There's a gentle hand on my shoulder. "I think you were having a nightmare."

I blink a few times and realize what's happening. I'm at home. We were at a bar, and ... oh, god, I don't want to think about that. Ronan is sitting on the edge of my bed, his face almost lost in the darkness.

I take a few breaths, trying to calm down. "What happened? Did I wake you?"

"No, I wasn't asleep," he says. "I heard you cry out, so I came to see if you were all right."

"I'm so sorry." A wave of embarrassment washes over me. This night just keeps getting worse.

"Don't be," he says. "Were you dreaming?"

I pull the sheet up higher. I'm only wearing a thin tank top and panties, and I'm suddenly very aware of Ronan's closeness. "Yeah."

"About what happened?"

I nod. "I can't seem to get rid of it. Every time I close my eyes, it's like it's happening all over again."

Ronan takes a deep breath. "Scoot over."

"What?"

"Scoot over," he says, lifting the sheet.

I move and he slides into bed with me.

"What are you doing?" I ask.

He lies down. "Come here."

I hesitate, still holding the sheet.

"I swear, Selene, you can trust me. I just want you to feel safe tonight."

I move in toward him. He puts his arms around me, and I lay my head on his shoulder. His body is so warm, his arms strong. He brushes my hair back from my face, careful not to touch me where I'm hurt.

God, he feels so good. I squeeze my eyes closed, willing myself to stop thinking about all the reasons this is a bad idea. Maybe I should have just let Braxton and Kylie stay, and insisted Ronan go home. He's my boss. I have to go to work on Monday. Am I supposed to pretend this didn't happen? I'm completely vulnerable—scared, hurt, and exposed—and in this terribly intimate moment, Ronan is here.

But his body next to me feels so right, I can't tear myself away. I'm melting into him, my limbs relaxing, my breath calming down. I hear his heartbeat, and mine slows to match his. Even with my brother's fierce protective streak, I've never felt as safe as I do in this moment, with Ronan's arms around me.

"What time is it?" I ask.

"A bit after two."

"You couldn't sleep?"

"Not really," he says.

"I'm sorry," I say. "You probably should have gone home."

"No," he says and his arms tighten around me. "You needed me here. Sleep now, Selene. Don't worry about tomorrow."

I keep my arm draped across his chest, my head on his shoulder. His clean scent fills me, and I let my eyes drift closed. The last thing I feel are his lips on my forehead as I fall asleep.

16

RONAN

*T*he eggs sizzle in the pan, and I flip them over. I have no idea if Selene likes eggs, but she had some in her fridge. The toast pops up in the toaster, and I pull it out, putting it on a plate.

She was still asleep when I woke up. I laid next to her for a while, just watching her breathe. In the dim light, it was harder to see where that asshole had hit her, although her lip still looked swollen. It pissed me off all over again, and any chance I might have had of going back to sleep was gone. I got up as quietly as I could, so I wouldn't wake her.

I take the eggs off the stove before they burn. I don't know what she's going to think about me sleeping in her bed last night. Before she woke up, I was too amped with adrenaline to sleep, so I paced around the house for a while, hoping I'd calm down enough to get some rest. Out of nowhere, I heard her cry out. She'd been dreaming. I knew she wasn't going to get a decent night sleep alone, and my desire to make her feel better was overwhelming. So I did the only thing I could think to do, and climbed in bed with her.

And fuck, she felt good in my arms. Too good. She was

barely dressed, her skin soft against mine. She relaxed quickly and fell asleep with her head on my shoulder. Not long after she drifted off, she draped her leg across mine, like she needed to get warm. I drew her closer to me, breathing in her scent. It was so intimate, yet I wasn't tempted to do anything other than hold her. Part of that was knowing what almost happened last night. The last thing she needed was another man slipping his hands, or his dick, where they weren't invited. But more than that, it felt so good just to have her near me.

I feel like I cheated—like I got away with something I wasn't supposed to. A night like that should be reserved for a man who has her trust. Maybe her heart.

I wasn't sure what to do this morning. I could have gone home, and called her later to see how she's doing. Her brother and his wife live right around the corner. If she wants company, she has them. God knows they almost didn't leave last night.

But I don't want to go. I want to see her come down those stairs and smile at me. I want to touch her face and check her bruises. I want to spend a leisurely morning with her over coffee and breakfast.

I want to stay.

I get another hit of fear. It tightens my chest and makes me feel like I can't get enough air. What the fuck is that about? I wasn't afraid when I went after that douchebag last night, and he got in a good shot. I touch my jaw and move it around a bit. Definitely sore, and my knuckles are bruised from hitting him. Apparently jumping in to save a woman from being attacked isn't cause for fear, but the idea of spending a quiet day with her is what's going to scare me? There's definitely something wrong with me. I imagine what Sarah would say. Or my brother. They'd tell me I need therapy again.

Fuck that. I need to go jump out of an airplane. That will get my head back on straight.

Selene comes down the stairs, tying a lightweight robe around her waist. She smiles, but her brow furrows a little. God, I could get used to that sight. I'm so fucking glad I stayed.

"Morning," I say, and push a plate across the island toward her.

"Wow, thank you." She sits down on a stool and I pour her a cup of coffee.

"I don't know how you take it," I say as she takes the mug from me.

"There's cream in the fridge," she says.

I get the cream for her and she pours a splash into her mug. I pour myself a cup.

"Did you sleep at all?" she asks.

"Enough."

She takes a sip and looks at me over the rim of her mug. "Ronan, I need to thank you for last night."

"It's all right," I say.

"No, I mean it. And, um..." She pauses, looking away. "I'm glad you stayed."

I walk around the counter and touch her chin with two fingers. "Let me see how this is doing."

She lets me turn her face. I gently brush my thumb across her lip and along her jaw. There's still a bit of swelling, and her skin is discolored, but it doesn't look as bad as I thought it would.

"Does it hurt?"

Her tongue runs along her lip and she winces. "It's sore, but not too bad."

My eyes lock on her mouth and I slide my hand around the back of her neck. I keep my grip gentle. If she pulls away, I'll back off, but my need to touch her is overwhelming. "I'm so sorry this happened to you."

"It could have been worse," she says, her voice soft.

I brush my nose against hers. Being near her feels so good. My craving for a hit of adrenaline is suddenly sated, although there's no rush going to my head. I'm calm and relaxed, but just as alive as when I'm hanging off the side of an airplane eighteen thousand feet above the ground. It's the strangest thing. I can't remember the last time I felt this way when I wasn't in mortal danger.

"I'm staying with you today." There's no question in my mind. I can't leave her. What happens tonight, I don't know, but she's going to have to kick me out on my ass if she thinks I'm going anywhere now.

"You really don't have to do that," she says.

I brush her hair back from her face. "I know."

She looks down and I can feel her hesitance.

"I want to kiss you." Ordinarily, I wouldn't ask this way, but I'm so aware of what she must be feeling after last night. She's like a cracked piece of glass—still strong, but liable to break if I'm not careful.

Her eyes meet mine, full of fire. She wants me, too. I can see it. "We shouldn't do this."

My body aches for her. The hours spent holding her while she slept, the feel of her skin, her scent in my nose, all come crashing down on me. I don't just want her. I *need* her.

"You're fired."

"What?"

"You're fucking fired," I say. "I'll hire you back on Monday."

I surge in and press my lips to hers, soft at first so I don't hurt her. She grabs my shirt and pulls me closer. Her mouth opens for me and I slide my tongue in, deepening the kiss. My jaw aches, but it's nothing compared to the feel of her lips. I hold the back of her head, twining my fingers through her hair, and slide my other hand up her thigh.

Leaving her mouth, I trail kisses down her neck. She leans

her head to the side, her hair spilling down her back. I reach around and grab her ass, scooting her forward on the stool. She tips her knees open and wraps those mile-long legs around my waist.

"Selene, I need you right now," I say into her neck. My blood burns, desire running hot through my veins. I grind my hard cock against her and she moans, her fingers digging into my back.

This big house is full of bedrooms, but they're all too far away. She drops her feet to the ground and stands, our mouths meeting again. We stagger toward the living room, yanking off each other's clothes as we go, our lips only parting long enough for us to pull off our shirts. I'm on fire for her, my hands all over her body, insatiable.

The backs of my legs hit the couch and I stop. I cup her breast and kiss my way down her neck, past her collar bone. I run my tongue along her nipple until I feel it harden, then graze it with my teeth. Selene shudders.

"On your back," I say.

She complies, lying down on the L-shaped sectional. She slips her thumbs into the waistband of her panties, but I gently grab her wrist.

"I'll do it."

She drags her teeth over her bottom lip and lifts her arms over her head, ceding control to me.

God, she's spectacular. The smooth lines of her neck and shoulders, her full round tits, narrow waist, protruding hip bones. I get on my knees in front of her and lean in, running my tongue down her belly. I pull her panties off and slide them down her legs, kissing as I go. I let them drop to the floor and turn my attention back to her phenomenal body.

"Where should I start?" I ask. I pull down my underwear,

releasing my very solid erection. I love Selene's hungry expression as she looks at me.

"Ronan, you better put that cock in me," she says, her voice breathy.

I climb onto her and lean down, pressing the tip against her opening. She widens her legs, tilting her hips into me.

"Do you need me to get a condom first?" I ask, speaking low into her ear.

"I have it covered," she says. "I need you. Now."

I thrust into her and she clutches my back. I groan into her neck. Holy fuck, she feels good. Even better than I remembered. How is that even possible? I'm overcome, consumed with a heady surge of passion. I slide out, reveling in the feel of her sweet folds surrounding me, and plunge in again. I don't want to lose myself too quickly, but she's intoxicating.

"I don't think I can do slow and sweet with you."

"I don't like slow," she says, meeting my eyes, "and I'm not sweet."

I keep my cock buried in her, as far as I can go, and kiss her mouth. Her tongue slides along mine, hungry for me. "I don't want to hurt you."

"I don't care," she says, her voice tinged with urgency.

I hold myself up with one hand and grab her ass with the other. She pulls her knees up higher and groans as I start moving in and out.

The rush overtakes me, sending me flying. I want to make this last, but her heat beckons me on, and I thrust faster.

"Fuck, Ronan," she says.

Her pussy tightens around me and I almost unleash. I slow my pace, drawing out the agonizing bliss. I'm ready to burst inside her, my cock pulsing. I almost can't think, my mind and body consumed.

Selene's eyes are half-closed, her lips parted. I devour her mouth, the pain in my jaw disappearing in the mind-numbing flood of pleasure. She presses her hands into my back and grinds her hips against me as I pound her.

An orgasm hits me out of nowhere, knocking the breath from my lungs. My body stiffens as I release into her and I feel her pussy pulse around me, heightening the pleasure. I keep thrusting while she calls out, the waves of my climax washing over me, filling me with ecstasy. I don't stop until she's finished, plunging into her over and over while she comes.

I touch her face with a gentle hand while we catch our breath. I'm as high as I've ever been on a wingsuit jump, but it's more than the euphoria of adrenaline and danger. I'm sated and content, but still fully alive. I don't understand how she makes me feel this way.

"God, Selene, I've wanted to do that for so long." I kiss her lips softly, careful not to hurt her. I'm still inside her, but I'm not ready to break free. "You're incredible."

She kisses me back, running her hands through my hair. I enjoy the feel of her for another moment before I get up. She stands and smooths down her hair.

"I'll be right back." Her eyes linger on mine for a moment before she heads for the bathroom.

17

SELENE

I slip into the bathroom and close the door behind me. I'm somewhere between "floating on air in bliss" and "banging my head against the counter at my stupidity."

I just fucked Ronan. My boss. On my couch.

And holy hell, he was incredible.

All that pent-up desire I've been trying to deny flooded through me at his touch. I knew I was a goner as soon as I came downstairs and saw he'd made me breakfast. After the way he comforted me last night and held me while I slept, a crack in my carefully crafted facade began to grow. I could feel it opening, letting in Ronan's heat. It made me crave him all the more, and when he touched me, I was done for.

But I might have just made a very big mistake.

I take my time cleaning up, to give my head a moment to clear. I want to tell myself the only reason he rocked my world is the fact that it's been so long since I've been with someone. My self-imposed dating moratorium, and subsequent time spent dating Aidan, means it's been months—a lot of months—since I've had sex. But I'd be kidding myself if I try to believe that. I know it isn't true. Ronan got under my skin five years ago, and he just reminded me why.

I come out of the bathroom to find him back in the kitchen, dressed in just his boxers and open button-down shirt. God, he looks sexy like that.

He gives me a relaxed smile. "I think our breakfast got cold. Maybe we should just go out."

I smooth down my hair, although I already fixed it in front of the bathroom mirror. I feel like I need to keep a little distance between us, so I sit down on the bar stool across the island.

"Sure, we could do that."

He pauses with his hands resting lightly on the countertop, and meets my eyes. "Are you okay?"

"Yeah, I'm fine."

He comes around the counter and runs his fingers through my hair. "You're beautiful, but you're definitely not fine." He leans in to kiss me, and my doubts fade a little at the feel of his mouth on mine.

"I know what you need," he says when he pulls away.

"Other than a lot of coffee?"

"I'll get you any coffee you want," he says and kisses my forehead. "But I know what else you need. New rules."

I can't help but laugh. "I don't know, I think we were doing pretty well with our old ones."

"Speak for yourself," he says. "Your rules were torture. Although my rule still stands."

"No dating anyone else?" I ask.

"You bet your ass," he says, slipping his hands around my waist. "I don't share."

"I guess the *no sleeping together* rule is thrown out?"

"It better be," he says.

"Okay, new rules," I say. "No sex in the office."

"Not a chance," he says.

"You're supposed to agree."

"There's no rule that says I have to agree to your rules." He plants a soft kiss on my lips before I can argue. "I already told you I'm going to fuck you on top of my desk. I intend to make good on that promise."

My heart flutters a little at the thought. Fuck, he's hot. I almost hate that he can make me feel this way. "We at least need to be careful at work."

"Wait, I thought I fired you."

"You're hiring me back on Monday," I say, "and when that happens, we need to be careful."

"Define careful," he says.

I sigh. He keeps shifting closer, and I can't seem to stop myself from touching him. I slide my hands up his chest. "People are going to freak out if they think I'm sleeping with the boss."

"You *are* sleeping with the boss."

"Correction," I say, adding a little wickedness to my tone. "I slept with the boss. It doesn't mean I'm doing it again."

He grips the sides of my robe at my waist and pulls me closer. "You're sleeping with him. As often as possible."

I laugh. "Let's just take things slow at the office. You're the boss, so no one can give you too much shit. But people are going to think ... they're going to think a lot of things about me."

"Who gives a fuck what they think?"

"I do," I say, leaning back. "This is my career, Ronan. I have to work with these people every day, and I don't have the benefit of being the one to sign their paycheck."

"All right," he says. "But it's going to be very hard to work with you all day and keep this in."

"Do your best." My phone buzzes with a text. I have a feeling it's either Braxton or Kylie. "I should check that. If it's my brother and I don't answer, he'll come busting through that door in about three minutes."

I grab my phone and check. Sure enough, it's Brax.

You OK? Text me back now or I'm coming over.

I'm fine. You don't need to come over.

U sure?

I shake my head and reply. *Positive. TTYL*

"Your brother?" Ronan says.

"Of course," I say. "I told him he doesn't need to come over."

"He's going to hate me, isn't he?" Ronan asks. By his tone, he doesn't seem too concerned about it.

"Not necessarily," I say, although that's kind of a lie. Braxton doesn't like anyone I date. "But you can expect him to give you the suspicious side-eye a lot."

Ronan laughs. "All right, since the old rules are gone, that means I don't have to keep ordering dinner in the office to get you to go out with me."

"So you admit those dinner meetings were all a ruse to get me in bed," I say.

"They were much more than that, Selene," he says, his voice throaty. He runs his hand through my hair. "So much more."

I stare at him. What does he mean? Is this the same man who walked out on me five years ago? Do I dare believe he could be different now?

What the fuck am I doing?

"I'm coming on too strong, aren't I?" he asks.

"No, I just..."

"You have doubts," he says.

"Ronan, what is this?" I ask, leaning away. "If I'm just your latest conquest—"

He puts his finger to my lips. "No, Selene. I told you that when this happened a second time, it wouldn't be a mistake."

I open my mouth, but I'm not sure what to say.

Ronan lowers his voice. "I blew you off once. I'm not stupid enough to do it again."

It feels good to hear him acknowledge what he did—like we aren't hiding from it.

"So, we're ... dating," I say. "Sleeping together. Exclusive."

"Yes," he says, grabbing my hair at the base of my neck, just hard enough that I can't pull away. It sends a tingle through my whole body. "Label it however you want. Just tell me I'm staying with you today, and I can sleep with you again tonight."

My mouth curls up in a smile. "Your place or mine?"

RONAN and I grab breakfast at a little restaurant not far from my house. I'm grateful Brax and Ky don't text again. I'm dreading explaining this to Kylie. She's my best friend, and she'll support me. But she won't bullshit me either, and she's going to give me an earful for sleeping with Ronan. Especially when I tell her I fully intend to do it again. Often.

Because holy shit, whatever else is going on between Ronan and me, the sex was unbelievable. And that's enough for now. Although I'm dreading facing the office on Monday.

Right as we're leaving the restaurant, I get a call from the police. They want me to come in and give a statement. Ronan takes me, and insists on coming inside the police station with me. I speak with an officer; he asks me to describe what happened, taking notes with clinical efficiency. He tells me they searched the bar, but didn't find anyone matching the description, and no one seemed to be missing one of their group. It's likely whoever the jackass came with got him out of there before the cops showed up.

It's disappointing, but not surprising. I give the officer what I can, answering his questions with an increasingly large pit in my stomach. Talking about it is uncomfortable, but I get through it. The officer assures me he'll be in touch if there are any new developments. I figure I probably won't hear from him again.

Outside the police station, we get back into Ronan's car. I breathe out a long breath and rub my temples. Ronan puts a hand on my leg. His touch is so comforting.

"We should do something to get your mind off this," he says. "What do you normally do when you're stressed?"

"I don't know. Drink with my brother and Kylie, mostly," I say with a laugh.

He shrugs. "Well, it's kind of early, but we could get started."

"What do you do when you're stressed?" I ask.

He turns toward me. "Jump from high places."

"Right, the skydiving and all that," I say. "You're an adrenaline junkie, aren't you?"

"I have been called that many times."

"I don't think your way would help," I say. "I'll stick with gin and maybe a cheesy rom-com."

He looks at me, his gray eyes eager. "You know what else helps with stress?"

My lips turn up. "What?"

He leans in to kiss me. "How about we swing by my place so I can get some clean clothes, then we'll go back to your house. I'll bartend after I fuck the hell out of you again. I did not get enough of you this morning."

His voice is like a lightning strike to my core. I'm not sure I want to wait to get back to my house. His hand slides up my thigh, and he kisses me again.

"You better start driving," I say, "or we're going to get into a lot of trouble out here in front of the police station."

18

SELENE

*T*ake a deep breath as I step out of the elevator. It's the same hallway I've been walking down for four years, but everything looks different this morning. The soft beige walls, the large photos of Puget Sound, the line of office doors—I know it's all the same as it was last week. It's me that's different.

Despite being assaulted in the back of a bar—a reality that seems so surreal, it's almost like it happened to someone else—my weekend was pretty fantastic. Ronan and I spent Saturday together at my house—watching TV, drinking gin and tonics (he is an excellent bartender), and fucking each other's brains out. The man was insatiable—and I admit, so was I. It was like we were making up for the months we've spent denying ourselves. We went to bed exhausted late that night, tangled in the sheets together. I woke up Sunday to find he'd gone out and gotten me coffee and breakfast. He even put a little birthday candle in my cranberry scone.

I tried to put Braxton and Kylie off, but it was our birthday, and I couldn't go all day without seeing my brother. Ronan seemed to realize that I wasn't quite ready to tell them about us, and bowed out of dinner, saying he had work to catch up on. I had a nice dinner with Brax and Ky, and amazingly, they didn't prod me for too much information. They were more concerned about how I was doing after the events of Friday night than what might have happened with Ronan staying at my house. I'm pretty sure Ky is on to me, so I'll have to come clean soon. After she and Braxton hid their relationship from me, and all the trouble that caused, we all appreciate more honesty from each other. I won't keep it from her, but I do need a little time to think before I tell her.

Whether Ronan actually had work to catch up on, or was simply perceptive enough to realize I needed space, I was both grateful for it and sad to see him go. I had a hard time falling asleep last night, alone in my big house again. It was so tempting to text him and ask him to come over, but in the end I decided I need to be careful. Part of me is ready to jump in with both feet, but the other part is worried. I very clearly agreed to date my boss, and now I have to start dealing with the consequences of that choice.

I set my things down on my desk and pull my laptop out of the case. I'm tense with anticipation. What is Ronan going to do? What's he going to say? Will it be awkward to see him here? I told him we need to take it slow at work, and I think he understands why, but I have a feeling he's not going to be quiet about us. Not for long, anyway. I feel like I need to have a short sound bite for when people ask what's going on. I'm not sure if I should simply be honest, or try to downplay things. *Why yes, I am having crazy hot sex with the boss man. Is that a problem?*

I put a hand to my forehead. When he and I were together this weekend, my concerns were there, but it was easy to push them aside. It wasn't just that the sex was incredible—though it was. But it simply felt good to be with him. Easy. We chatted and joked and drank a little too much, and it was fun. *He* was fun.

Our verbal sparring transformed into playful banter, and we had a great time.

My message notification lights up as soon as I'm online, and I get a tingle in my belly.

Morning. Can I see you in my office?

I smile. God, it's been less than twenty-four hours since I saw him, but I missed him. I am in so much trouble.

Sure. Be there in a minute.

I head down to Ronan's office. Sarah isn't at her desk, and I'm grateful. I feel like as soon as anyone looks at my face, they're going to see it. They're going to *know*. Especially his assistant.

Ronan is at his desk. His attention is on his computer screen, and he's got that sexy groove between his eyebrows. He keeps almost nothing on his desk, save his laptop and sometimes his phone. His office is all clean lines and uncluttered spaces. There are a few bookshelves, but everything is placed neatly. The pictures on the walls are hung in precise order. His condo was the same—orderly almost to the point of being stark.

I'm hit with a sudden flutter of nervousness. It's so silly. I'm a grown woman, not some little girl. I take a deep breath and knock softly. "Morning."

He looks up at me and leans back in his chair, a hungry smile crossing his face. "Morning, gorgeous."

"You needed to see me?" I ask.

"It's not even eight, and already you're all business," he says. "Come in."

He stands and walks over to meet me, slipping his hands around my waist. He kisses me and I take a quick glance over my shoulder.

"No one's here yet," he says. He slides his thumb over my lip and tilts my face to the side. "This is healing pretty fast. I doubt anyone will notice."

His touch makes me heat up and I resist the urge to clench

my thighs together. "I hope not. I don't really want to have to explain it."

"How was the rest of your birthday?" he asks, putting his hands on my waist again.

I glance back at the door. "It was nice."

"Did you miss me?" he asks, quirking an eyebrow.

He's so fucking sexy. I'm ready to melt into a puddle at his feet—but damn it, I haven't even made it to eight o'clock on Monday morning. What am I doing?

As if he can sense me about to pull away, he dives in, planting a hard kiss on my mouth. His hands slide around to my back and he presses me against him.

"Yes, I missed you," I breathe when he finally pulls his mouth from mine.

"Good. I missed you, too." He reaches out behind me and shuts the door, then fumbles with the lock while he kisses my neck.

"I don't think we should do this here," I say, but there's no conviction behind my words. He grabs my ass and presses his erection against me.

"We definitely should," he says, his voice thick and raspy.

He pushes my skirt up and reaches between my legs, rubbing me through my thong. My eyes roll back in my head as he massages my clit, sending shockwaves through my whole body.

"The blinds," I say.

He doesn't stop teasing my clit through my panties. His teeth graze down the side of my neck. "I'll get it."

He pauses, leaving me breathless, and takes a remote out of a desk drawer. A click of a button, and the blinds close.

"Come here," he says. His voice is hard, commanding.

I'm throbbing with need, and the fact that we're in his office in the early morning is starting to matter a whole lot less in the wake of his fiery touch. I want his hands on me again. Hell, I want all of him on me, and I want it right now.

I walk over to his desk and he moves his laptop onto the shelf behind it, leaving the desk clear. He pulls me close and kisses me hard. It sends a jolt of pain through my jaw, but I don't pull away. The pain doesn't matter.

He hikes up my skirt and spins me around, pinning me down on his desk. One hand presses into my back, bending me forward, while the other yanks down my thong.

My breath comes in ragged gasps and I hear his zipper. I flip my hair and look back at him over my shoulder. He slides his fingers into me and pulls them out again, rubbing my wetness around the tip of his cock. The sight of his hand on his hard cock makes me desperate. I definitely no longer care where we are.

He teases his cock along my slit and I rock my hips back, trying to make him slide it in.

"You want this, don't you?" he says. "That's my dirty girl." He grabs my ass with one hand, his cock still in his other, and rubs the tip against me. "Are you sure? You said no sex in the office."

"I lied."

He licks his lips and keeps rubbing his cock up and down, never quite going in. "I don't know. Rules are rules."

"Fuck the rules," I say.

I expect him to ram his cock into me, but he slides in, almost gentle. He holds there for a long moment, grabbing my hips, his eyes half-closed.

He fills me up, stretching me open, but it's not enough. I try to move my hips to get the friction I desperately need, but he pins me hard against the desk.

"Not yet, my dirty girl," he says. "I'm the boss. I'm in charge here."

His hand travels up my back and he grabs my hair. I tilt my

head up and move with him as he starts to thrust, letting him control me. I arch my back, trying to get him in deeper, but he keeps it shallow, teasing me. Torturing me.

"I love being inside you, Selene," he says, his voice gravelly. He thrusts a little harder. "I love the way you look, bent over my desk." He thrusts again and pulls my hair. "I love having you at my mercy."

Every nerve in my body sparks. I'm spiraling, losing control, my thoughts fleeing on a wave of ecstasy. I don't know how he does it, handling me like he *knows*. He straddles the line between pain and pleasure, keeping me just on the brink of both. No man has ever made me feel this way. I can't get enough.

He pushes in harder, his hands rough on my body, and picks up the pace. The tension in my core rises, my muscles clenching deep inside.

Ronan groans. "You like that, don't you?"

"Yes."

My pussy heats up, every move bringing me closer to release. I'm losing control, only just stopping myself from crying out, calling his name.

He pulls out and the breath rushes from my lungs. His hand lets go of my hair, and I look at him over my shoulder.

"Turn over," he says.

I straighten up and he guides me with his hands on my hips, helping me to sit on the edge of his desk. He tips my knees open, sliding his hands up my thighs, his cock glistening wet in front of me.

Stepping closer, he pushes his cock inside while I wrap my legs around his waist. He grabs my thighs, his strong arms helping hold me up. His mouth finds mine and our tongues lash against each other, firm and aggressive. He drives his cock in and out, harder, faster. I cling to him, my arms around his neck, and rock my hips against him with every thrust.

Ronan growls into my ear. "What do you want, baby?"

"Come in me," I say. I drag my teeth along his earlobe. "Come in me hard."

His first pulses send me over the edge. The ground opens up beneath me and I'm falling. I throw my head back, clinging to him for dear life, overtaken. My orgasm sweeps me away, blurring my vision. Ronan moans into my neck, pounding furiously while he empties himself into me.

He slows down and finally stops. I can barely breathe. He takes my face in his hands and kisses me, soft and tender.

"Do you know how unbelievable you are?" he asks, leaning his forehead against mine.

I kiss him so I don't have to answer. There's something in his voice that sends another crack snaking across my facade, threatening my protective shell.

Suddenly the fact that I'm sitting on the edge of his desk, my skirt hiked up around my waist, comes crashing in on me.

"Fuck, Ronan, someone probably heard us," I say.

He just smiles and lets go of my legs. I stand up and push my skirt down.

"You can clean up in the bathroom if you want," he says. He grabs my thong off the floor and hands it to me. His eyes look a little glassy.

I duck into his bathroom and shut the door. I don't want to admit how much I loved what he just did to me. I love how he makes me feel when he's aggressive, grabbing me and making my body do what he wants. I love relenting, ceding myself to him. I've never let a man do that to me before. I've always maintained control of myself, even in the moment of climax. With Ronan, I don't want to. I want to let him have his way with me— take me somewhere I've never been.

How does he make it so easy to trust him like this?

I clean up, and fix my clothes and hair. My face is a little flushed, but luckily my olive skin hides it reasonably well. Once I feel presentable, I come out and find Ronan standing next to his desk, fully dressed, adjusting the cuffs of his sleeves. He gives me a lazy smile and comes over to slide his hands around my waist.

"That's a good way to start the week," he says.

My brow furrows with concern and my eyes flick to the still-closed door.

"Don't worry," he says. "Sarah isn't here yet. And people are going to find out eventually."

"It's one thing to find out we're together," I say. "Quite another to hear you fucking me in your office."

He kisses me again. "No one heard anything. It's going to be fine."

I let myself relax a little. I ought to at least enjoy the post-sex glow. I can almost still feel him inside me.

"Okay," I say.

He gives me a wicked smile, his hand sliding around to squeeze my ass. "Now get back to work."

"You too, boss man."

He smiles again and goes back to his desk. I unlock the door and open it, glancing out. Relief washes over me at the sight of Sarah's empty desk. I take another cleansing breath and go back to my office, hoping what I just did isn't written all over my face.

19

RONAN

*A*fter a fucked up day of bad news—delays and roadblocks for both dev teams—I leave the office without talking to Selene. I'm in a shit mood and I don't want to subject her to it. I send her a quick text so she doesn't think I'm blowing her off like a total asshole, and go home for a much needed drink.

Sitting alone in my condo, clutching a glass of bourbon, I wonder if I made the right call. I'm wound up as tight as a fucking spring. Maybe spending the evening with Selene would have helped me relax. I've been working too much lately, but nurturing the right relationships to get this contract is a full time job in and of itself. Add to that running two separate companies, and making subtle changes that will allow me to integrate some of the research and development people—without pissing them off and making everyone quit—and it's no wonder I feel like hell.

The bourbon goes down easy, sliding down my throat with a pleasant burn.

My phone rings. It's Damon. I decide to answer, hoping he's not calling to give me shit about not seeing our parents.

"Hey," I say.

"Hey," Damon says. "How's Seattle?"

"Good. Definitely the right call." For so many reasons.

"Glad to hear that," he says. "Talked to Mom and Dad lately?"

"Is that why you called?" I ask, not bothering to hide the annoyance in my voice.

"No, man," Damon says. "It was just a question. I'm not trying to guilt trip you. Have another drink or something."

"What's up, then?" I ask.

"I'm going to be up your way soon," he says. "Just thought I'd give you a heads up, see if you wanted to get together while I'm in town."

That actually isn't a terrible idea. I wouldn't mind seeing Damon. He knows how to piss me off, but he's a good guy. "Sure, just keep me posted."

"Great," he says. "So, jumped off any bridges or whatever recently?"

"No, not lately," I say. Aside from rock climbing in Denver, I haven't done any of my usual sports in a while. It's odd, but I don't have the all-too-familiar itch, the craving for soaring through the air.

"Too busy with the ladies?" Damon says with a laugh.

"Not ladies," I say. "Just one."

"One? You're kidding."

"Not in the least," I say.

"You mean one this week, right?" Damon asks.

"Fuck off," I say with a laugh.

"Seriously, though, do you mean you have an actual girl-friend?" he asks.

"Yes, I guess that's what I mean."

"Holy shit."

I'm kind of irritated at Damon's reaction, but I suppose it's warranted. It's been years since I've been with a woman and called her my girlfriend. Not since college. Not since Chelsea.

She's the last person I want to think about, so I take another swig of bourbon. "Is that all, Damon?"

"Yeah, I'll text you when I have travel plans," he says.

"All right, talk to you later," I say and hang up.

I finish the rest of my drink. What I need is a day off. I've been working my ass off without much of a break. I get an idea and send a text to Sarah.

Anything on my schedule I can't blow off tomorrow?

I wait a few minutes for her reply. *No, I can move stuff. You ok?*

Fine. Won't be in tomorrow.

I bring up Selene's number and hit send.

"Hi," she says when she answers.

Just hearing her voice starts to uncoil the tension in my back. "Hi, gorgeous. Sorry I left the office without saying goodbye."

"It's all right," she says. "I'm still here, actually."

I glance at the time. It's nine fifteen. "What are you doing at the office?

"Having dinner with Justin from Sales," she says.

She delivers the line totally deadpan, and for a second, I wonder if she's serious. "Excuse me?"

"I'm working, obviously," she says with a laugh.

Now I'm even more sure my idea is the right thing. She needs a break as much as I do. "Pack it in and come over. Bring something casual to wear tomorrow. You're taking the day off."

"What?"

"You heard me," I say.

"I can't take tomorrow off," she says. "I have way too much to do."

"I'm your boss, and I'm telling you that you're taking tomorrow off."

She's quiet for a moment. I think she's trying to decide whether or not to argue with me.

"Selene," I say, my tone serious. "I'll call building security and make sure they escort you out if you try to get in the building tomorrow. You're banned from the office for the next twenty-four hours."

"You won't call security," she says.

"No?" I say. "Show up at work tomorrow and test me."

She sighs. "Okay, if I'm not working tomorrow, what am I doing?"

"I don't think I'm going to tell you yet."

"Come on, Ronan," she says. "If I don't know what I'm doing, how will I know what clothes to wear?"

"Pretend it's a weekend," I say. "Pants, not a skirt or dress. Although I do love the access a dress gives me."

"Ronan."

I laugh. "Bring a coat in case it's cold."

"Anything else?"

"Just get that hot ass over here," I say. "There are some things I'd really like to do to you tonight."

WE WAKE up early and grab breakfast on the way out of town. I still haven't told her what we're doing. I like keeping her in suspense. She asks questions as we drive down the freeway, trying to get me to let something slip, but I just smile at her. Eventually we settle into a comfortable silence. I put my hand on her thigh, and she lays hers on top of mine. There's something soothing about the low hum of tires on the road, my hand touching her. Normally I'd be feeling the first pings of adrenaline, knowing where we're going. But I'm calm, my mind completely clear. I'm excited for what I have planned, but the deep need I typically feel isn't there.

I'm not flying down the freeway in a hurry to get to my destination, itching for the high I know is coming. I'm sated. Relaxed. Alive.

I glance over at Selene, wondering how she has this kind of magic over me. It's not just the sex, although I could fuck that woman every day for the rest of my life and never get tired of her.

That thought comes out of nowhere, hitting me like a train. Goddamn, I really could. Usually, I'm all about the chase. I love it when a woman is a challenge, or when there's a hint of danger in being with her. My statistics professor senior year at Stanford. The daughter of the CEO at my first job after college. Women I work with. Women who don't want to give me the time of day, until I convince them otherwise. I go after them, loving every minute of the prowl. Once I have them, though, the excitement wears off pretty quickly. A few weeks. A couple months. There's a reason my brother was surprised to hear me call Selene my girlfriend. That implies a level of commitment I don't usually bother with.

But not only do I not want to share Selene with anyone else, my interest in her isn't fading. If anything, the more time I spend with her the more I want her around.

And yes, it scares the fuck out of me. Genuinely scared, and I don't do fear. Maybe that's what this is—the intrigue of the fear. Maybe that's what keeps driving me to be with her. To see her again. To spend my nights with her. To walk by her office just so I can get a glimpse of her. I'm driven by the strangeness of the fear, just like I'm usually driven by the thrill of the chase.

That must be it, because the only other explanation is something I'm not ready to contemplate.

We drive down a long road through empty fields, and the airstrip comes into view.

"Ronan," Selene says, her voice betraying her anxiety, "what are we doing here?"

I grin at her. "Have you guessed yet?"

I find a parking space and we both get out. Selene stares up at the huge hangar, at the words *Skydive Kapowsin* in big red and blue letters.

"I am not jumping out of a perfectly good airplane," she says.

I walk around the car and take her hands. "Yes, you are."

"No," she says, shaking her head. "No way."

I put my fingers through her hair at the base of her neck. "Selene, you're going to do this. Trust me."

Her eyes lock with mine. "Okay," she says. "I trust you."

Suddenly the fear is so strong I almost get back in the car. She does trust me. She's trusted me with her body in more ways than I expected—letting me touch her, hold her, pin her down, control her. I've tried to remain true to that trust and never hurt her, never push her past her limits.

But right now, she's not just trusting me with her body. She's trusting me with her life. And for a moment I'm not sure I want that responsibility.

Then I'm flooded with satisfaction, like the verbal confirmation of her trust was something I desperately needed. I kiss her, my fear melting in the face of my excitement.

"You don't have anything to worry about," I say. "I've done this hundreds of times. We'll do a tandem jump. That means we'll be harnessed together and I'll have control of the chute. I'll keep you safe."

She bites her lower lip and smiles. I lead her inside and talk to Sam, the owner. I already made the arrangements for our jump. Normally they only let their own instructors do tandem jumps, but I have more than enough experience and the necessary certifications to make it legal.

They take Selene through the customary training session. It's not long—with a tandem jump, there's a lot less for a beginner to learn. We both get suited up and head out to the airstrip. Selene grips my hand as we walk toward the twin engine aircraft. She's dressed in a bright blue skydiving suit with the harness that will attach her to me. I feel the weight of the gear on my back and adjust the straps on my shoulders. My heart starts to pump as we get in the plane. A tandem jump seems tame after some of the things I've done over the last couple years, but sharing it with Selene brings a whole new element to the experience.

The plane takes off and Selene keeps a death grip on my arm. The jump coordinator goes over some last-minute instructions and helps us get the harness connected. We get up to jump altitude. He double- and triple-checks everything and then opens the door.

Selene twists her head around. "I don't know if I can do this."

I put my arms around her and plant a kiss on her cheek. "Yes, you can. I've got you."

We move toward the open door, Selene strapped in front of me. I have to push her forward, but I'm not letting her change her mind now. The wind rushes past, almost deafening. I adjust my goggles and take a deep breath, feeling the adrenaline pumping through my veins. Fuck, I love this shit.

"Ready?" I yell above the noise. I put my hand on her forehead and tilt her head back against my shoulder so her neck doesn't jerk when we hit the air. "Let's do this."

Then I grab the bar and hoist us out.

Suddenly we're falling, plummeting through the air. We accelerate, and I deploy the drogue chute. It's small, and doesn't slow us down; it's there to ensure proper deployment of the main canopy.

I hear Selene's voice, flying past me on the wind. I spread my arms and legs wide, keeping Selene steady beneath me. We slice through the air and it feels thick, like water. My lungs burn a little, and the heady excitement sends a flood of euphoria through my mind. My entire body is teeming with vitality, tingling from my scalp to my toes.

The freefall is over too quickly, but I won't take chances with Selene's safety. I deploy the main canopy and there's a jerk, as though we're suddenly being pulled upward. Our descent slows as the chute billows out above us, and we go from horizontal to vertical, our legs dangling in the open air.

I pull the lead on one side and guide us toward the landing zone. Freefalling is my favorite part, but even the slower ride down is a rush. Everything looks tiny below us, but grows quickly as we get closer. The wind roars past, loud in my ears, and it feels like we're floating. I tug on the lines to steer us in the right direction, reveling in the feel of flying through the air.

The descent is about five minutes, but it feels much longer. Time seems to slow, and the weight of the world is nothing while I'm out here in the chill air, gliding toward the ground. I reach around to give Selene a thumbs up. She throws her arms up in the air, leaning her head back against me, and shouts into the wind. Her enjoyment pulses through me and I wish we didn't have an hour's drive to get back to my place. I'm so fucking turned on.

The ground gets closer and I ready myself for the landing. "Pick up your legs," I shout and adjust so we're straight. My feet hit the ground and I take a quick step forward. Selene hollers again as we hit the dirt. The chute drops behind us, pulling us down, and we fall backward onto the ground.

The staff is there to help with the gear, and I unfasten Selene from the harness. We get to our feet and she turns to me, throwing her arms around my neck.

"Oh my god, I can't believe I just did that," she says, her voice trembling.

I slide my hand to the back of her neck and kiss her mouth. "What did you think?"

"That's one of the most amazing things I've ever done," she says.

I can't keep the wide smile off my face. I feel so free, so alive. Selene's eyes sparkle and she laughs, giddy as a little kid.

"Now are you glad I made you do it?"

"Yes," she says, looking deep into my eyes. "I'm glad about everything."

20

SELENE

*M*y phone lights up, and I take a deep breath before answering. It's Kylie. I shouldn't be nervous to talk to my best friend, but I know she's going to give me an earful about Ronan. I'm probably a wimp for telling her over the phone instead of in person, but I just want to get it over with.

"Hey, Ky."

"Hey, babe," she says. "Got your message. What's up?"

Might as well get right to the point. "I have a confession."

"You're sleeping with Ronan, aren't you?"

I open my mouth but nothing coherent comes out right away. "How did you know?"

"What?" she asks, her voice almost a squeal. "I was kidding! You *are*?"

I groan and cover my eyes with my hand. "Yes."

"Hold on a second here, Ms. Taylor," she says. "Do you mean you slept with him, as in it happened once? Or you are sleeping with him, as in this is now a regular occurrence."

"The second one."

"Oh my god," she says.

I take a deep breath. "I know. He's my boss. He blew me off once before. I know you're going to think I'm crazy, or stupid, but this isn't like that. Yes, when he first showed up at my office, he probably just wanted to get in my pants. But I feel like there's something more. A lot more, Ky."

"I don't think you're stupid," she says. "Crazy remains to be seen. But, really? So it's official now? Dating, the whole thing?"

"Yeah," I say. "We're ... together."

"All right," Kylie says. "So do we get to meet him again soon? The night of your birthday thing wasn't exactly the best introduction."

"Yeah, I want you guys to meet him," I say. "But you have to make Braxton behave."

"Since when do you think I can *make* Braxton do anything?"

"I don't know," I say. "Promise him something kinky if he's nice to Ronan."

Kylie laughs. "That might actually work."

"Gross, now I'm getting a mental picture."

"You said it, not me," she says. "So, you're sure about this?"

"Honestly?" I say. "Not really. This could turn out to be a huge mistake. But he's kind of amazing."

"Wow," she says, her voice soft. "Okay, babe, I'll trust you on this. Just be careful."

"I know, Ky," I say. "I will."

～

I LOOK DOWN at the long list of unanswered emails. I'm still playing catch up after our impromptu skydiving trip last week. Every time I think about how it felt to jump out of that plane, I get a renewed rush of exhilaration. I never would have done something like that on my own. My mind was racing with excuses the entire time, but it was incredible. The whole world was stretched out below us, tiny and insignificant. And when we jumped—oh my god. It was fun and terrifying and thrilling all at once.

The sex when we got back to Ronan's place wasn't bad either.

I'm still a bit tense at work. We aren't exactly hiding our relationship, but we're not being completely open about it either. That's at my insistence. He still swears it won't matter—that any gossip will blow over quickly. But I'm not so sure. I'm pretty certain Sarah knows. She gives me odd looks whenever I come out of his office—even if nothing was going on behind his closed door besides a meeting. Which is usually the case.

Not always. But usually.

I really need some coffee, so I head to the break room. The stuff in the cafe downstairs is better, but I don't want to take the time. There's usually a line. I turn the corner and hear voices coming from the small kitchenette.

"Like it isn't obvious?"

I recognize Kelly's voice. She's in Marketing.

"Come on," someone else says. "There's no way she's with him."

I peek around the door and see Kelly talking with Lydia, who's also on the marketing team, and Justin from Sales. Something makes me hesitate—are they talking about me?

"There's totally something going on between them," Kelly says.

"Selene?" Justin says. "I don't know."

Fuck. They *are* talking about me.

"Oh yeah, he's definitely sleeping with her," Lydia says. "Shelley Johnson said she saw Selene come out of his office the other day with sex hair."

"In the office?" Kelly says, her eyes lighting up like it's the best thing she's ever heard. "Oh my god, that's crazy."

"I know," Lydia says. "You'd think Selene would know better."

"Well, come on," Kelly says. "It's Ronan Maddox. Who could resist him? Not me."

"I hope your husband doesn't know that," Lydia says with a laugh.

Kelly laughs right back. "Seriously, that guy is so hot, he's definitely on my list."

"Your list?" Justin asks, sounding clueless as usual.

"Yeah, you know, the list of people you'd get a pass to sleep with if you ever had the chance," Kelly says. "Usually it's celebrities and stuff, but Ronan Maddox is on mine. Damn, that man is fine."

"I don't care how hot he is," Lydia says. "I wouldn't do it."

"Why are you all judgy about it?" Kelly asks. "You dated that sales guy for a while."

"He wasn't my boss," Lydia says. "There's a big difference. Selene already thinks she runs this place. If she's sleeping with the boss, that's only going to get worse."

"She's not that bad," Kelly says. "Now you just sound jealous."

"I'm hardly jealous," Lydia says. "But watch. Selene's going to get some big promotion, and we're going to know exactly why."

I back away from the room, a sick feeling in the pit of my stomach. This is exactly what I was afraid of. I hurry back to my office. I don't want one of them to come out into the hallway and realize I heard. I'm embarrassed enough as it is.

Sex hair? Fuck.

When I get back to my desk, I have a message from Ronan. *Can I see you in my office?*

Ordinarily, that little message would fill me with anticipation. He might just need to chat with me about something business-related. Or, he might be standing in his office with a velvet rope, ready to tie up my hands and fuck me on his desk. But right now, I don't want to play his games. We've been pushing the boundaries of what's appropriate at work way too much.

Is it urgent? I type back. *Busy.*

It can wait. Lunch?

That probably means it's business. *Sure.*

I don't get much done in the two hours leading up to lunch. I keep going over what I heard in the break room. I just met with the development team the other day, and filled them in on the new direction for VI and the integration with Edge. Do they know about us too? Were they sitting there thinking, *Of course Selene is encouraging us to trust Ronan. She's banging him, so...* Is everyone going to see an ulterior motive in everything I do?

This is one of the reasons I always stuck to my rule about dating coworkers. Things can get so awkward in the office.

And like Lydia said, I'm not just dating a coworker. I'm dating my *boss*. Everyone's boss.

God, what am I doing?

Ronan knocks on my door and pokes his head in. "Ready? I was thinking Indian sounds good."

"Can we just meet here really quick?" I ask. "I have a lot to do." *And I don't want to be seen leaving for lunch with you. Again.*

His brow furrows. "What's going on that has you so busy?"

"Nothing," I say with a wave of my hand. "Just the usual."

"Then I'm pretty sure you can come have lunch with me," he says.

I keep my eyes on my computer screen. "No, I really can't."

He quietly shuts the door and takes a seat across the desk from me. "Selene, what's going on?"

"Nothing."

He rests his elbow on the arm of the chair and puts a hand to his chin, looking at me with those piercing gray eyes. "Yes, there is. Tell me."

I don't know if I want to discuss this with him. He's set above the world of office gossip. Untouchable. He won't care what people say about him because he's the owner. What are they going to do? They have to respect him. Not to mention there's a maddening double standard. In the minds of most people in the office, Ronan sleeping with me makes him, at worst, an opportunist. He's a man, having sex with a woman. Not a slut or a whore. But me? Oh, they'll think all sorts of things about me, none of them flattering.

"I heard some people talking in the break room," I say. "About me. About us."

"What did they say?" he asks, his voice completely neutral.

"They were speculating as to whether we're sleeping together," I say. "Apparently people are saying I came out of your office the other day with sex hair."

The corners of his mouth turn up. "You probably did."

"Fuck you, Ronan," I say, a flash of anger burning through me. "This isn't a joke."

The lines of his jaw stand out and his eyes narrow. "I don't consider it a joke."

"I work my ass off for this company," I say. "I earned every bit of respect I have from the team. But now people aren't going to see Selene Taylor. They're going to see Ronan Maddox's fucking mistress."

I regret the words—and my tone—as soon as I say it. I shouldn't lash out at him. It's not his fault. He was persistent, but I made my own choices.

"All right," he says, and stands. "I'll back off."

His tone is so cold, it's like a slap to the face. He walks out of my office and shuts the door behind him.

I lean my head back against my chair and breathe out a heavy sigh. Fuck. I just made that situation worse.

Maybe Ronan and I should have been more open about our

relationship from the beginning. The fact that we've been more or less hiding it makes the potential for gossip even higher. People love to think they've discovered a dirty secret. If I'm going to date Ronan—if we're going to have an honest to goodness relationship and not just a hot fling—I'm going to have to live with what some people in the office think. I can't control their opinions, and what they think of me shouldn't matter so much. But it does. I've spent my entire career navigating the ins and outs of snap judgments and misinterpretations of who I am.

I'm aware of what I look like. I'm tall and beautiful, and there's no conceit in me knowing it. But it means a lot of people don't take me seriously. I can't count the number of times I've been told I should "go be a model." Sometimes it's meant as a compliment, but often buried in the comment is the implication that my best assets are my face and my body. That the fact that I have long legs, big boobs, and a fortunate bone structure means there must not be much more to me.

There's some irony in complaining about being beautiful. I understand that plenty of women would kill for a body like mine, and I appreciate it for what it is. But I've always felt like I have to work a little harder to earn the respect of my coworkers, and I hate that dating Ronan is jeopardizing that.

Is there a way to make this work? And *is* this more than a hot fling? Am I putting my career at risk for a man who's going to chase the next sexy pair of legs that catches his eye?

I close my laptop and unplug the power supply. I need to get out of here. I send a quick text to Kylie, telling her I need to talk, and gather up my things. I'll probably get more work done at home anyway. At least I won't be wondering what everyone is saying about me on the other side of my door.

My focus isn't much better sitting at my dining table than it was at my desk. Around five, I give up and pour myself a glass of wine. I'm not being very productive, so I figure I ought to stop staring at my computer screen.

There's a knock at my door. I'm expecting Kylie, but not till later—and she would just use her key. I set my wine glass down on the coffee table and go to answer the door.

I open it to find Ronan standing on the other side, still dressed in his button-down shirt and slacks, his hair slightly unkempt. He looks like he came straight from the office.

"Can I come in?"

"Yeah, of course."

I close the door behind him and we walk into the kitchen.

"Drink?" I ask.

"Sure."

He leans against the counter, his hands in his pockets. He seems so distant. I know I owe him an apology, but I hate that he didn't touch or kiss me when he first walked in. Maybe I did more damage than I realized.

I pour him a glass of bourbon, and he takes a sip while I refill my wine.

"I'm sorry for what I said earlier," I say. "I was upset, and I took it out on you."

His face softens a little. "You don't need to apologize. I was worried this afternoon when I saw you'd left."

"Worried about what?"

"That you might quit."

"I'm not quitting my job," I say, my voice sharp.

"Don't get defensive," he says. "I don't say that because I think you would make a decision like that lightly. I say that because I need to make sure it doesn't happen."

I watch him for a moment, turning my wineglass in my hand. "Why?"

"Because you're the reason I bought VI."

"What do you mean?" I ask. "You didn't know I worked there when you bought it."

"You're right, I didn't," he says. "But I know that a lot of what made VI worth buying was you. Your fingerprints are on everything. Yes, Brad put together a good team, but it was you who held things together. It was you who drove the company's direction as much as Brad. Maybe more."

I stare at him, not sure what to say.

"I know that I'm walking a line with you," he says. "I don't know what's stronger—my respect for you as a professional, or my feelings for you as a woman."

"Are you saying you think you have to choose between our working relationship and our personal one?"

One corner of his mouth turns up and he walks over to stand in front of me. "I'm saying I'm greedy, and I want both. I love working with you. You're focused and passionate, and you care about your work. And I love..." He stops and sets his drink on the counter. He looks deep into my eyes, and something stirs inside me—a mix of fear and longing. "I think I'm falling in love with you, Selene."

My mouth drops open and my heart races. Did he just say what I think he said? I blink, trying to see the pretense in his eyes, but there's nothing but raw honesty.

He licks his lips and touches my face. "I didn't think you'd say nothing to that."

"I'm sorry," I say, slightly breathless. "That was unexpected."

I need to say something else. The crack in my protective shell widens as his eyes bore into me. Can I really let him in? Can I risk this?

My voice is barely a whisper. "I think I'm falling in love with you too."

An easy smile spreads over Ronan's face. His lips come to mine and he kisses me, deep and slow, tangling his fingers in my hair. I'm lost in the feel of him, falling through the air like we just jumped out of a plane. He wraps me in his arms. His kiss is luxurious. I run my hands through his hair and press my body against him.

Whatever else happens at work, I'm too far gone to stop this now.

21

RONAN

I hang up the phone after what may prove to be the most important phone call of my career. The meeting is on, and we'll have the chance to pitch our plan to get the biggest contract I've ever gone after. My thoughts swirl and I lean back in my chair, putting a hand to my chin. I'm feeling a little invincible right now.

I get a sudden craving for speed. For freefall. But I'll have to wait to indulge it, because I have a shit ton of work to do and several meetings that are too important to miss.

I can't wait to tell Selene. Her hard work is as much a part of this as anyone's. My hand hovers over my keyboard, about to type a message asking her to come to my office. But we have a meeting in ten minutes; knowing her, she's already in the conference room preparing. I'll wait. Maybe I'll tell her over dinner.

Just thinking about Selene sends a strange warmth through me. I'm still reeling from the fact that I told her I'm falling in love with her. I didn't plan on saying that. That wasn't why I went straight to her house when I found out she'd left work early that day. I knew she was upset about the rumors, and I had to make sure it wasn't going to drive her away. On the way to her house, all I thought about was what the company would do if we lost her. I didn't let myself think about what *I* would do. I couldn't. Wrestling with that would mean I'd have to face what I was feeling. And that was too fucking much.

Until the words came out of my mouth.

It was a rush just to say it. To admit what I've known for quite some time. Selene isn't a game. She's not a prize, or an accomplishment I can add to my trophy case. She's an unbelievable woman—smart, funny, sexy as hell. She's opened up a place inside me that I didn't think was there anymore. I thought it died a long time ago. But somehow, she found it. She drew it out and made it live again.

The fear is still there. But I've never been one to shy away from fear. I use it. Embrace it. So I pushed past it and admitted that I love her. And fuck, I'm glad I did. I do love her, and hearing her say it back made it worth the risk to bare my soul to her.

Sarah knocks on my door. "You have a minute?"

"Sure, come on in."

She takes a seat across my desk. "Well?"

I can't help the smile that crosses my face. "We got it."

"Are you serious?"

"Completely," I say. "They're coming here next month. We have a lot to do to prepare, but we have our shot."

Sarah shakes her head slowly. "I almost can't believe you're pulling this off. But then again, you are ... you."

I smile again. "Anything else? I have a meeting and then I'm ducking out early. I think I deserve it."

"I'd say so," she says. "If that's the case, mind if I head out when you do?"

"Hot date?"

"Yes, as a matter of fact, I do have a hot date," she says with a smile. "What about you? Seeing Selene tonight?"

I lean back in my chair. "Yes."

She raises her eyebrows. "We're admitting to this now?"

I shrug. "I've never denied it."

"You haven't exactly been forthcoming."

"You didn't ask," I say.

"All right, I'm asking," she says. "And not as your assistant, but as your friend."

"Asking what? There wasn't a question."

She rolls her eyes. "You're such an ass. Are you in a relationship with her?"

"Yes."

"So, is this the usual thing?" she asks, her voice hesitant.

"What does that mean?"

"You know what it means," she says. "How long is this going to last?"

"Are you asking me to put a time limit on my relationship?"

"No, I'm asking you if you're serious about her."

"Why?"

She sighs. "Because we've been friends since we were nineteen, Ronan. Sometimes friends talk about things. In sentences. Without deflecting by asking more questions. So I'll ask you again. Are you serious about Selene?"

"Extremely."

She raises her eyebrows again. "Extremely? Now you need to tell me what that means."

I look away. I'm usually pretty open with Sarah. She's known me long enough. "She's different. It's been a long time since I saw myself having a future with someone."

"Since Chelsea?" she asks, her voice quiet.

"Yes, since Chelsea," I say. For the first time, saying her name doesn't hurt. "Fuck, Sarah, I'm not going to lie to you. I'm crazy about her."

"Wow," she says. "I'm really happy for you."

"What are people in the office saying about her?" I ask.

"In regards to the two of you?" she asks. "People are just speculating. You don't exactly hide the way you look like you want to eat her for dinner. The problem is, people fill in the blanks. Your reputation followed you back to Seattle, so people make assumptions."

"My reputation?"

Sarah tilts her head and raises her eyebrows. "Come on, don't tell me you've never heard what people call you."

I'm not sure I want to hear this. "I don't believe I have."

"CEPD?"

"What the fuck are you talking about?"

"Chief Executive Panty Dropper," Sarah says.

In another context, that might be funny, but I don't find it amusing. "That's idiotic."

"Yes, it is," she says. "It's immature and silly. But you asked what people are saying. Office buzz is that you're having a sort-of-secret fling with Selene. Mostly people wonder if she'll quit when—or, I guess, *if* it ends between you."

I shift in my chair. That's about enough sharing for today. "All right, get out of here. Have a good date."

She shakes her head. "Okay, you too. And congrats on the meeting."

"Thanks."

Sarah leaves, and I close my laptop and grab my phone. The meeting is in the large conference room. I brought up some of the key people from the dev team in San Francisco, and they'll be reporting their progress on the work they're doing with the developers here.

As I suspected, Selene is already here, standing at the front of the room chatting with one of the dev guys. I hesitate just inside the door, looking at her. She's wearing a fitted cream blouse with the top two buttons undone, a dark gray pencil skirt, and a pair of sexy black heels with straps across the tops of her feet. The strappy shoes put some interesting thoughts into my head.

I step to the side and people file in, taking their places around the table. Selene glances over and meets my eyes with a little smile, just the slightest curve to her lips.

The things I want to do to that mouth.

I take a seat at the back and rest my elbow on the armrest, my fingers on my chin. This project is becoming Selene's baby as much as mine, so I'm content to let her take the lead.

She starts the meeting with her usual relaxed efficiency, revisiting the goals we've laid out for the company, and summarizing the progress we've made. Her eyes sweep over the entire room, but I catch her gaze at every opportunity. I'm mesmerized, watching her lips as she speaks, her hands gesture, her legs move, pressing against that skirt as she takes slow steps across the front of the room. And those shoes. Fuck, she looks hot in those heels.

When she finishes, she gives the floor to the lead developer, and comes to the back of the room, taking a seat in the opposite corner.

My attention should be on the front of the room, but Selene crosses her legs and blood rushes to my groin. Her eyes flick over to me and she gives me that sultry almost-smile again. She shifts in her seat and slides a hand up her thigh, to the hem of her skirt, and pushes it up, just a little. Her fingers swirl across her skin, dipping beneath her skirt and out again. I have to stop myself from groaning.

With her face still pointed dutifully at the presentation, she lifts her hand to her neck and traces the line of her shirt collar.

She trails her hand down and brushes the backs of her fingers across her nipple, setting me on fire with lust. I suck in a breath and give the room a quick glance. Everyone's backs are to us. My dirty girl knows exactly what she's doing and it's driving me crazy.

Still not looking at me, she leans down, as if she needs to adjust her shoe. She runs her fingers up her leg, ankle to skirt hem, reminding me of the silky feel of her skin. I can't even pretend I'm paying attention to the meeting, and my dick is so hard I'm going to have to be careful when I stand up so I don't cause a fucking scene.

Selene flips her hair over her shoulder and brings her hand to her chin. Slowly, she slides her fingers up to her mouth and her tongue darts between her lips. My heart races, the blood pumping so hard I can feel it in my temples. She dips the tip of her index finger into her mouth and sucks, just for a second, then draws it out again. She pauses, her eyes still on the front of the room, then does it again. In, and out, her tongue flicking across her lips.

Adrenaline bursts through me. My eyes are locked on Selene, the droning voice at the front of the room fading in the wake of the desire I can barely contain.

She brings her hand to her neck and trails her fingers down between the open top buttons of her blouse. Tilting her face toward me ever so slightly, she meets my eyes and blinks, then licks her lips with exaggerated slowness. She drags her teeth over her bottom lip and holds my gaze. I can see her unspoken words written all over her face. *I'm going to fuck you later.*

Oh, no, my dirty girl. I am going to fuck *you* later. And I'm going to make you pay for this torture session.

Selene stops her little game, and I'm mostly grateful because I'm so fucking turned on I can barely see straight. I wait in the back of the room, watching her while she finishes up the meeting and chats with a few people as the rest file out and go back to their desks. Her gaze flicks to me a few times but I just stare at her, unwavering. It gives me time to think of all the things I'm going to do to her when I get her alone.

The last person leaves the room, and Selene picks up a stack of papers. Her back is to me and I quickly cross the distance between us. I lean my face into her neck so I can speak directly into her ear.

"You're a naughty little minx, my dirty girl," I say, my voice breathy against her skin. "You think you can get away with playing with me like that?"

I can almost feel her hard swallow, the stiffness of her body, the quickening of her breath. I stand behind her, not quite touching. My hands ache to be all over her, but I hold back. I have something special in store, and it begins right here.

"You need to be reminded who's the boss," I say.

"Do I?" she breathes.

I spare a quick glance out the door to make sure we're truly alone, then grab her hair and lean her head to the side, baring her neck to me. "Yes, you do. Be at my place at six on the dot. You earn an additional punishment for every minute you're late." I graze my teeth across her skin. "And wear these shoes."

I let go and walk away without looking at her, high as fuck on the feeling of dominance she's giving me. I'll show her who's boss, and she's going to love every second of it.

22

SELENE

*M*y hands tremble and my heart wants to crack my ribs wide open. I pull out my phone and glance at the time. Five fifty-nine. I stand in front of Ronan's door, waiting to knock. He didn't say anything about being early, but he did say six on the dot.

I'm not quite sure what I'm getting myself into tonight, but his little chat with me after the meeting had me almost panting with desire. I think my game in the conference room might have worked too well. He watched me like a predator sizing up his prey, his gray eyes so intense I was sure anyone who looked at him could read his (very dirty) thoughts.

After the meeting, I went back to my office, my vision blurry, and pretended to work until I could leave. The throbbing between my legs hasn't let up since, and I almost got myself off in the shower when I was getting ready. I stopped, though. I want him to do it. I want to come to him hot and wet and ready.

None of which is going to be a problem.

Six o'clock. I knock on his door.

He opens it, dressed to the nines in a slate-gray suit, complete with tie. I feel a momentary pang of disappointment.

Are we going out? We're meeting Braxton and Kylie for drinks later, but maybe he wants dinner first. I'm not really dressed up —I'm wearing a fluttery gold halter top with distressed jeans and the heels I wore to work—and I wonder if I missed a text from him, telling me what the plan is for tonight.

His eyes rove up and down and he steps aside, gesturing for me to come in. He closes the door behind me and grabs my wrist.

"Are you ready for this, my naughty girl?" he says into my ear.

I gasp a little breath, and my back tightens. Maybe he doesn't want to go out. "Yes."

His lips brush my neck. "If I do anything you don't like tonight, tell me to stop, and I will. You're safe with me."

I swallow hard and nod. He steps away, letting go of my arm.

"You seem to have forgotten that I'm the boss," he says, his voice going icy cold. "I'm in charge. From this moment forward, you will not speak unless I tell you. You will not move unless I tell you, and you will move only as instructed. Is that clear?"

I nod again, practically shivering, and bite the inside of my lip. My panties are completely drenched already, and he's barely touched me.

"You thought your little game in the conference room was fun, didn't you?" he asks, taking slow steps in front of me, his hands clasped behind his back.

He didn't tell me to speak, so I wait, my eyes locked on his face.

Instantly, he's right in front of me, his hand an iron grip on the back of my neck. "That was very naughty, Selene. You made my cock so hard I couldn't think. All I wanted was the feel of your skin. The taste of your pussy. The heat of your body. I can't work like that, dirty girl. I lost my whole afternoon to fantasizing about what I'm going to do to you."

He pulls his hand away, sliding it along the base of my jaw. I want to grab his tie and force his mouth to mine, but he didn't tell me to move, and I'm determined to play his game.

"Good," he says, holding my eyes. "Come in."

He walks into his condo and I follow. The lights are low, and soft music drifts from the speakers. It would be a relaxing scene, but for the fire racing through my body.

Ronan stands a few feet in front of me and puts his hands in his pockets. "Strip."

I try not to smile—I'm not sure if I'm allowed—and put my purse down on a side table. Slowly, I reach behind my neck and unfasten the clasp that holds up my shirt. I pull it over my head and let it drop to the floor. Ronan watches me, unmoving, but I can see the hunger in his eyes. I unzip my jeans and slide them down.

"Leave the shoes."

It's a little awkward getting my jeans over my heels, but I manage to do it while still feeling like a sex goddess. I stand in front of him, wearing only my lacy strapless bra and matching thong. He raises an eyebrow and I reach back, unhooking my bra, and let it drop. Then I slide my fingers beneath the waist of my thong and push it slowly down my legs, kicking it off when it gets to my feet.

I stand up again, naked save for my shoes. He licks his lips.

"Touch your nipples," he says. "Slowly."

My mouth drops open, but I comply, rubbing my fingers over my nipples, and feel them harden.

"Slide your hands down," he says. "That's it, dirty girl. All the way down."

I move my hands down my body to my hips, and angle them in.

"Keep going," he says. "Touch yourself."

I find my clit with two fingers and rub a slow circle. My heart beats faster and heat rises between my legs.

"Stop," he says, his voice still like frozen steel. "Bedroom."

I take a deep breath and walk past him toward the bedroom, but he keeps his hands in his pockets and doesn't touch me. I notice the blinds are already closed throughout his whole apartment. My heart is beating wildly as I stop in front of the bed.

He comes in and takes off his jacket, laying it on the back of a chair. Then he loosens his tie. "Sit down."

I lower myself onto the edge of the bed, and he stands in front of me. I watch his face, struggling to contain myself. He unfastens his tie and slides it through the collar of his shirt, then loosens the top two buttons.

Fucking hell, he looks so sexy like that.

"Hands," he says.

Oh my god. I hold out my arms, wrists together, trying not to shake. He binds my wrists, just tight enough that I know I won't be able to get free.

"On your knees, facing the headboard," he says.

I comply, although putting my back to him sends a renewed flurry of nervousness through my belly. He climbs onto the bed and ties my wrists to the headboard. His hands finally touch my skin again, grabbing my hips. He eases me backward so I'm bent at the waist, my arms stretched out.

He rubs one hand up the back of my thigh and palms my ass. My breath starts to go ragged and my pussy throbs again. I tilt my hips to the side, trying to force his hand near my center, but he squeezes my flesh.

"No moving until I say so," he says. "Don't worry, I'll give you everything you want, Selene. Everything you need. But I have to punish you first."

Never in my life did I think those words would elicit the flood of lust that overtakes me. I am not a child—if any man before Ronan had used the word *punish* while I was naked and bared to him, I would have been out so fast he wouldn't know what happened.

But Ronan ... I want him to. I want to play this game. I want him to make me pay for being naughty, like the dirty girl I am. It's a thrill I've never had before.

"Do you know why you're being punished, Selene?" he asks. "Answer."

"For teasing you at work," I say.

"Exactly," he says, rubbing his hand up and down my ass and lower back. "Don't make a sound." He smacks my right cheek, and I bite my lip against the sting. Immediately his hand rubs the spot. "Ooh, poor baby. Did that hurt?"

I nod.

"Do you want another?"

I nod again.

He smacks the other side, the light sting sending a jolt of electricity through me. It doesn't hurt enough to be upsetting, just a sharp burn that fades quickly. He rubs it with a gentle touch.

"I don't want to hurt you," he says, his voice low. His fingers brush my folds and I try not to moan. "But I will drive you crazy, like you drove me crazy today."

He slips a finger inside and I arch my back, trying to get more. He presses against my ass, not letting me move.

"Not yet," he says, circling his wet finger around my clit. I shudder and bite my lip again. "Fuck, Selene, I want to taste you. Look at me."

I turn my head over my shoulder and watch as he slides his fingers into me, then brings them to his mouth and licks. His eyes flutter closed for a second and I see the tight grip he's trying to maintain on his self-control start to waver. He puts his fingers in again, rubbing me just how I like it, hard against the front of my pussy where I'm so sensitive. Relief floods through me as he rocks my hips back and forth, letting me grind against his hand.

"Is this what you need?" he asks.

"God, yes."

He slides his fingers out and I'm left panting, my arms starting to ache. A whimper escapes my lips.

The bed shifts beneath my knees and suddenly Ronan is lying on his back, his head between my legs.

"Get down here," he says. "I want my mouth on you."

He pushes my knees apart, widening my legs, until I'm straddling his face. The new angle relieves the strain on my arms, but his mouth on my pussy almost sends me tumbling over a cliff. His velvety tongue slides up and down, putting exquisite pressure on my clit. I moan as he licks me, clamping my mouth shut so I don't make too much noise. I'm afraid if I talk, he'll stop what he's doing, and I need him to make me come. I need it so bad I can hardly think.

He drags his tongue in and out of my pussy, his hands grabbing my ass, rocking me back and forth over his mouth. I'm rolling toward climax, my core clenching. He sucks on my clit and I throw my head back, unable to contain the shriek that rips from my throat.

He stops, holding me right on the edge, his tongue suddenly soft and gentle. I try to grind into him, but he grips my ass with hard fingers and stops me from moving.

"Not yet, dirty girl," he says, and flicks my clit again. "You didn't have my permission to make noise."

He gets out from under me while I take panting breaths. My entire body aches for release. I'm so desperate I'll do anything he asks.

He runs his hands along my arms and loosens the knot at the headboard. With my wrists still tied together, he turns me over onto my back and kneels in front of me. He still has his pants on, although at some point he took off his shirt. I don't remember him doing it. He leans forward and kisses down my arms. "Do your arms hurt? Is this better?"

I nod, still breathing hard.

"Tell me what you need," he says.

"I need you inside me," I say, barely able to get the words out.

"What do you need inside you?" he asks, brushing his fingers up my thighs. "My fingers? My tongue?"

"No."

"Tell me."

"I need your cock inside me," I say. "Please, Ronan."

"I need it, too," he says, his voice a low growl. "I've needed it all fucking day."

He pulls off his pants, his thick erection springing in front of him, and sinks on top of me, his chest over my hips. He runs his tongue up my stomach as he crawls forward. When he gets to my breasts, he lingers, tracing my nipple with his tongue.

"Fuck, Ronan, please," I say.

He kisses higher, and I feel the tip of his cock teasing outside my opening. I want to grab his hips and push him into me, but my wrists are bound. I'm helpless, totally at his mercy. He nibbles my collarbone, digging in his teeth until it almost hurts.

With a hard thrust, he plunges in. I close my eyes, reveling in the feel of his thickness stretching me open, filling me completely.

"Are you okay?" he asks, speaking low in my ear.

His sudden concern for my well-being unmakes me, opening me to him more fully than I've ever been. "Yes," I say, almost breathless. "Just make me come. Please. I can't stand it anymore."

"Neither can I," he says. "I'm going to make you come. Then I'm going to come in you *so fucking hard*."

He picks himself up, holding onto the headboard with one

hand, giving me a perfect view of his exquisite body. His broad
chest, muscular arms and shoulders, the hard edges of his abs.
He drives into me, fierce and frenetic. I lose myself, any sense of
control I had completely gone.

"Yes, fuck yes, harder," I say. There's no more punishment for
talking. He gives me what I need, his cock so deep, his pelvic
bone grinding against my clit with every thrust. My eyes roll
back in my head, and the power, the agony, the bliss all sweep
me away. My muscles tense, so tight I can't breathe.

And then, the release. Blinding waves of pleasure tear
through me. Ronan's cock pulses and we both call out, primal
and unrestrained. I'm soaring, free-falling through nothing.
Ronan doesn't stop, his hips driving hard.

I'm lost. Taken. Completely his.

Eventually the pulses subside, and he lowers himself over
me. He puts one hand on the side of my face and stares into my
eyes. His lips meet mine, so soft and sweet.

"I love you," he says, and kisses my cheeks and my forehead.

His sudden gentleness disarms me and tears spring to my
eyes. "I love you, too."

He rests his forehead against mine. "Thank you for trusting
me."

"Thank you for letting me."

23

SELENE

*I*t feels like I'm coming to after losing consciousness, but I don't think I was asleep. I blink, looking up at the ceiling. I'm lying on my back, splayed across the bed. My body is so spent I'm not sure if I can move.

Ronan props himself up next to me and reaches for my hands. He unfastens the knot, slipping off the tie, and brings one arm to his mouth. He kisses the vulnerable skin on the inside of my wrist, rubbing the base of my palm with his thumb.

"Are you all right?" he asks.

"Yes. You didn't hurt me."

"Good." He kisses my other wrist, his lips warm on my skin. "Did you learn your lesson?"

My mouth turns up in a smile. "Yes."

"Are you going to be a naughty girl again?" he asks.

"Definitely."

He laughs and kisses me again. "You're the most amazing woman I've ever known, Selene Taylor."

"And you are nothing like I thought you would be, Ronan Maddox."

I glance over and look at the time. "We should probably get up. We're going to be late."

Reluctantly, we both get up and get dressed to meet Braxton and Kylie. I'm hit with another flutter of nerves. Back before Brax and Ky got together, the triple date test was always important to me. The three of us are so comfortable with each other, hanging out is as natural as breathing. But anytime we added a boyfriend or girlfriend to the mix, the dynamic changed. I insisted we get together as couples to make sure we could all still hang out—that if one of those relationships turned out to be *the* relationship, it wouldn't separate us as friends. Since Braxton and Kylie married each other, the worry over whether either of them will wind up with someone the rest of us don't like is gone. Now it's down to me.

I'm in so deep with Ronan; I'm worried I've fallen too fast. He hasn't passed what's now the double date test. He met Braxton and Kylie the night I was assaulted, but that wasn't under regular circumstances, and he and I were still dancing around our attraction to each other. Or rather, I was dancing around my attraction to him, keeping him at a distance, while he made it abundantly clear what he wanted from me. But tonight is the test. Braxton is always suspicious of the men I date, so I don't expect them to be fast friends. But will there be a glimmer of hope that the four of us could spend time together and it wouldn't be strained?

I don't know if I've made it completely clear to Ronan how important Braxton and Kylie are to me. They're almost the entirety of my family. Brax and I don't have anyone else left. Our parents died, and our one living relative was the aunt who raised us. She died years ago, and it's been just the two of us ever since. The two of us, plus Kylie and her dad, Henry. That's it.

We have friends, and coworkers, and people who have moved in and out of our lives over the years. But aside from that, there's no one else. I can't have a future with any man who puts a wedge between my brother and me. And as I freshen up in Ronan's bathroom, I find myself desperately hoping that tonight goes well. I want to keep the flame of hope alive, that Ronan is something special.

We get to the restaurant later than planned, but Brax and Ky aren't here yet either. We find a booth in the bar and order drinks.

I still feel flushed from earlier. Ronan leans back in his seat, looking completely relaxed, his arm stretched out behind me. He didn't put the suit back on, nor *the tie*, opting instead for a casual blue top with three buttons at the collar, layered over a crisp white t-shirt, and a pair of muted green slacks. My hair doesn't look quite as nice as it did when I first arrived at Ronan's place, but I managed to tame it down and fix my makeup. I put my gold halter top and jeans back on, and feel reasonably put together for a Friday night out.

Braxton and Kylie show up a few minutes later. Brax is sporting his fifties bad boy look with a black leather jacket over a white t-shirt and a pair of jeans. Kylie is cute, as usual, in a pale blue top and little black skirt, her dark hair down around her face.

"Hey, sorry we're late," Kylie says.

"It's fine, we pretty much just got here," I say. "So, you guys met Ronan once, but Ronan, this is my brother Braxton and his wife, Kylie. Guys, this is Ronan Maddox."

Braxton looks Ronan right in the eyes and gives him an easy smile while they shake hands. "Nice to see you again."

Kylie smiles and greets him warmly, and they both slide into the booth across from us.

Brax sits back, his face totally relaxed, and drapes his arm across the seat behind Kylie. "Did you guys order yet?"

"Just drinks," I say. I keep waiting for the tension to rise, but

Brax looks ... happy. He plays with Kylie's hair and asks Ronan a few questions. The two of them start chatting about football—one of Braxton's favorite subjects—and Kylie gets up.

"I just need to run to the ladies' room," she says. "Can you order for me?"

"Sure, baby girl," Braxton says, his mouth turning up in a lazy smile.

I get out of the booth and meet Ronan's eyes. "I'll be right back."

I follow Kylie to the bathroom, grateful there's no one else in there when we get inside.

Kylie looks at herself in the mirror and fluffs her long, dark hair. "Sorry, I'm um ... a little warm." She fans herself.

"Are you okay?" I ask.

"Yeah, I'm great." She turns to look at me. "I just, you know, didn't want Braxton coming to dinner with a loaded weapon, so..."

I laugh. "Gotcha."

"You know, the only thing that sucks about being married to your brother is that I can't talk to you about my sex life anymore," she says.

"That does kind of suck," I say. Kylie and I were always really open about that sort of thing. We told each other everything. More or less. "You know what, talk to me anyway. We've been sharing this stuff with each other since ... well, since there was anything to share."

"You sure?" she asks.

"Positive," I say. "Maybe just stop yourself from describing anything where I have to generate a mental picture."

She laughs. "That's fair." She takes a deep breath. "So, he does this thing where he goes down on me and gives me two orgasms, one right on top of the other. And that's all before he even, you know, has his turn. And usually there's another one when he goes. But fuck, it's kind of exhausting. I feel like I want to crawl in bed right now instead of sit in a bar. I meant for it to be a quickie before we left, but he doesn't really do quick."

"Damn," I say. "No wonder you married him."

She lifts her eyebrows. "Right?"

I lick my lips, and my mind goes to the mild ache between my legs.

"You obviously fired the cannon before you guys came," Kylie says with a knowing smile.

"Is it that obvious?" I ask.

"On you? Only because I know you," she says. "Ronan though. Look at his face when we come out of the bathroom. I bet you twenty bucks he and Braxton are wearing identical expressions. It must have been pretty good."

I roll my eyes upward. "God, Kylie, it was ... holy shit. He..." I stop and purse my lips together.

"Oh, now you really have to tell me," she says.

"He tied me up and punished me."

Her mouth drops open. "Holy shit."

"I know," I say. "He didn't hurt me or anything like that. But god, it was phenomenal."

"I kind of want more details because that sounds fun," she says.

"Just imagine a necktie, a headboard, and being told not to speak or move without permission. Then there was some spanking, and a lot of touching and teasing before we finally got to it."

"Damn, that's hot," she says. "You were good with all that? Were you worried he'd take it too far?"

"No, I wasn't worried at all. I trust him." I pause again. "Ky, he said the L word."

She gasps. "What?"

"I know," I say. "He did. He said he loves me. He's said it more than once."

"Wait, when you were tied up?" she asks.

"No, he said it for the first time last week."

"And did you say it back?" she asks.

I know her question means more than whether or not I said the words. She wants to know if I meant it. "I did."

She puts a hand to her mouth. "Selene, this is a big deal."

"Yeah, it is."

"That's not what I expected you to tell me tonight," she says. "But I'm so happy for you."

"Thanks, Ky." I glance at the door. "We should probably get back to them. Unloaded weapons or not, I don't want to leave Brax alone with Ronan for too long."

"Good plan."

We come out of the restroom and make our way back to our booth to find drinks on the table and the two men chatting amiably. Kylie was right, they do have identical expressions on their faces. They both look laid-back, almost tranquil. We take our seats, and Ronan is telling Braxton about Edge Gear and their recent breakthroughs in technical fabrics. After a while, the conversation turns back to sports. Braxton is fascinated by Ronan's extreme sports passion, and Ronan listens with rapt attention as Braxton talks about some training techniques that could improve Ronan's rock climbing.

We all have a few more drinks and chat late into the night. I try not to stare at Braxton, but I'm amazed. His easy mood is not just the result of recent sex with his wife, regardless of how hot or kinky it might have been. I'm almost afraid to think it, but Braxton seems to like Ronan. He never likes men I date. I didn't think he'd be any different with Ronan. It isn't like Ronan doesn't have the same reputation for arrogance and womanizing that the last few guys had. But Braxton never gives him the glowering stare I'm so used to seeing.

We're all pretty tipsy by the end of the night, but we're

walking distance from my house, and Brax and Ky don't have to drive home either. We get up from the table and Ronan excuses himself to the bathroom, so the rest of us wait in the lobby.

I look up at Braxton. He's one of the few men I know who is actually tall enough that I have to look up, even when I'm wearing heels. "So, say something."

He gives me an easy smile. "About what?"

"About Ronan."

"He's a good guy," Braxton says with a nod.

"That's it?"

"What am I supposed to say?" he asks with a laugh.

"What you think of him," I say. "You didn't glare at him across the table all night, and I want to know why."

Braxton looks at me for a long moment. "He protected you when you needed help. That earned him a lot of points in my book. And he looks at you the way a man should look at you."

I'm about to ask what he means when Ronan returns, putting a gentle hand on my elbow.

"Ready?" Ronan asks.

"Yeah."

Ronan takes my hand, twining our fingers together. We say goodbye to Braxton and Kylie outside, and walk back to my place in a comfortable silence.

24

RONAN

*S*elene and I get out of my car and head into the hangar. After our last skydive, Selene decided she wanted to do it again. I hardly need an excuse to take to the air, so I was thrilled. Since she wanted to be able to jump on her own, she took the five hour skydiving course a week ago. The weather didn't cooperate that day, so we didn't get to jump. But today dawned clear, and the forecast calls for nothing but sun. It's the perfect day to fly.

After a quick safety overview, we get geared up and head out to the plane. The air is chilly, and it will be colder up high, but my blood pumps hard, warming me. Selene's eyes sparkle with excitement. I love sharing this with her, although I feel an unfamiliar twinge of fear as we board the plane. I'm not scared for myself—I'm buzzing with adrenaline in anticipation of the rush I know is coming. I'm worried about Selene. I know she can handle herself, and she's been through the proper preparation. Yet I can't shake the slight feeling of darkness that threatens my euphoria.

The plane takes off, the engines roaring. We watch the ground fall away below us through the window. Selene clasps her hands together and chews on her lower lip. I know she's nervous. We'll be jumping together, and I'll be in constant physical contact with her until we deploy our chutes. She also has a radio in her helmet, connecting her to someone on the ground who will help guide her landing. It allays my fear a bit to know I'll be with her the whole way down.

We circle wide, giving us a chance to appreciate the incredible views. My limbs tingle and I'm getting restless.

"You okay?" Selene asks, pitching her voice to be heard above the noise of the airplane.

"Yeah," I say. "You ready for this?"

She nods and smiles, giving me a thumbs up.

We get to altitude and the jump coordinator opens the door. My heart thunders. Selene and I get into position, holding the bar above the opening. I meet her eyes, grab the strap at her hip, and give her a nod.

She lets go and we both tumble out of the plane. I could have let her jump without me holding her jumpsuit. I know how to navigate while free-falling, and I could have moved to her once we were in the air. But I want the security of my hand on her suit the whole time.

We spread out, horizontal to the ground, our arms and legs held up by the rushing air. Selene hollers with joy as we fall, and I let the high take over. There's nothing like free-falling. High above the world, you're flying, soaring through the fucking sky.

I check my altimeter more than usual, even though I know Selene has a voice in her ear, telling her what to do. I work my way around so I'm holding her arm, but in front of her so she can see me. She smiles, the air buffeting her face, and gives me another thumbs up.

We have about ten seconds before she needs to pull the chute. I'll free-fall a little longer so I get below her and can land first. I want to be on the ground when she comes down in case she has any problems.

I motion to her to pull the cord and let go of her arm. My heart is in my throat, waiting for it to deploy. She pulls the cord and the lines shoot out around her. They're tangled—turned in the wrong direction—and her chute isn't opening properly. It jerks her up and I keep falling, but I can see the chute isn't slowing her nearly enough. I turn so I'm facing skyward, but I can't do anything but fall.

Fuck. Panic constricts my chest, and I can't breathe. She's going to hit the ground. She's going to hit the ground and fucking die because I took her up here.

Deploy the reserve, Selene. I will her to remember what to do, to listen to the instructions I'm sure she's hearing through the radio in her helmet. *Deploy the reserve. Do it, Selene. Don't keep falling. We're getting too low, goddamnit. Deploy the fucking reserve.*

Her main chute jettisons, flying away above her, and the reserve deploys. It opens perfectly, jerking her body, and her legs dangle below her.

I check my altimeter. I'm getting dangerously low. I turn over so I can pull the cord, deploying my own chute, and steer toward the landing zone.

Normally I wish the glide down would last longer, but this time I need to get on the fucking ground. I come in faster than I should, my feet pounding on the dirt as I land. The chute falls, and I unhook the straps, disentangling myself as quickly as I can.

I turn, desperate to see her land safely. She comes in perfectly, guiding her direction with the lines on each side, just like they taught her. The landing crew helps her down, ensuring she doesn't hurt herself when her feet touch. She takes a few quick steps forward and stops, her chute deflating behind her.

I'm on fire with panic and adrenaline as I run over to her. I grab her and crush her against me, fear saturating every fiber of my mind and body. She could have died. Right here, in front of me. She could have died because of me.

I can't live through that again.

I hold her tight and she wraps her arms around me.

"Fuck, are you okay?" I ask.

"Yes," she says. "I'm fine, Ronan. I was scared for a second, but they told me what to do. It was okay."

She tries to pull back, but I can't let her go. Not yet. My body shakes and I can't get enough air. For the first time since I started skydiving all those years ago, I'm not buzzing after a jump. My limbs are heavy and my chest feels like there's a weight sitting on top of it. I wonder if my heart is going to explode into a bloody mess.

"Ronan," she says, pushing against me. "Stop. I'm fine."

I drop my arms, but looking at her doesn't help. She takes off her goggles and smiles, but I can't see her expression. All I see are her eyes wide with fear when the tangled lines twisted around her, the realization that something had gone wrong.

And there was absolutely nothing I could do about it.

Anger flares and I storm into the hangar, looking for Sam, the owner.

"What the fuck happened up there?" I say when I find him at his desk. "She's a fucking beginner."

Sam stands up. "Listen, Mr. Maddox, we've never had a main chute fail in a beginner jump before—"

"I don't give a shit," I say. "You just had one. Who packed her chute?"

"Mr. Maddox, her reserve chute clearly deployed exactly as it was meant to—"

"Fuck the reserve chute," I yell, cutting him off again. "It shouldn't have been necessary. You could have killed her."

I hear Selene running up behind me. "Ronan," she says. "Stop."

"No," I say, a hard edge to my voice. "You sent her up there with a faulty chute. A fucking beginner."

"She was completely safe," Sam says. "Our ground crew was in constant contact, relaying instructions, and Selene handled herself perfectly."

"She was not safe!"

Selene puts her hand on my arm but I shrug her off. I'm so angry, I want to kill these assholes. I whip around and rip my jumpsuit off, tossing the last of the gear on the floor as I make my way to the exit. I have to get the fuck out of here before I hit someone.

I sit in my car, gripping the steering wheel, until Selene comes out a few minutes later. She gets in the car and fastens her seat belt.

"Ronan—"

"No." I don't want to hear her tell me she was fine. She was not fucking fine.

She closes her mouth and sits back in her seat. I start the car and drive out of the parking lot, heading toward the freeway.

Selene is quiet on the drive back to Seattle, looking out the window with her fingers resting against her lips. I almost can't look at her. The quick glances I take out of the corner of my eye make me feel like I'm going to lose control and panic again.

Logically, I know Selene was okay the entire time. A reserve deployment isn't uncommon, although it's unusual in a beginner jump. I'm still livid that they gave her that chute. An experienced jumper can handle a reserve deployment. It happens to anyone if you jump often enough. I've had five, but I've jumped hundreds of times. But she never should have had to face that.

But logic doesn't fucking matter. I saw her. She was free-falling well past the right altitude. If she hadn't been able to get her reserve chute to deploy, if anything else had gone wrong, she would have crashed to the ground, breaking every bone in her body. The image of her lying on the ground, bloody and broken, won't leave my mind.

I can see it all: The blood marring her face. The limbs at odd angles. Her blond hair matted.

No. Selene doesn't have blond hair. That was Chelsea.

Fuck, I'm losing my mind. I haven't let myself think about that in years. Now the vision of Chelsea mingles with the nightmare of Selene hitting the ground. I can't separate them. I turn, forcing myself to look at Selene. She's not dead. She's not hurt. She landed perfectly. But I blink, and the image is there. Pain. Blood. Death.

I can't get it out of my head.

25

RONAN

*B*ourbon isn't helping.

I took Selene home after the skydiving incident yesterday and made an excuse about not feeling well. I went home and tried to bury myself in the bottom of a bottle, but I woke up this morning both hungover and still panicked. My attempts at distraction did me no good, and I couldn't bring myself to send Selene a text asking her how she's doing, let alone see her.

I lean my head back against the couch cushion and close my eyes. The weight of her trust sits heavily on my chest. It's not just that she trusted me enough to jump out of an airplane with me. Maybe if this had happened earlier, before I realized how vulnerable I'd become with her, it wouldn't be hitting me so hard. She's trusted me with everything. Her career. Her body. Her heart. Her life. Her entire fucking life. There's nothing she has that I don't permeate, now that I've broken in.

Because *break in* is exactly what I did. She put up a wall between us when I first came back to Seattle. Brick by brick, I pulled it down, never taking no for an answer. Fuck, she was dating some other guy, and I still pursued her. I got her to agree to stay single. I maneuvered to have lunches and dinners with her as often as I could, pushing against the boundaries she tried to set between us. I wormed my way in, sure that she would be glad when I did. When I conquered her.

When I won.

And once she let me in, I took everything. I'd like to think I earned her trust, and remained worthy of it, but looking back, I don't know. I tempted her, teased her, convinced her to do things she might not otherwise have done. I tied her up and had my fucking way with her, and I loved every second of it. But she let me. She gave me that power. She handed it to me willingly.

Just like she followed me onto that airplane.

The responsibility is too much. I hold her life in my hands and if I fuck this up, in any one of a million ways, I could destroy her. I could ruin her career. Maybe I already have. Did her coworkers lose all respect for her because they know I fucked her on top of my desk? I could break her heart. I've never been a man who could commit. I've always lived for the chase, the thrill of a challenge. What do I do now that the pursuit is over? Now that I have her, what is left? I don't know how to be that guy. I've never done it before.

I could have killed her.

She's made me afraid, something I haven't felt since I was a stupid kid. I used to feed off the fear, but since it left me, I've thrived. I've taken risks no one else will take, and many of them have paid off. They've paid off big, and I can't afford to be weak now.

I swallow the last of the bourbon, my head swimming. I can't be responsible for someone else's career, their life, their happiness. It's too damn much. I know how easily it can be taken. It can all be gone in a second. One fucking second and everything changes.

One second, and everything is gone.

26

SELENE

*R*onan's office door is closed, and Sarah isn't at her desk. It's early, so she's probably not here yet. I stand outside his door, wondering if I should knock. Or just go in. I haven't heard from him since he dropped me off after skydiving on Saturday. No calls. No texts. Ordinarily, that wouldn't be a big deal. But he also wouldn't look at me when he took me home, just mumbled a goodbye, and said he wasn't feeling well. Since then, silence.

I know he was angry about the chute failure. Hell, I was terrified. Those lines sprang up around me, one slapping me across the cheek and snaking across my goggles, and I knew something was wrong. Everything was twisted, and I didn't feel the harness tighten around me. The chute wasn't opening.

The voice of the ground crew was calm and focused. It took me a few seconds to recover, but once I did, I followed the instructions. I remembered the training, and jettisoned the main chute. I pulled the reserve, and it did exactly what it was made to do. It opened above me, and I was jerked upward, slowing dramatically. The rest of the jump went perfectly, with the ground crew guiding me down.

It was a frightening experience, but the fear was already dissipating by the time my feet hit the ground. Until Ronan. I'd never seen him like that before. Wild-eyed, panicked. I can understand that he was worried, but he's an experienced skydiver. He knows that sometimes you have to deploy the reserve. He told me that himself. I was prepared. I knew what to do, and the crew knew how to get me to the ground safely. Everything was fine.

Ronan apparently did not think it was fine. But that doesn't explain why he went dark on me. Why he didn't return my call yesterday.

I'm worried about him. He was so tense, so out of control. I figured he just needed some time to himself, but as I stand here in front of his door, I have a sinking feeling in the pit of my stomach. I wonder if something else is going on.

I take a deep breath and knock. No answer. I know he's here. I'm not too proud to admit I circled the parking garage, looking for his car when I arrived. I knock again. Maybe he's in the building but not in his office. He could have gone down to the lobby for coffee. Or be talking with someone from one of the other departments. He isn't *always* in his office.

But it's barely after seven. Hardly anyone else is here.

Although it feels like an intrusion, I grip the door handle and push. Locked.

Either he's locked himself in, or he's not in there. I go back to my office and send him a message. *Hi. Can we talk?*

I get caught up with work for a while, although the fact that my message goes unanswered isn't far from my thoughts. I walk by his office again, on my way to the copy machine, and Sarah is at her desk. Ronan's door is still closed. I almost ask Sarah if he's in, but for some reason, I can't make myself do it. The longer I go without hearing from him, the more anxious I get. I'm afraid of what she'll tell me.

I have an afternoon meeting, and I glance at the list of invitees after I get back to my desk. Ronan is listed as attending. I wonder if he'll show up.

He's not in the conference room when I arrive at two. I take my seat and scroll through my emails while I wait for it to begin.

The meeting gets going, and Ronan finally slips in, taking a seat in the back of the room instead of at the conference table. I glance at him, but he doesn't meet my eyes. My stomach turns sour. What is going on with him?

I try to pay attention, but I'm too preoccupied. Ronan sits where I can't see him without turning all the way around, but I feel him there. I can picture him leaning back in his chair, his elbow bent, his hand on his chin.

Finally, the meeting ends. I get up and turn in time to see Ronan's back, heading out the door.

What the fuck?

This is getting ridiculous. I follow him back to his office, forcing myself to walk normally so it doesn't look like I'm chasing after him. I don't want to look pathetic in front of the whole staff, but my stomach churns with worry and a dark sense of foreboding follows me. I can tell by the rigid set of his shoulders that something is wrong.

Very wrong.

He passes Sarah without a word and goes into his office, shutting his door behind him. I follow, struggling to keep my composure. He better not lock the damn door.

I turn the handle, and it opens.

He's already sitting at his desk. I don't wait for an invitation. I walk in and shut the door behind me.

Ronan looks up at me, but doesn't hold my gaze. He goes back to something on his laptop. A sudden flash of anger replaces the worry.

"Are you serious?" I ask.

"Excuse me?"

"You're going to completely ignore me?" I ask. "I'm standing right here."

"I know you're there," he says.

"Well, say something. What's going on?"

"Selene, I'm very busy this afternoon," he says. "Can we talk later?"

His voice is so cold, I'm instantly chilled. "Is this about Saturday? Because honestly, I'm fine. It was a little bit scary, but nothing bad actually happened."

"It isn't about Saturday."

Something about the way he says that makes my shoulders tighten. It means I'm not imagining things. There's an *it*. A problem.

I have a feeling I'm about to get hurt.

"What is it, then?" I ask.

"I really don't think we should do this right now—"

"Yes, we should." I cross my arms and stand my ground. He's going to tell me what's going on, and he's going to do it now.

He rubs his chin. "Saturday made me realize something. I crossed a line with you that I shouldn't have."

"What are you talking about?" I ask. "Skydiving was my idea—"

"It's not the fucking skydiving," he says, his voice low. He gets up and turns to the window. "I'm not what you need, Selene. I can't be what you need."

My chest tightens. "What are you saying?"

He puts his hands in his pockets and stares out the window. "I'm not right for you. I can't be the man you need me to be."

I stand there like an idiot, watching him, my mouth hanging open. He's breaking up with me. He's fucking breaking up with me.

Tears burn my eyes, but I swallow hard to regain my composure. I refuse to lose my cool in the office, no matter what happens. I take a deep breath to make sure I'll be able to speak clearly.

"Why?" My own question takes me by surprise. It isn't what I meant to say.

"I just can't."

"That's not an answer." I can't keep the edge from my tone.

"It's all I have. I made a mistake with you. We work together, and I pushed you into this. I shouldn't have."

"So, that's it?" I ask. "You're ending it, just like that?"

He doesn't answer. Just stands there, looking out the goddamn window.

If he won't answer me, I won't say anything else either. I turn and walk out the door.

By the time I get to my office, I'm shaking. I don't even pretend I'm going to stay. I gather up my things and head straight for the elevator. My heart races and I feel like I can't breathe, but I keep my face completely still. I'm sure I have massive resting bitch face right now, but it's a hell of a lot better than breaking down in tears in front of everyone I work with.

I get home, and rather than feeling like I need to have a sob fest on my couch with a bottle of wine and a tub of ice cream, I'm strangely calm. Empty. I'm hollowed out, like I left everything in Ronan's office. He gutted me with those words, and didn't leave enough behind that I can feel anything anymore.

Usually when I get dumped, the first thing I do is call Kylie. She comes over and we drink too much and badmouth the asshole who screwed me over. But this time I leave my phone in my purse, and don't even text her.

This time, it's different. Ronan was different.

I've heard men tell me they were crazy about me. I've had men promise me the world. Even when I thought I was crazy about them too, I never really believed them. Deep down, I saw them for who they were. I knew they'd wind up leaving me. But when Ronan said it—when he said he loved me—I actually believed him.

Out of nowhere, the tears come. I sink down onto my couch and close my eyes, letting them trail hot tracks down my face. I've never been hurt like this before. Not by the guy who was cheating on me. Not by the guy who ditched me for his ex while he was on a date with me. Not even by the guy who planned to move in with me, then decided he couldn't handle the commitment. I thought I'd had my heart broken before, but none of those men had my heart to begin with. They couldn't break it. I was disappointed and hurt when those relationships ended, but I was usually more upset with myself for trusting them in the first place.

Ronan had my heart. I bared my soul to him, offered him all of me. I thought he wanted it. I thought he'd take care of me, be gentle with my fragile pieces.

Apparently he can't.

27

SELENE

$\mathcal{I}$ don't go into the office for the rest of the week. I can't face it. I work from home just enough to keep up, but it's hard to stay focused. Kylie and I do our usual get drunk after a breakup thing, and Braxton fumes with anger for a while until we convince him to drink with us. But my heart really isn't in it. I don't want to sit around and badmouth Ronan, and I wake up with a wicked hangover the next day. I love Ky and Brax for it, though. They're always there when I need them.

Some people say rules are meant to be broken—or at least bent—but in this case, I should have stuck to my no dating coworkers rule. I don't care how intense an attraction I felt for Ronan. It blew up in my face, exactly like I thought it would.

Back at work on Monday, I have a momentary panic in the elevator. Is everyone going to know? Are they going to watch me walk by and turn to whisper to each other as soon as they think I'm out of earshot?

Did you see Selene Taylor? She was having this crazy affair with the boss, but he dumped her, and then she showed up at work a total mess.

No one gives me a second glance as I walk through the

hallway toward my office, so I figure I must appear more or less normal. I'm dressed in a fitted white blouse tucked into a slate-gray pencil skirt and my highest heels. It's actually one of my least comfortable work outfits—the skirt is a bit too short for my long legs, and I have to be careful about how I sit. But there's something about it that feels like armor. I might be crumbling to pieces inside, but on the outside I look fierce.

I haven't made a final decision about my job, but I clearly have a choice to make. Do I stay, and try to find a way to work with Ronan? Or do I leave a job I really love and find something else?

I'm honestly not sure what I should do. I'm extraordinarily fortunate in that I don't have to worry too much about money. I own my house outright, and my parents left Braxton and me a trust fund. I'm seriously considering taking a few months off, just to figure out what I want to do next. I thought VI was my future, but I screwed that up when I screwed the boss.

That's a mistake I'll never, ever make again.

If I do decide to leave, it won't be until after our big presentation. That isn't about Ronan anymore. I've been spearheading the project as much as he has, and the development teams for both companies are counting on me. I can put any awkwardness between Ronan and I aside long enough to get through that meeting. But afterward ... I'll have to decide what to do.

I figure my best bet today is to caffeinate heavily and focus on my work—and avoid walking by Ronan's office at all costs. The morning goes by in something of a blur. The lead engineer comes to me with issues, so we have an impromptu meeting with some of his staff and get the details hashed out. Before I know it, I've worked well past the lunch hour and haven't heard a word from Ronan. It's like he's not even here.

This is good. The less I see of him, the better.

Then, at the end of the day, there's a soft knock at my door. I look up to find Sarah.

"Come on in," I say.

"Thanks." She sits down across my desk from me and crosses her legs. "I'm sorry to bother you, but I was wondering if you know what's going on with Ronan?"

"I..." I falter for a second. "I don't know what you mean."

"Look, I'm not very good at dancing around a subject," she says. "I know you were keeping it quiet, but he told me about the two of you. And I know you've been out of the office, but he has been an absolute nightmare to deal with since last week. I'm probably really stretching the limits of appropriateness here, but I was hoping you might know why. He isn't telling me anything, and ... to be honest, I'm kind of worried about him."

I take a breath. I suppose I might as well be honest. "He ended it with me last week."

Sarah lets out a heavy sigh and pinches the bridge of her nose. "That asshole."

I raise my eyebrows. "That's not the reaction I would expect from you."

"You think I'd take his side?" she asks. "I've been his friend for a long time, so he does deserve some loyalty. But this is just him being stupid."

"I don't think it's stupidity."

"Call it what you want, he's being an idiot," she says. "Do you mind if I ask what happened?"

I lean back in my chair. "He told me he crossed a line with me and he shouldn't have. That he can't be the man I need."

"He said that out of nowhere?" she asks.

"Well, not exactly." I tell her about the skydiving trip.

She nods her head slowly for a moment. "Things are starting to make sense."

"What do you mean?"

"Did he ever tell you about his accident?" she asks. "The one that happened when he was in college?"

"Not really," I say.

"He's probably going to fire me for telling you this, but you deserve to know," she says. "In college, Ronan dated my roommate, Chelsea. I was dating this guy named Mike, and the four of us became good friends. Mike and Ronan were both kind of crazy and loved outdoor sports, so we did a lot of stuff on the weekends—hiking, rock climbing, that sort of thing. Nothing like what Ronan does now, of course. Anyway, we had a climbing trip planned. Ronan and Mike scoped out a location out in the middle of nowhere. We were excited, because our usual climbing spots were getting really busy. At the last minute, I had to cancel because my mom had to go to the hospital, but I insisted the rest of them go. I told them they could find out if the location was any good, and we'd all go the following weekend."

Sarah takes a deep breath and re-crosses her legs. "They left early in the morning, and the route was up this mountainside on a road that was barely a road. I don't know why they swerved. Ronan wasn't driving, and he always said he didn't see. But they ran off the road, and there wasn't anything on the side. It was literally a cliff. The car rolled all the way to the bottom."

"Oh my god."

"Yeah, it was bad," she says. "Mike never regained consciousness. Ronan tried to revive him and when he couldn't, he did his best to keep him hydrated while he waited for help. Chelsea was awake for a while, but they determined later she was bleeding internally. There was nothing Ronan could have done. He had a broken arm, and cuts and bruises all over. Even with climbing gear, he couldn't get back up to the road. Not that it would have mattered. There wasn't any other traffic. They were too far out."

"Chelsea didn't make it?" I ask quietly.

"No," she says. "I don't know how long she lasted, but I'm

pretty sure he stayed with her for a long time after she was gone. Eventually, he figured he had to move or he was going to die, too. I was at my folks' until well into the following week, and it wasn't until Tuesday that anyone even knew they were missing. We got a search party going, but I only had a vague idea of where they went. There was so much ground to cover."

"How did they find him?" I ask.

"A trucker picked him up on the side of the road, and called 911," she says. "He walked thirty miles in two days to find a highway with traffic. He was dehydrated, sleep deprived, and injured, but he was alive."

Sarah pauses and takes a deep breath. "He was never the same. He was always pretty adventurous, but after that, he started taking bigger and bigger risks. Rock climbing turned into cliff diving, which turned into skydiving, and BASE jumping, and who knows what else. His family was afraid he was trying to kill himself, but he always insisted he wasn't. He pushes himself in every aspect of his life. He takes risks no one else will take, and he does it without flinching. When he took over Edge, everyone thought he was nuts. Same with buying VI. But he does that. He doesn't see the world the way most people do anymore. If he's not tackling some new challenge, he isn't really living."

Ronan makes a lot more sense now that I know what he's been through—but Sarah's story also confirms everything I thought about why he left me. "And I was a challenge. I was hard to get, and he couldn't resist trying."

Sarah's eyebrows draw together. She looks uncomfortable. "I know that's how it seems."

"Are you really going to tell me that isn't what happened?" I ask. "Did Ronan tell you everything about me? How we spent a night together before he moved to San Francisco? How as soon as he saw I worked for him here, he started pursuing me? How he pushed against all my boundaries, found loopholes in the rules I set for working together? He wanted me because I told him no."

"If you were any other woman, I'd have to grudgingly agree with you," she says.

"What does that mean?"

"I've known Ronan for a long time," she says. "I'm well aware of how he is with women. And it's nothing like how he was with you."

I shake my head. "That's what we always want to believe, isn't it? That we're the special one? With everyone else, he's a player who gets what he wants and moves on. But with me? Oh, I'll be different. Do you know how many times I've told myself that? How many men have screwed me over because I bought their bullshit? Ronan is not the first. But he's certainly going to be the last."

Sarah takes another deep breath. "I'm sorry, Selene. I really didn't mean to stick my nose in your business. He's just ... he's not okay. But now at least I know why."

My heart aches at the thought of him hurting, and I'm angry at myself for caring. He should be hurt. He crushed me. It would be worse to hear he was happy, wouldn't it? At least maybe I can believe he misses me.

No, I don't want to believe that. I've been naive for too long.

"He's probably just stressed about landing this contract," I say. "We're all working too much lately."

"I suppose," Sarah says. "Can I ask you one more question? You don't have to answer if you don't want to, and regardless of what you say, this is confidential. I won't tell him."

"Sure."

"Are you going to quit?"

I look away. "Honestly, I don't know what I'm going to do."

"Well, for what it's worth, I hope you don't," she says. "But I'll understand if you do."

"Thanks, Sarah."

She smiles and leaves.

I wonder what she meant when she said Ronan isn't okay. Does he regret what he said to me? Or is he just working too hard?

I'm tempted to go talk to him. I'm hurt and angry, but I can't help that I still care about him. I glance at the clock. It's after five, but I'm sure he's still here.

I grab my things, but I head for the elevator. He made himself clear. I can't indulge in any stupid fantasies about him changing his mind at the sight of me in his office. It's been a week. If he had any doubts about what he said to me, I'm sure he would have told me by now.

28

RONAN

*T*here's a knock at my door and I look up from the paperwork I've been perusing. Damon sticks his head through the crack. Fuck, I forgot he was coming.

"Hey, brother," he says.

I lean back in my seat and rub my temples. This fucking headache will not go away. "Damon."

He raises an eyebrow at me and comes in, shutting the door behind him. He's dressed in a faded green t-shirt and jeans. "Sarah said I could just come in. Am I interrupting?"

"I'm just working."

"Right," Damon says. He takes a seat across the desk. "You forgot I was coming, didn't you?"

The bullshit line I'm about to give him fades before I say it, and I decide to be honest. "Yeah, I forgot."

"I figured you would," he says.

I narrow my eyes at him. "What's that supposed to mean?"

"Nothing," he says. "You're busy and I know how you get caught up with work."

I take a deep breath. I don't need to be an asshole to my brother. He's a decent guy, and he's always had my back when it counted. "Sorry, Damon. Things have just been kind of fucked for me lately. I have you on my calendar, but I wasn't expecting to see you until tonight."

"Yeah, I took an earlier flight," he says. "I'm the dick for showing up early."

"No, it's fine," I say.

Damon rubs his smooth jaw. "So, there's something I need to talk to you about, and I sort of want to get it over with."

"What?"

"Something happened, and I think you're going to be pissed," he says.

The tension in his voice makes my back clench. "What happened?"

"Mom has breast cancer."

The words drop onto me like a boulder. "Cancer? What the fuck? When?"

"She found out a little over a month ago," he says.

I almost fly out of my chair. "A month? Are you fucking kidding me? Why didn't anyone tell me?"

"Slow down," he says. His tone is infuriating. "They didn't want to tell you until they knew for sure what was going on. They ... well, they know how you handle this kind of thing."

"What the fuck does that mean?"

Damon sighs. "They were worried you'd flip out and go dive off the Golden Gate bridge or something."

"You can't jump off the Golden Gate," I say.

"See, the fact that you know that is part of the problem," he says. "They didn't want you to go do something stupid."

"What the hell are you talking about?"

"Come on, Ronan," he says. "Remember when Dad had that scare a couple years ago? When we thought it might be his heart? What did you do?"

I pause, thinking back. "I went BASE jumping in Nevada."

"Exactly," he says. "And you almost fucking died that trip. Mom has enough to deal with right now without worrying that you'll try to kill yourself."

"I'm not trying to kill myself," I say.

"Could have fooled the rest of us."

I get a grip on my anger with a deep breath. "How is she? What's the prognosis?"

"She's fine," he says. "They caught it very early, and it's not aggressive. She had a lumpectomy two weeks ago, and the surgeon was really happy. She starts radiation in a few weeks, but really, that's more of a precaution than anything. She's going to recover."

"I can't believe they didn't tell me."

"Well, I'm telling you now," he says. "Call her. Talk to her. She misses you."

I'm overdue for a visit to my folks. "I'll go. I don't know when I can get away, but I'll get down there as soon as I can."

"Good," Damon says. "Honestly, you don't need to worry about her. She feels great, and there's every indication she'll make a complete recovery."

I nod. "Good."

"So what's the plan for tonight? Do I get to meet this mysterious girlfriend of yours?"

That word is a stab to my gut, and my voice goes icy cold. "She's not my girlfriend."

"Sorry, last time we talked, you said—"

"She's not."

Damon takes a deep breath. "I know it's usually a bad idea to poke a wounded animal, but what happened?"

There was a time when I might have talked to Damon about this. He knew all about Chelsea. I even talked to him about how I felt afterward. He helped get me through one of the worst experiences of my life. "Things just got really intense."

"How so?"

"You know what? It's nothing. I made a mistake with her. And I've been so fucking buried with this meeting we have coming up. When it's over, I need to get out of town for a while. Blow off some steam."

"Right, blow off steam."

"Do you actually wonder why I don't come around?" I ask, unable to mask the irritation in my voice. "I get the same thing from you every time. From Mom and Dad, too. Stop with the passive-aggressive bullshit. I know none of you approve of me—but none of you understand me, either."

"I understand you a lot better than you realize," Damon says.

I shake my head. "I don't need you to come here and psycho-analyze me."

"Actually, I think you do," he says. "I didn't come up here intending to bust your balls, but I think I'm overdue. I haven't been much of a brother to you all these years, and I'm sorry for that. But every time life gets hard, you can't go dive out of a goddamn airplane or whatever it is you do."

"It's not about life getting hard," I say.

"Then what is it about?" he asks. "What is it that makes you do all that stupid shit? Mom thinks you have a death wish. She's convinced it's survivor's guilt and you're trying to tempt fate or something."

"I'm not trying to die," I say. "This is what I mean. You look at me and you think you understand what I went through, or what it did to me. No one does."

"Then enlighten me," he says. "What's it like to be you? Why do you take such stupid fucking risks with your life?"

"Because that's the only time I feel alive," I say. "Right now, sitting here? I'm half dead. I don't feel much of anything. I don't jump off cliffs or out of airplanes, or climb rock faces, because I want to kill myself. I do it so I can stay alive."

Damon gapes at me for a long moment. "You're a fucking mess. You know that, right? The only way you're ever going to get better is if you find something to make you feel alive that isn't going to kill you."

"What did you say?" I ask.

"Which part?"

I put a hand to my chin and look away.

Something that makes me feel alive, and won't kill me.

I had it. That's exactly what she was.

"What?" Damon asks.

"No, it's nothing," I say.

"Fuck that," Damon says, his voice sharp. "I'm sick of sitting on the sidelines watching you self-destruct."

"Self-destruct?" I ask. "Look around you. This company is mine. I bought it because I had a vision that no one else had the guts to pull off. And I'm right on the brink, Damon. I'm one presentation away from making this happen."

"I know you're successful," Damon says. "I'm sure you have more money than you know what to do with, although you probably risked it all to buy this company."

I tip my head. He's right about that. I did risk it all.

"But here's the thing, Ronan," he says. "No risk is ever going to be enough for you. You can keep betting it all and hoping you come out on top, but one of these days, you're going to be fucked."

"Is that your professional opinion?"

"Don't be an ass," he says. "It's the truth. I know you hate it when I do this, and I've always backed off. Just ... tell me one more thing."

"What?"

"What was that a second ago?" he asks. "I said something about feeling alive, and your face changed. What went through your mind?"

I'm not one of his goddamn patients. But he struck a nerve, and I'm compelled to tell him. "Her name is Selene."

"Tell me about her." He settles back in his chair and I can imagine him sitting in his office, talking to his patients in the same, soothing voice.

"She works for me," I say. "She's amazing at her job—smart, passionate, driven. She's one of those women that makes every man stare."

"And you were in a relationship with Selene?" he asks.

I pinch the bridge of my nose. Fuck this headache. "Yes."

"That's past tense," he says. "You're not with her now."

"No."

"Can you tell me what happened?"

For reasons I can't fathom, I tell him everything. How I pursued Selene relentlessly. How she made me feel. I tell him about taking her skydiving, and her chute failing. About how it made me realize I had to end it with her, even though now I feel so dead inside I'm not sure why I'm even here.

Damon doesn't say anything for a long moment, and I start to regret telling him. He's probably diagnosing me right now.

"Chelsea wasn't your fault," he says finally. His voice is quiet.

"Excuse me?"

"What happened to Chelsea wasn't your fault," he says. "I don't think you realize that. I think you're carrying the responsibility for her death on your shoulders. You need to let it go."

"I wasn't talking about her," I say.

"No, but that's where this comes from," he says. "You just admitted to me that you fell in love for the first time since Chelsea, but you broke up with her. Why do you think you did that?"

"Because she deserves better. If I stay with her, everything in her life would be wrapped up in me. Her career. Her happiness.

Her fucking life. I'm never scared for myself when something goes wrong out there. But I was scared shitless for her."

"But that's a completely normal reaction to a person you love being in danger," he says.

"It isn't about the jump," I say.

"No, I know it isn't. It's about realizing that someone trusted you deeply, and being afraid that you aren't worthy of that trust."

I want to argue with Damon, but he's making a little too much sense.

"She's going to quit," I say.

"That bothers you as much as anything, doesn't it?"

"Yes," I say. "This is where she belongs. The company won't be the same without her."

"Neither will you."

I look away. He's right. I'm not the same. Selene cut through me, to my core. She found a part of me I thought was dead. I thought it died the day Chelsea did, at the bottom of that cliff. But whether or not Selene is good for me isn't the point. I can take risks with my own life, but how can I take them with hers?

29

RONAN

*S*arah texts me to say they're ready for me in the main conference room. A buzz tickles the edges of my mind. This is it. Everything I've done, bringing these two companies together, comes down to today. I have so much riding on this deal that failure isn't an option.

I'm not worried. I'm finally feeling awake again. The thrill of victory is so close I can almost taste it.

I have no idea if Selene is going to show. The thought of doing this without her kills my buzz a little, but I won't blame her if she doesn't come. I'm prepared to go over her material if I need to. I try to push thoughts of her out of my mind.

Maybe it's better if she's not there. I won't be distracted. Today, I need to be focused. On point. Ready.

The air in the office tingles with electricity. People watch me as I walk to the conference room. Everyone knows what this meeting means. I feed off the tension, letting it drive me. It feels as good as a plane climbing, or standing on the edge of a cliff, ready to jump. This is what I do. This is what I live for.

I'm in my element, but there's a hollowness to it.

I should be sharing this with her. But I can't.

I walk in and greet our guests. Ten men and women sit around the table, several in highly decorated uniforms. Sarah sits at the table, along with two of our lead developers.

Selene isn't here.

"Good morning," I say. "Welcome to Vital Information and Edge Gear."

The door opens. From the corner of my eye, I see Selene walk in. Her entrance almost shatters my concentration into a million pieces, and I falter for half a second while I regain my composure. She quietly takes her seat, but doesn't meet my eyes.

I recover quickly and move on with the introductions while Sarah passes out packets. The beginning of the presentation was always mine, so I continue on. I can't read anyone's faces. If they're impressed by my speech, they're not showing it. I click through the slides, giving an overview of our company and products, as well as background on some of the developers and engineers who have particularly impressive resumes. I empha-size the team aspect, and talk about how we've brought together the two teams to achieve something completely new and extraordinary.

I get to the point where Selene should take over. She's here. Does that mean she plans to go through with her part of the presentation?

I shouldn't even have wondered. She stands up on my second-to-last slide and eases her way to the front, unobtrusive so as not to interrupt me. She still won't look at me, but she takes the remote from my hand and smoothly launches into the next part of the presentation.

She's perfect. She holds her audience in rapt attention while she talks about the technologies involved and how we're bringing them together to provide state-of-the-art protective gear with both military and law enforcement applications. Her intimate knowledge of the team—and the tech—shines through in her words. Selene is an excellent speaker, and I see interest playing in the eyes of several of the people sitting around the table.

I realize after several minutes that I'm not watching her. I'm listening, but my eyes are on the other people in the room. I don't want it to be noticeable, so I force myself to look up at her.

In the dim room, with the projector screen glowing behind her, she's framed by a soft glow. Fuck, she's beautiful. I'm mesmerized by the way her mouth moves when she talks. The straightness of her posture. The way her neck looks so soft with her hair pulled up.

But more than anything, I'm so fucking proud of her. She is nailing this presentation in every way possible. Her points are spot on. Her excitement for the project shows. There's no question she knows her shit. She's making me look like a rock star for having her on my team.

If we close this deal, there's no way I can claim credit. She's owning this room right now, and I'm in awe of her performance.

She finishes her part, and opens the floor to questions. She and I hadn't planned the meeting beyond this point, but she stays up front, taking questions and directing them to the engineers when necessary. I let her take the lead. She's relaxed and competent, and there's nothing more I need to do until the hand-shaking at the end.

I take it as a good sign that they have so many questions. I answer a few, and the engineers get a chance to talk about their recent developments. I sense a great deal of interest. We don't have an agreement yet, but we will. I can sense the deal closing.

It will take weeks before we have a signed contract, but it's going to happen. I can feel it.

I should be in the midst of an adrenaline rush, fueling my high. But Selene's voice lodges itself deep inside me, her proximity like a tiny hammer knocking inside my skull. I realize I'd counted on her not being here. She's hardly been in the office, and I've been waiting for her to turn in her notice any day. I certainly haven't given her any reasons to stay.

But here she is, knocking the socks off everyone in this room, myself included. And I'm hit with such a raging storm of emotions, it's all I can do to say the right things to close up the meeting and assure them we'll have copies of the official proposal to everyone by morning.

After what feels like an eternity, the meeting ends and our guests file out. Selene lingers, standing at the head of the large table, thumbing through her notes like she has a reason to stay. I wait behind, nodding to Sarah as she heads back to her desk, and close the door behind her.

Selene looks up at the sound of the door closing. Her eyebrows lift, like she's surprised I'm still here.

It all came to me in a rush as I watched her. I know what I need to do.

"Can I talk to you?" I ask.

"Sure," she says.

"Selene, I realize this has been difficult," I say. "But there's something I should have done a while ago."

She keeps her eyes on the table. "What's that?"

"I want to offer you a promotion," I say. "Make you VP of Operations."

Selene turns her face toward me, her brow furrowed. "What?"

"After that presentation, no one will question where this is coming from," I say. "You deserve this. It's what you do already; I'm just catching up with your title."

"Is this supposed to fix everything?" she asks.

"This isn't about us," I say. "This is about you and the company. This is where you should be. You're the heart and soul of this place."

"I'm leaving," she says. "I was going to wait to tell you, but I'm planning on giving my notice."

I don't just hear her words; I feel them. Right in the center of my chest, as if they reverberate through me. I knew this would happen, but I hoped I could head her off. I hoped I could salvage this before she left for good.

Fuck.

"Don't do that, Selene," I say. "Don't leave because of me."

"You tell me you love me, then you break up with me, and now you want to promote me?" she asks. "You're insane, Ronan. I don't know how you think I can trust a word you say."

"I never lied to you."

"Don't," she says, holding up a finger. "Don't even do that to me. The game is over, so you can cut the bullshit. You wanted what you couldn't have, and once you got it, you were ready to move onto the next challenge."

"That's not true—"

"What happened, then?" she asks. "Because from where I'm standing, things got too intense for you, and you bailed."

She's hitting way too close to the truth. Smack in the middle of it, in fact. But she still has the wrong idea. I don't have an answer, so I just turn away.

"You don't want a future with me, fine," she says. "But how you think I could stay here is beyond me. I don't give a shit what titles you dangle in front of me."

"I'm not fucking with you," I say. "This promotion is what you deserve for your work here. It doesn't have anything to do with what happened between us."

"Why do you want me to stay, Ronan?" she asks, meeting my eyes.

It's hard to hold her gaze. "Because you're what this company needs," I say.

She shakes her head. "The company. Of course. But not you. I'm not what you need."

"Have you not heard a word I've said?" I ask. "I can't be what *you* need. Not the other way around."

"Why?"

I look away.

"No? You claim to fear nothing, but you're too scared to tell me the truth," she says. "And who are you to make that choice for me? You don't get to decide what I need. I get to make that call. God, I'm so fucking sick of men who think they know what's best for me. What am I, some sort of fragile little flower? I'm a grown woman, Ronan, and I'm perfectly capable of making my own decisions."

"If I had any doubts about you, I wouldn't be offering you this position," I say. "You are a strong, competent woman, and we need you here."

"The company does. But not you."

"This isn't about me. This is about the company." I'm barely holding on to the threads of my temper. "What the fuck do you want me to say?"

Selene puts her hands on her hips. "I want you to tell me how you can look me in the eyes and tell me you love me, and then days later push me aside like I mean nothing to you."

And there it is again. The crushing weight. The fear. The certainty that I can never be the man she needs. She waits, her eyes intent on me, but I don't answer. I don't know how to make her understand.

"No? I didn't think so. I'll stay as long as it takes to pass off my responsibilities to others, but then I'm leaving. Believe me, this is not what I wanted. I loved it here. But there is no way I can come to work every day and see you. I thought maybe I was strong enough to do it, but I'm not."

She walks over to her chair and leans down to pick up her

things. I catch sight of something at her throat, just beneath her shirt collar.

"Goodbye, Ronan," she says.

I watch her go, but I saw it, and it's like getting hit upside the head with a board. She's wearing the necklace I bought her.

30

SELENE

I already regret this date.

In a fit of anger after Ronan *dared* to offer me a promotion, I accepted an invitation to dinner from a guy I met in a coffee shop near my house. I'd seen him there before, but never talked to him. When he asked if I'd join him for dinner, I was still so pissed off at Ronan that I said yes.

Josh seems like a nice guy, but I never should have come out with him. I was honest about the fact that I literally just got out of a relationship, and he said he didn't mind. If anything, he looked relieved. Even though he's the one who approached me, I get the feeling he's as reluctant about going on a date as I am. In a way, that was part of what made me accept. I felt like he and I could have a pleasant meal together without there being pressure to worry about what would come next.

But he had to choose the restaurant where Ronan interrupted my date with Aidan all those months ago. And the hostess just seated us at the same table.

I feel like this is a really bad sign.

My phone dings and I pull it out of my purse. "Sorry, I should have turned the sound off." It's a text from Kylie.

Where are you?

"Let me guess," Josh says. "You have a friend ready to text you with a fake emergency in case you need an excuse to leave."

I laugh while I send Kylie a reply. *Date. Chase's Bar and Grill. Why?* "Not exactly. It is my friend, but she was just asking where I am. She probably stopped by my house and wondered."

Josh rubs his chin and looks away. "Listen, I need to be honest with you. I know this is strange, considering I invited you, but I'm not sure I should have done that."

Despite the fact that I'm not sure either, it's still a little disappointing to hear. "Oh, I'm sorry. I guess ... we don't have to do this if you don't want to."

"I'm crazy, right?" he says. "I mean, look at you."

I glance down. I'm wearing a simple black dress with the necklace Ronan gave me at my throat. I should probably stop wearing it, but the meaning is so special. I think of my parents every time I put it on, and not in a way that makes me sad. It makes me feel like they're still watching out for me, strange as that sounds.

"You're really, really beautiful," Josh continues. "But things in my life are uncertain right now, and I'm not sure if dating anyone is a good idea. I feel bad, because I asked you to dinner, and now here I am telling you I probably shouldn't have. I'll be honest, my brother has been pressuring me into dating and that's why I asked you."

I laugh and Josh's eyebrows raise in surprise. "I'm sorry. I'm not laughing at you. I was just sitting here thinking I probably shouldn't have agreed to come out with you tonight. It's way too soon for me."

His shoulders relax and he smiles. "Tell you what, then. We're here. We might as well eat."

I glance at my phone one more time, wondering what's up

with Kylie, but she hasn't replied. I put my phone back in my purse and go back to perusing the menu.

Josh and I order and start to chat. He confesses that his wife left him and their divorce was finalized recently. I find myself telling him about Ronan—some of it, at least. I don't mention the fact that he was my boss, nor that I told Ronan I quit but haven't yet put in official notice. I should. I need to be able to tell the rest of the office that I'm leaving, but I haven't been able to bring myself to make the announcement yet.

Josh is sympathetic and understanding. Our food arrives, and it's quite good. Despite the fact that neither of us want this to be a date, it's nice to be out of the house and having a conversation with someone. I feel a bit more like myself than I have in a while.

"Excuse me," someone says behind me, and I almost drop my fork.

He can't be serious.

Josh looks up with raised eyebrows.

"Sorry to interrupt," Ronan says, sliding a chair up to our table. "Actually, I'm lying. I'm not sorry." He looks at Josh. "I hope you weren't expecting to get lucky tonight. The lady's coming home with me."

My mouth drops open and I sputter, so angry I can't get a word out.

Josh looks bewildered, and maybe even slightly amused. "Is this him?" he asks.

"Yes," I say through gritted teeth, my eyes on Ronan. "And he's definitely not staying."

"Selene, we need to talk," Ronan says.

"You cannot just show up here and interrupt my date," I say.

Josh puts up a hand. "It's not really a date."

I glare at him. "You're not helping."

"Of course it's not a date," Ronan says, his eyes twinkling.

"What is that supposed to mean?" I ask.

"You can't date him when you're in love with me."

I shake my head slowly. "You're unbelievable, you know that? *You* left *me*, in case you've forgotten already. That was your decision. Now you need to live with it." I stand up and root around in my purse for a second, then toss some money on the table so I don't stick Josh with the bill. "Josh, I'm very sorry about this. Dinner was lovely, but I have to go."

I push past Ronan, ignoring what he says to my back as I walk away. I cannot believe he would show up here like this. First he says he can't be what I need, and now suddenly he wants to waltz back into my life?

He follows me out, but doesn't seem to be trying to catch up. I hurry to my car, grateful that Josh and I decided to meet here and I don't have to ruin my dramatic exit by going back to ask for a ride home, or stopping to get a cab. I get in my car and leave, checking my rear view mirror for signs that Ronan is following me. There's a car behind me for a while, but it doesn't look like his and it turns down a side street before I get home.

Without really thinking it through, I drive past my house and don't stop. He's going to come here. If he was brazen enough to interrupt my date, he'll certainly try to find me at home. Seeing him made me so angry—he's so smug and fucking arrogant.

The lady's coming home with me. What an asshole.

I do not want to admit how hearing that sent a lighting strike straight to my core.

After driving around aimlessly for a while, I find a parking spot on the street in front of a random restaurant and go in. I don't even know what I'm doing. The host shows me to a table, and I order a glass of wine.

Reluctantly, I check my phone. I have a string of texts from Ronan.

I'm sorry. I tried your house. You weren't home.

Kylie was there. She said you were on a date.

This is my fault.

Please, can we talk?

I need to see you.

Where are you? I'm getting worried.

I put my phone down on the table and take a sip of my wine. What the hell am I doing? I just let him chase me out of a restaurant and now I'm avoiding my house.

My phone dings again. *Get. Your. Ass. Home.*

Oh, no he fucking didn't.

Furiously, I type out a reply. *Are you kidding me? FUCK YOU*

I drop my phone back onto the table, but it dings again almost immediately.

I knew that would get you to answer.

I grind my teeth together. He is so damn infuriating.

He texts again. *Please, Selene. Come home.*

Should I? Should I hear what he has to say? I'm hurt, but he's right about loving him. I don't think that will ever go away, regardless of what happens between us. I'll carry a piece of him with me for the rest of my life.

What happened to him? The last time we saw each other, he had that haunted look in his eyes. Tonight, he was back to his old confident self. I can't shake the feeling that the only reason he's interested again is because he doesn't have me. He's back to chasing what he can't have—once again, I'm a challenge.

I nurse my wine for a while, listening to the soft hum of conversations around me. Ronan texts a few more times, asking where I am, if I'm okay, and whether I need a ride. Those are followed by another plea to come home. I don't answer.

After paying my bill—the waiter seems a little perplexed that I didn't order any food—I decide I ought to go home. I briefly consider going to Braxton and Kylie's place instead, before realizing how ridiculous that is. If I don't want to talk to Ronan, I can simply tell him to leave. I don't have to let him in.

But as soon as I see him sitting on my front porch, I know I will.

The collar of his shirt is unbuttoned and his hair looks unkempt as usual. Somewhere between here and the restaurant, he lost some of his confident swagger. There's concern in his eyes as I walk up the sidewalk.

He stands as I approach. "I was getting worried."

I'm still not sure I want to talk to him. Without a word, I sweep past him and go inside. But I leave the door open.

I hear the door close as I drop my purse on the counter.

I whirl on him. "What the hell are you doing here?"

"I need to talk to you," he says.

"What makes you think you have the right to barge in on me like that?" I ask. "I was out with someone, and you just walk up to my table? Again?"

"Come on, that wasn't really a date," he says.

"I don't care what it was," I say. "I could have been planning on fucking that guy's brains out tonight. You had no idea."

A flash of anger crosses his features. He did not like hearing that.

"But you weren't," he says, stepping closer. His calm tone is maddening. "And we both know why."

"So, what is this?" I ask. "Do you consider this an apology? Because you're terrible at it."

"I haven't even started to apologize," he says, his voice low. He gets closer. "I have a lot of apologizing to do."

The heat between my legs only makes me angrier. He should not be able to make me feel this way. "You are such an asshole."

He stands right in front of me. I should move. He's so close, I can feel his body heat. He wraps his hand around the back of my head, twining his fingers through my hair. God, I love how he does that.

No, I don't. I'm angry. Furious.

"Listen to me," he says. "I told you the second time we got together it wouldn't be a mistake, and it wasn't. I'm the one who screwed up, and fuck if I don't know it. This is all on me, Selene, and I will literally do anything you want if you'll just listen."

"Fine, talk."

He doesn't let go. His face is so close our noses nearly touch. "I know I don't have the right to kiss you yet, but fuck, Selene, I missed you so much."

I almost kiss him, right there—my body aches for him—but I can't let this be about sex. I move back, and he lets go.

"You said you wanted to talk," I say.

"Do you want to sit down?" he asks.

"Not really."

He lets out a breath and I try to keep my eyes away from his crotch, but he's standing at attention and it's so distracting.

"What?" I say when he doesn't start talking. "Out with it."

"I was scared," he says. "You scared the fuck out of me, and I literally haven't been scared of anything since I was in a car accident in college."

"What are you talking about?"

"Sarah said she told you about the accident, so you know what happened," he says. "The bottom line is, Mike and Chelsea both died, and there was nothing I could do for them. I tried everything to keep them alive. I've never felt so helpless. And afterward, Selene, I should have died, too. I walked for two days to get help and my injuries were infected. When that trucker found me, my fever was so high I was delirious."

"You shouldn't feel guilty for surviving," I say. "It wasn't your fault."

"I know," he says. "I've never thought of it as guilt. But that

accident changed me. I stopped feeling fear. I guess I figured if I
lived through that, nothing was going to kill me. So I started
taking bigger and bigger risks. The rush was addicting. It was
the only time I felt real. The only time I felt alive. I started
chasing the high, going after bigger and bigger challenges. It
wasn't just the sports, although it felt like nothing would ever be
high enough, or fast enough. I lived for any kind of challenge. It
was the only thing that made me feel like I hadn't died at the
bottom of that cliff."

"Then why were you scared of *me*?"

"Because you trusted everything to me," he says. "Your
career. Your body. Your life. Your heart. After we went skydiving,
all I could think about was how I failed Chelsea. I didn't save
her. What if it happened again? What if something happened to
you? I didn't think I could live through that again."

"Ronan, you can't expect to protect me from everything," I
say. "Even if I never jump out of an airplane again, I could get
killed just driving home from work."

"I know. It wasn't just the thought of you dying. I realized
how deep I was with you. Your whole life was wrapped up with
mine. It scared the shit out of me, and I'm a man who hasn't felt
fear in years. I didn't know how to cope with it. But the truth
is..." He gets close and wraps his hand around the back of my
neck again. "No matter how much you scare me, you're the only
thing that's ever made me feel alive that isn't likely to kill me."

"I don't understand."

"Since the accident, I've fluctuated between feeling dead
inside and being high on adrenaline. There was no in between. I
was either riding a rush, or craving the next one. With you, I feel
calm but alive. I feel whole. Balanced. And the longer we were
together, the longer that feeling lasted. It wasn't just when you
were near; the feeling would stay. Normally I'd be jumping out
of airplanes or off of cliffs every chance I get. But you were

magic, Selene. I don't know how, but you smoothed out all my edges."

His lips brush against mine, just a whisper. "I am so sorry for hurting you. I let fear get the better of me and I acted like a complete asshole. You're beautiful and perfect, and fuck, I love you so much." He closes his eyes. "Please let me kiss you. I'll go if you tell me to leave, but god I need to kiss you right now."

I give him the slightest nod and his lips come to mine. He lights me up; my body comes alive at his touch. He doesn't hold back. He coaxes my lips apart with his tongue, opening me to him. His kiss is deep and pure.

He pulls away and touches my cheek. "I'm sorry it took me so long to realize the truth."

"What truth?"

"That you're the only risk worth taking."

He kisses me again, and I thread my arms around his neck. All the tension I've been carrying melts away at the feel of his body pressing against mine. He wraps me in his arms, holding me close.

"Are you sure you're not just chasing what you can't have again?" I ask.

"No," he says, looking me in the eyes. "When it comes to you, I don't need the chase. I love you, Selene. I always will." He leans his forehead against mine.

I smile. "I love you too, Ronan. I love you too."

EPILOGUE
SELENE

$\mathcal{T}$he hum of the airplane engine roars in my ears and my heart beats fast. I get a familiar tingle in my limbs as we gain altitude. Over the last six months, I've jumped with Ronan nine times. Today is number ten.

I've gotten good enough that I can jump on my own, without Ronan or an instructor. It's literally the last thing I ever thought I'd enjoy doing, but I love it. I love every second of it, from the moment we get on the plane to the moment we're on the ground.

I've long since settled into my new role as VP of Operations for VI. Ronan has to split his time between the Seattle office and Edge in San Francisco, so I run things in Seattle. There was plenty of water cooler talk about the two of us when he announced my promotion, but it was followed closely by the announcement of our three-hundred-million-dollar government contract, so the rumors didn't last. Everyone knew my role in getting that contract, so it was clear the promotion was not the result of me fucking the boss.

Not that I mind fucking the boss. Not one bit.

Kylie looks at me with wide eyes. Braxton has been up with

us several times, but it wasn't until today that we finally talked Kylie into jumping. One of the instructors will jump with her, and she has a radio in her helmet with a crew member on the ground to help guide her down. But I can see the nervousness on her face.

"You're going to be fine," I say, pitching my voice to be heard above the engine.

"I'm scared," she says. "And excited. And fucking scared."

I laugh. "I know. But this will be amazing. Trust me."

Braxton turns around and checks her harness again. He's usually as amped as Ronan for a skydive, but I think having Kylie here is making him nervous. He's run his fingers beneath the straps at her shoulders at least a dozen times, making sure they're tight enough.

Ronan takes my hand and brings it up to his lips, kissing the backs of my fingers. I smile and we both look out the window. There are a few puffy white clouds high above us, but otherwise the sky is clear. He was in San Francisco until late last night, and I still feel the relief of being together after missing him all week. I'm glad he doesn't have to go back for a while.

Some people might get sick of each other when they're together pretty much all the time. But Ronan and I have settled into working and living together, and I can't imagine it any other way. He moved into my house a few months ago, after we both admitted he more or less lived there already. We have plenty of room at home, so we both have our own spaces. I insisted he take my dad's old study and make it into an office, so he has a place to work and unwind. I love that the room is being used again. It was always so sad and dusty before, with no one who needed it. My whole house feels better with two of us living there. It used to be too empty, just me with all these rooms. Now I have someone to share it with, and I know my parents would be happy to see us there, living and loving in the space where they lived and loved Braxton and me.

Ronan keeps staring out the window. He seems quiet today, like he has a lot on his mind. It's hard to have a conversation with the noise of the airplane, so I figure I'll ask him about it after the jump. Maybe he just needs his adrenaline rush. He doesn't seem to crave danger nearly as much as he used to, but he does get antsy if we spend too much time working without doing something to blow off steam. Maybe he had a stressful week in San Francisco. He looks at me again and smiles, bringing my hand up to his lips for another kiss.

We get to jump altitude and the door is opened. The noise level rises with the air whipping past. The first couple of jumpers take their positions and go, disappearing from sight. Kylie's instructor eases her out to the jump spot, and when she nods that she's ready, they both take the leap. I'm so excited and nervous for her that my heart feels like it's going to thump right out of my chest.

Braxton turns and gives me a wink before he throws himself out of the plane, right behind Kylie.

Ronan and I move toward the open door. We both hold on to the bar, but before we can jump he turns to me.

"When we get on the ground, I have something for you," he says.

"What is it?" I ask. It's a little hard to hear him with all the noise.

He gives me a smile that makes my core tingle, and unzips the top of his jumpsuit. He reaches inside and pulls out a small box.

It's a jewelry box.

Oh my god. Is that what I think it is? My tummy does a belly flop and my mouth drops open.

He slides the box back in and pulls up the zipper, giving me a sly smile.

He raises his voice above the noise of the engine. "Marry me?"

Then, with another smoldering smile, he tumbles out of the airplane.

I gasp and jump out of the plane after him.

ALWAYS EVER AFTER

Braxton and Kylie have been married for over a year, and Kylie is busy helping Selene get ready for her upcoming wedding. Kylie and Selene go out of town for a bachelorette party weekend, and Kylie gets a little—or maybe it's a big—surprise.

But springing the news on Braxton is harder than Kylie thought. In the week leading up to Selene and Ronan's wedding, Ky and Brax both have things to share, and life as they know it is about to change forever.

This is a short follow-up novella of about 16,000 words, and takes place after the books ALWAYS HAVE and ALWAYS WILL. It contains spoilers, as well as the couples, from both books.

1

BRAXTON

I nod to the bartender as he slides over my glass of whiskey. "Thanks, man." The first sip goes down nice and smooth, sending a trail of heat to my gut. My phone vibrates and I take it out of my pocket, hoping it's a text from Kylie. I'm kind of bummed to see it isn't, but I wasn't expecting to hear from her until later tonight anyway.

Instead, it's Ronan, my twin sister Selene's fiancé. *We still on for tomorrow?*

Ronan and Selene's wedding is in a week, so we're going skydiving for his bachelor party. Both Ronan and I like women as much, or maybe more than, the next guy, but he's not really into the whole strip club thing. He's more of a *put himself in mortal danger* kind of dude, so skydiving it is. Works for me. I'd never tried skydiving before I met Ronan, but fuck it's a rush. I've gone up with him quite a few times since he started dating my sister. It's fucking awesome.

I text back: *You know it.*

I wonder if he's doing the same thing I am—feeling sorry for himself because his woman is out of town without him—and send another text: *I'm at Phinney Tavern if you're bored.*

Selene and Kylie went away for Selene's bachelorette party weekend, and won't be home until Sunday. Ky was really looking forward to this, so I'm glad she gets to go have some fun with my sister. But fuck, I miss her. She's been gone for maybe twelve hours and I already hate it. We haven't been apart, except to go to work, since we got married—hell, not since we got back from London, when I proposed to her. When I almost lost her.

I shudder at that memory. What a fucking nightmare that was. I was such a dumbass for lying to my sister about our relationship.

I know Selene feels bad about what happened, but I've never blamed her. She did make me promise not to hook up with Ky, and like an idiot I broke up with Kylie over it. But Selene had no idea how I really felt about Kylie. When I finally stopped lying, and told Selene how much I loved Kylie, she was ready to do anything to help me get her back. She even flew to London with me when we realized Kylie had gone away for New Year's Eve.

I know Selene was only trying to protect Kylie, and protect their friendship. She had every reason to believe I'd hook up with Ky and leave her—it's what I'd done with all the women who came in and out of my life before.

But Kylie was always different. She was always the one I wanted.

And the look on Selene's face when Kylie and I got back to our hotel in London, and Kylie was wearing my ring? Fucking priceless.

Thinking of that makes me smile a bit, and I take another sip of my drink.

Ronan texts back. *Nah, I'm wiped from work. Calling it a night.*

Ronan's a good guy. I wanted to tear his arms off when he broke up with Selene, but in the end, he came around. I'm happy for my sister. I've been anxious to see her with the right guy for years, and I'm relieved she found someone who's so good for her. It's satisfying to know she's not living alone in our childhood home anymore.

"Braxton Taylor," a voice says behind me. I cringe. The voice is familiar, but I'm not quite sure who it is. The way she said my name makes me think it must be one of my exes, or at least a girl I slept with once or twice. I glance over my shoulder, hoping I remember who she is. I'll feel like a dick if I have to ask her name.

It's Hope, a girl I dated for a couple months not long before I finally got together with Kylie. I'm relieved I know her name but, if I remember correctly, Hope had a temper.

I decide to play it cool and pretend this isn't going to be awkward. I turn around and give her an easy smile. "Hope. Good to see you again."

"How nice," she says. "You actually remember me."

Did I really date her? What was I thinking? "Yeah, of course. What are you up to tonight?"

She shrugs and slides up onto the stool next to me. Uh oh, what is she doing? "Nothing much. I just moved to an apartment around the corner from here. I came in with some friends and saw you. Figured I'd come say hi."

"Um, hi." Now I *am* feeling awkward. Hope is clearly checking me out. Her eyes move up and down, lingering on my crotch longer than necessary. When she looks up, she holds my gaze. I know that look. She wants to hook up with me tonight. I'm guessing she just wants a casual fuck, but there's no mistaking her expression. She's giving me the *I'm going to fuck you later* look.

There was a time when she'd have been right. I'd have taken her home, and not worried too much about the consequences. But now? Hell, no. Those days are long behind me, and I'm fucking ecstatic about it. I don't care who I was before Kylie. I'm all Kylie's—now, and for the rest of my life. There isn't a woman on this planet who could even tempt me.

Hope's got a lot of skin showing, and by all accounts she's an attractive woman. My dick? Doesn't give a shit. All I can think about is how to get out of this situation.

"So, are you here all by yourself?" She licks her lips. "That's not like you."

My mouth turns up in a half smile. "Actually, my wife's out of town, so I'm just killing time."

Hope's eyes widen and her mouth drops open. I shift on my stool so I can lean my arm on the bar, my left hand in plain sight. Her eyes dart to my hand. *Yes, Hope, that's a wedding ring you're looking at.*

"*You* got married?" she asks.

I keep smiling. This just got fun. "Yes, I did. Over a year ago."

"What, did you knock her up or something?" Hope asks.

My face goes still. "No, I didn't marry her because I got her fucking pregnant."

Although come to think of it, I sure wouldn't mind getting Kylie pregnant. We've talked about it a little bit, but we haven't made any definite plans. I've been thinking about it lately, and the more I do, the more I like the idea—and that's the weirdest thing, because it wasn't long ago that *pregnant* was the most terrifying word imaginable. But Kylie pregnant with my baby? I like the sound of that. A lot.

Hope leans away and crosses her legs. "Hey, sorry. I just figured she must have roped you in somehow."

"No, she didn't have to rope me in."

"Well, who's the lucky girl?" Hope asks. "Anyone I know?"

And I'm smiling again. "You remember my best friend, Kylie?"

"Yes..." Hope says, her voice hesitant.

"Kylie's my wife." God, I love saying that. It's my favorite fucking sentence.

Hope's mouth drops again. "You have got to be kidding me." She rolls her eyes and laughs. "I knew it. The whole time we were dating, I knew she was trying to get her claws into you."

"That's not what was going on." I turn back to the bar and take a sip of my drink. "But you can think whatever you want."

She gets down from the stool. "Well, congratulations to both of you. And good luck to her." She flips her hair over her shoulder and walks away.

Good luck to her? That was a bitchy thing to say, but I just shrug and go back to my drink. It doesn't matter what Hope thinks. All that matters is that I married the best fucking woman in the world, and I get to love the shit out of her forever.

Except when she's out of town. Which sucks.

I finish my whiskey and decide to head home. I wonder what my girls are doing tonight. They drove out to a resort in the mountains, and Kylie said there's going to be a lot of spa treatments and booze. I'm glad they didn't go more than a few hours away. Yeah, I'm acting a little crazy about Ky being out of town, but I like that if I had to jump in the car to get to her, I could.

I love my girl. So sue me.

My phone buzzes with Kylie's text right as I walk in the door of our condo. *Miss you, baby.*

I toss my coat on a chair and sink down onto the couch. *Miss you too. Call me? I want to hear your voice.*

My phone rings right away. "Hi, baby girl."

"Hi," she says. "How was your day?"

"Not bad," I say. "You?"

"It's been good," she says. "So relaxing, and the restaurant here is amazing."

"Awesome, I'm glad you're having a good time. What are you up to now?"

"Nothing much," she says. "Selene went back to her room for a while, so I'm just lying here."

I perk up at that. "Lying where?"

"On the bed."

"Alone?"

"Yeah."

"I wish I was there," I say.

"Me, too," she says. "What would you do if you were here?"

"What are you wearing?" I lie down and get comfortable. "I need a visual."

"Well, jeans," she says. "And a gray shirt. I guess I should do better than that, though."

"No, that's fine," I say. "But take off the jeans."

"Okay." There's some muffled noise before she gets back on the line. "Now I'm in a shirt and panties. They're light blue with a bit of lace."

"Mm, I love the light blue ones," I say. "They look good against your creamy skin. I want to nibble down your thighs until I get to those panties. Then I'd tease you through them, pressing my tongue against you until you beg me to fuck you with my tongue."

"Holy shit, Brax," she says. "Are we doing this?"

"Yeah we are, baby," I say, my voice going rough and low. "Put your fingers in those panties and tell me what you feel."

I hear her sharp intake of breath. "Oh god, Braxton, I'm already wet."

My eyes roll back and I unzip my pants. "Fuck, Ky, I'm so hard right now. My dick is aching for you. I want to taste your sweet pussy. I want to flick my tongue on your clit and make you call my name."

"I love your tongue on my pussy," she says. "I'd put your cock in my mouth and suck you so fucking hard. I'd take you all in, and my mouth would be so warm and wet. You'd fuck my mouth, in and out, until you're ready to burst down my throat."

I get Kylie's lotion off the coffee table and put a little in my hand. It smells like her. It's not the same as having her here, but it's going to make jacking off to the sound of her dirty mouth a hell of a lot hotter.

"That's right, baby." I slide my hand down the shaft and get my cock nice and slick. "Before I come, I'd pull out and throw you down onto your back. I'd push your legs wide open and bury my dick in you." I start to stroke, not too fast at first, and groan into the phone. "I can feel you all over me. You're so tight. Tell me what you're doing."

"I'm putting my fingers in my pussy," she says. "I'm getting them wet. Now I'm rubbing my clit and ... oh fuck, yeah, there it is."

"Imagine my cock inside you." I pick up the pace, stroking faster. "I'm pounding you so hard. So fucking hard, Kylie. You're going crazy underneath me."

"Tell me what you're doing," she says.

This is so hot. I'd rather be fucking her for real, but this is good, too. "I'm rubbing my cock, baby. I'm as hard as if I was inside you right now. I have your lotion on me, so I can smell you."

"Rub faster," she says. "Do it faster."

I stroke faster and groan again.

"You're inside me, Braxton, and I'm so hot," she says. "I'm clenching around your thick cock. Fuck, it's so good."

"Harder, baby girl." I pick up the pace, feeling my balls tighten.

She whimpers into the phone. "Brax, I want to come."

"Do it, baby." I take a second to put her on speaker so I don't have to hold the phone. "I'm stroking it fast. Rub yourself faster. Imagine it's me. It's my cock in you."

"Holy shit," she says and the urgency in her voice gets me closer. "Yes, fuck. Yes."

I really go for it, leaning my head back and closing my eyes as I rub my dick faster, listening to her breathing heavily into the phone.

"I'm so close," she says. "Talk to me. I'm so close."

"I'm going to fuck you so hard when you get home," I growl at her between breaths. "I'm going to pound you with my cock until you can't breathe."

She whimpers and moans. "Brax, I'm gonna come."

"Come, baby girl. Let me hear it."

She moans again and her voice goes higher, sharp spasms of sound in time with her orgasm. Just the sound of it sends me off the cliff. I stroke a few more times and burst, come spurting out of my dick. I don't hold back, groaning with each pulse, letting her hear me lose my mind with her.

The climax subsides and I take a few deep breaths, my eyes closed. I can hear her breathing hard.

"Wow," she says. "I didn't think I could do that."

I laugh and open my eyes. Shit, I made a mess. I didn't plan that very well. There are splotches of come all over my shirt. But it was worth it.

"Fuck, Kylie, you're not even here and you know how to undo me."

We both sit in silence for a moment. I can hear her breathing.

"Stay on the phone, okay?" she asks. "I'll be right back. I want to clean up a little."

"Yeah, me too."

I leave the phone sitting on the arm of the couch, and go wash up and change. I come back wearing just a fresh pair of underwear and take the phone to the bedroom. I climb in bed and roll over to Kylie's side. Her pillow smells like her, and I bury my face in it, breathing her in.

"You back?" she asks.

"Yeah," I say. "I feel better, but I still miss you."

"I miss you too, love," she says.

I roll onto my back and put an arm across my forehead. "Are you getting up again, or are you guys done for the night?"

"I'm pretty sure I got a text from Selene a few minutes ago," she says with a laugh. "She probably wants to go get a drink in the bar. I guess I'll tell her I was in the bathroom."

"Okay, well, you girls have fun tonight," I say.

"We will," she says. "I love you, Braxton."

A wide smile crosses my face. "God, I love you so much, Kylie. I'm so glad you're mine."

"Always," she says. "I'll call you in the morning."

"Night, baby girl."

"Night, love."

2

KYLIE

I touch up my makeup and fix my hair, although my cheeks are still flushed. I've never actually had phone sex before, but damn, that was hot. I didn't call Braxton with that in mind, but my panties were drenched as soon as I heard his voice.

God, that man. He can melt me with nothing but a word. It's really quite the talent.

We've been married for more than a year—a year!—and he still takes my breath away. I think he always will. We're just as crazy in love as we were the first night we were together. He was already my best friend—one of my two favorite people in the world—so being married to him is like all the best parts of our friendship, plus the best sex I've ever had.

Seriously, who gets that lucky? I have no idea what I did to deserve him, but I'm grateful beyond words.

I send Selene a quick text, telling her I'm ready. So far, our girl's weekend has been a blast. We have a couple of rooms at a beautiful resort in the mountains, and I planned us a weekend of pampering. Today we had facials, plus a delicious dinner in the restaurant downstairs. Tomorrow we have brunch, followed by mani-pedis, and massages in the afternoon.

I figure tonight Selene probably wants to hang out in the bar and have a few drinks. It's mellow for a bachelorette party, but it's what she wanted. I'm happy I get to spend so much time with her, just the two of us. With her wedding coming up, things have been pretty crazy. I think we both needed to unwind.

There's a knock on my door, and I answer it to find Selene. She's dressed in a mint green top and jeans.

"Ready?" she asks.

"Yeah, let me grab my purse." I make sure I have my wallet and room key, and follow her out into the hallway. We get to the elevator, and I notice she keeps messing with her hair. "You okay?" I ask.

"Yeah." She smooths her hair down again. "Is it warm up here? I'm a little warm."

"I guess. Maybe it's all the phone sex you were having with Ronan."

She gasps.

I glance at her. "Did you really?"

She touches her fingers to her lips and smiles. "Maybe."

The elevator opens and we both get in. Thankfully, there's no one else inside. "You little minx."

"Hey, don't judge," she says. "That man can do it for me from three hundred miles away. There's nothing wrong with that."

"I'm not judging," I say. "I may have been on the phone with Braxton when you texted, and..."

"Kinky," she says. "And, ew."

I laugh. "I won't give you details. Fuck, I miss him. Don't get me wrong, this weekend is wonderful. But he and I haven't really spent any time apart since we got married. Is that weird?"

"I don't think so," she says. "And it's sweet that you miss him. I miss Ronan too. I always do when he's gone."

Selene and Ronan are not only getting married, they work together. He has to spend some of his time in San Francisco, so they have weeks when they're apart. But they seem to have adjusted to their new life really well.

I could not be more excited for her to get married. I've wanted this for her for so long, and Ronan is amazing. He's kind of insane, what with his penchant for jumping out of perfectly good airplanes, and climbing sheer rock faces. But he's crazy about Selene, and I think she's just what he needs to keep him on his toes.

We get down to the hotel bar and find a small table. The bartender comes to take our order, and Selene asks for more time. He brings us a couple ice waters.

Selene fiddles with her necklace and keeps glancing away.

"What's going on with you tonight?" I ask. "Is it that hard to pick a drink? Just order a martini."

"I'm not sure if I want to drink tonight," she says.

"Okay," I say. "I guess there's no rule that says we have to get wasted this weekend. Although it would be fun. Are you sure you're feeling okay?"

"Yeah, I'm fine," she says. "Maybe I'll see if they serve dessert in here instead."

It's not that Selene and I are raging drunks, but we usually enjoy a cocktail or three together. And this is her bachelorette weekend. I assumed getting tipsy was on the agenda.

But it's her weekend, so I just shrug. "Okay."

The bartender comes back, and Selene orders a coffee and a slice of cheesecake. I decide to follow her lead and order the same. We chat for a few minutes, and our coffee and desserts arrive.

Selene picks at her cheesecake for a while, barely touching her coffee.

"Okay, babe," I say, putting my fork down. "What's going on?

Is it the wedding? Is something going on with Ronan? You've been acting weird all day. What's up?"

"No, Ronan is great," she says. "And the wedding ... it's basically done. I guess maybe I'm just nervous."

"It's going to be wonderful," I say. "I was nervous for my wedding, too, but I promise it will be amazing. And Ronan is so perfect for you."

"I know he is," she says. "It's not that at all. I want to marry him. I can't *wait* to marry him."

"Then what is it?" I ask. "I know you. Something is bugging you."

She takes a deep breath. "Ky, I'm late."

It takes me half a second to get her meaning, but then my eyes widen. "Oh, shit. Do you think—"

"I don't know," she says. "I bought a test before we left, and I was going to take it when we went back to our rooms earlier, but then Ronan called."

"So that's why you're not drinking," I say. "Oh my god, Selene, this is so exciting. Did you say anything to Ronan?"

"No, I didn't want to make him panic," she says. "We haven't really talked about having kids. Not seriously, at least."

"Are you worried he doesn't want to?"

"A little," she says. "He's never said he doesn't want children, but he's never specifically said he does. I know I really should have brought this up with him sooner. What if he doesn't want kids? And what if ... fuck, Ky, what if I'm pregnant?"

"Honey, there's only one way to find out," I say. "Did you bring the test?"

"Yeah, it's upstairs."

"Let's go do it," I say. "I know you're scared. I'll be with you the whole time, okay? And listen, Ronan loves you. If you're pregnant, even if it's a huge surprise to him, he's still going to love you. I bet he'll be thrilled."

I pay our bill and we head back upstairs to Selene's room. I put my purse down and sit on the bed while she goes into the bathroom. After a couple of minutes, she comes out.

"Okay, I did it," she says. "Now it says to wait three minutes. I'm terrified."

"Come here," I say. She sits down on the edge of the bed and I put my arms around her. "It's going to be fine."

"Ky, there are two tests," she says. "Go take the other one."

"What? Why?"

"I know it makes absolutely no sense," she says. "But please. Just go take it. It will make me feel better if we're doing this together."

I laugh and squeeze her. "Like when you got your period before me, and I wore a maxi-pad too, so you weren't the only one?"

"Yes, exactly."

"Okay, babe. I'll go pee on the stick if it makes you feel better."

I go into the bathroom. Selene's test is sitting on the counter with a strip of toilet paper over the top of it. I do my best not to laugh at her. She's so sweet. Poor thing. I grab the box with the other test in it and look at the instructions.

It's simple enough. I pee on the end and put the cap back on, then set it on the back of the toilet, so it's not right next to Selene's.

"There," I say when I come out of the bathroom. "Happy now?"

"Actually, yes," she says. "I'm still nervous, but this is better."

We're supposed to wait three minutes, so we sit in silence, both of us staring at the clocks on our phone screens.

"Okay, I think mine should be ready," she says, but she doesn't get up.

I squeeze her again. "Babe, you're so nervous. I'll go get it and tell you what it says."

She nods. I go into the bathroom and get her test off the counter. I grab the box, so I can compare what the results mean. There's one blue line in the test window, and according to the box, that means not pregnant.

I come out of the bathroom and smile. "Negative. You're not pregnant."

She puts a hand to her mouth and closes her eyes. I bring the test over and set it on the nightstand, in case she wants to see it.

"Are you okay?" I sit and put my arm around her again.

She takes a shuddering breath. "I don't know why I'm upset. I should be relieved. But ... I'm kind of disappointed."

"Aw," I say, and rub her back. "That's totally understandable. You've probably been working yourself up to it all day."

"Yeah." She sniffs. "Okay, go get yours."

I laugh. "Well, I know mine is negative, but I'll grab it, I guess."

I go back into the bathroom and pick up my test off the back of the toilet. I glance at it, and something catches my eye. It doesn't look the same as Selene's. I look again, and grab the box, holding up the panel with the instructions.

Wait, did I have that wrong? Does two lines mean negative and one means positive? Because mine has two lines, and Selene's only had one. Didn't it?

"Selene, I'm confused." I come out of the bathroom, my test in one hand and the box in the other. I toss her the box. "What does this mean? Did I read them wrong?"

She catches it and looks at the instructions. "One line is negative. Why, does mine have two, and you thought that meant negative?" She grabs her test and compares it to the picture on the box. "No, it says here one line means negative, and mine definitely has just one line." She meets my eyes. "Wait. What does yours look like?"

I stare at her, my eyes bugging out of my head, my heart racing a million miles a second. I swallow hard and look at the test dangling from my fingers. The test window is a little rectangle in the middle of the strip of plastic, and staring back at me are two very dark, solid blue lines. I turn it so Selene can see.

"Holy shit, Kylie," Selene says, her voice quiet. "I think you're pregnant."

3

KYLIE

"*W*hat the fuck is this?" I say, holding out the test. "These must be defective."

"Or you're pregnant," Selene says. "Are you sure that's yours, and this one is mine?"

"Absolutely. Yours was on the counter, and I put mine on the back of the toilet." My heart won't stop pounding and my hands are starting to shake. "How could I be pregnant?"

"I'm pretty sure you know how sex works."

"I know, but..." I look at the test again, hoping I'm seeing double. But there's only one test, and it definitely has two lines. "Why did you have to get this stupid thing with the lines? How do we know these are right? Maybe they're both defective."

"Is your period late?"

"No," I say, my voice emphatic. "I'm not supposed to start for another few days. Do these things even work before your period is due?"

Selene looks at the box and reads out loud: "*Test early, up to five days before your period is expected.* Yeah, I think they work."

"No way," I say, grabbing the box out of her hands. "This

must be wrong. I bet these got it backwards somehow, and you're pregnant and I'm not."

"Are you wishing this on me, now?" she asks with a laugh. "Because you're the one who's been married for a while. You must have at least talked to Brax about kids. Ronan and I haven't even gotten through our wedding yet."

I sink down onto the edge of the bed. "Yeah, we've talked a little. He seems pretty hesitant. Not *forever* hesitant, but I don't think he's ready for kids yet. He says he's happy to have me to himself right now, and we'll think about a family in the future. Honestly, that's how I feel too, so I haven't worried about it very much."

Selene takes a deep breath. "You know what? Maybe these *are* defective. We need to get more tests and do this again."

We head out to Selene's car—this isn't the kind of thing the resort gift shop carries—and find a little store a couple miles away. We end up buying several boxes of tests each, just in case, and the cashier doesn't even make small talk with us while we pay.

Back at the resort, we stop outside our rooms.

"How about we go into our own bathrooms, so we can take them at the same time," Selene says.

"Sounds good."

Our rooms are next to each other with an adjoining door, so we open it and both go into our respective bathrooms.

I pick a brand that has a digital readout. The damn thing will say either *Pregnant* or *Not Pregnant*, so that should be clear. And I think it's good that we're not taking tests from the same box. I bought enough that I can take more if this one is confusing.

My hands are shaking so badly I almost drop the stupid thing in the toilet. I follow the instructions and set it on the counter, putting a strip of toilet paper over the top so I can hide it until I'm ready to look.

I come out to find Selene pacing in between our two rooms.

"This is insane," I say. "How did we end up taking pregnancy tests on our girls' weekend?"

Selene stops. "I have no idea. I'm so sorry. I should have waited until we got home for this."

"No, I'm glad you brought it up," I say. "Fuck, Selene, I was going to get smashed with you tonight. And probably again tomorrow."

I glance at my phone, but it's only been two minutes. What if I *am* pregnant? I quit my job to do freelance graphic design full time about six months ago, and I was hoping to spend a couple years building up my client list. Having a baby now would change things. It would change everything.

What is Brax going to say? Is he going to be upset? We've never had an in-depth conversation about kids, but I've never felt like we needed to. He's always been so casual about it, with a shrug and a *sure, someday* attitude. And that was fine with me. I thought this would be something we would decide together, and plan for. Is he going to freak out?

"Okay, I think it's time," I say. "Go get yours and I'll get mine, and we'll look together."

Selene nods and we both rush back into the bathrooms. I grab the test, still covered. I come out of the bathroom and Selene and I stand in front of each other, pregnancy tests in hand.

"Are you ready?" she asks.

"I think so."

My heart is racing so fast I'm almost dizzy. I pull the test out from under the bit of toilet paper and force myself to look.

On the screen, in very clear letters, is the word *Pregnant*.

I meet Selene's eyes.

"Mine says *Not Pregnant*," she says.

I hold mine up so she can see it.

We stare at each other for a long moment. Selene blinks, her eyes filling with tears, and sets her test down.

"Kylie," she says, her voice barely above a whisper. "You're going to have a baby."

My hands tremble so much I drop the test. Selene rushes in and wraps me in a hug. I put my arms around her, so shocked I can barely think.

I'm freaking the fuck out, but I'm so glad I'm with Selene.

She pulls back and grabs my hands. "Oh, honey. What do you want to do? Do you want to call Brax? Should we go home?"

"No," I say, squeezing her hands. "No, I don't want to ruin your weekend. This is about you. And I don't want to tell him over the phone. I'll talk to him when I get back." I take a deep breath. "Let's just enjoy our day tomorrow. I think maybe I could use some time to get used to this before I tell him anyway."

"How about this," she says. "We won't stay tomorrow night. We don't have anything planned for Sunday as it is. We can either stay for dinner and head home then, or leave right after our massage appointments in the afternoon. It's up to you."

"Are you sure?"

"Positive," she says. "But honestly, if you want to go now, I'll drive. I don't even care."

"No, I don't want to leave now," I say. "But can I sleep in your room with you tonight? I don't think I want to be alone."

She hugs me again. "Of course. Come on. Let's find a movie to watch. I'd say let's get drunk, but I guess that isn't happening for a while."

We both change, and I get in her big king-size bed with her. I let her pick the movie; I doubt I'll be able to pay attention anyway. My eyes are on the screen, but my hand drifts down to my belly.

Is there really a baby in there?

This is so unexpected, and I'm kind of terrified. But there's also a new feeling blooming inside. It's warm—a deep sense of contentment when I think about what this means. Braxton and I having a baby together. My belly growing with the child we made. I smile a little when I think about it that way.

A baby. *Braxton's* baby. The more I think about it, the more I like the way that sounds.

4

BRAXTON

I set down my keys on the counter with a clink. Skydiving today was off the hook. The weather was perfect, and everything went according to plan. We went with a couple other guys Ronan knows, and afterward we all got dinner and beers at a great barbeque place. I'm still a little buzzed from the mix of adrenaline and alcohol.

I pause, noticing Kylie's purse is on the little table by the door. Is she home early?

She steps out of the bedroom, dressed in nothing but a lacy black bra and panties.

Fuck, yes.

"Baby girl, you are the best thing I've ever seen in my life." I strip my shirt off and toss it to the floor.

She laughs and curls a finger at me. "Come here."

I kick off my shoes and take off my pants as I follow her into our bedroom. I have to get my hands on her, but she keeps backing away.

"Get your ass over here." I pin her against the wall and kiss her mouth, gently caressing her tongue with mine. I take my time, feeling her body melt into me while I savor her.

I'm suddenly reminded of the first time I kissed her. God, she felt so good. I waited so long for that kiss.

I pull away and touch her face. "Is everything okay? You're home early."

"Yeah, everything's fine." She hesitates for a moment, running her hands up my chest and around to the back of my neck. "I need to talk to you about something, though."

"Okay. Sex first." I kiss her again, threading my fingers through her hair.

She laughs as I move her to the bed and lay her down on her back. "You're insatiable, you know that?"

"No, I'm just in love with you." I climb on top of her and graze her neck with my teeth. "Plus, you're so fucking sexy."

I get her bra and panties off, and run my hands all over her body. She lifts her arms above her head and closes her eyes while I caress her skin. I slide my tongue across one of her nipples, and she shudders.

"Baby, stop playing," she says, her voice breathless. "I need you inside me right now."

I lick her again and kiss my way up to her neck. She reaches into my underwear and wraps her fingers around my cock.

I groan into her ear. "What do you want, baby girl?"

She squeezes my dick. "This. Now."

I groan again and pull off my underwear. She opens her gorgeous legs for me and I settle in on top of her, sliding my cock in slowly. She grabs my ass and tries to push me in harder, but I resist. There's nothing like that first thrust, when her hot pussy envelopes me.

My desire to move slowly doesn't last.

She wraps her legs around me and I move in and out, pushing in as deep as I can go. Her hips move with me, and she digs her fingers into my back. I kiss her mouth, our tongues lashing together, as frantic as our bodies. I pick up the pace, pounding her harder. She moans and runs her hands along my skin, sending sparks through every nerve.

Nothing compares to this. To her. She feels so goddamn good. I know she thinks I have an unending sexual appetite—and to be fair, I probably do. But it's not just that. This is the best way I know to show her how I feel. I can tell her a million times that I love her. That she's my world. My life. And I do, every single day. But when I make passionate love to her—when I fuck her until she's breathless—I show her. Not just with words, but with my whole body. I can show her what she is to me, make her feel what I'm feeling.

With our bodies connected, we're completely in sync. She moves with me, moans with me, cries out in pleasure with me. I feel her climax building and I hold back, waiting for her to be ready. My cock throbs.

"Yes, baby," she says. "Right there. Oh, my god, yes."

Her voice goes high-pitched and her pussy tightens. My eyes roll back in my head and I explode inside her. The orgasm comes in hot waves, pulsing through me. For those blissful seconds, there's nothing else. Just the agony of release, the feel of her wet pussy, the sound of her voice as we come together.

I move off her and we lie together for a moment, catching our breath. She rolls over to kiss my shoulder, then gets up and slips into the bathroom.

She comes back a few minutes later, still naked. I pull her back into bed with me and wrap her in my arms, breathing in her scent. My eyes drift closed. I'm so relaxed with her body warm against mine that I could probably fall asleep like this, but I remember that I have some things to talk to her about.

"I heard back from the real estate guy," I say.

She lifts her head and props it up on her hand. "You did?"

"They accepted my offer."

I've been working for months on a deal to buy a new

building for my gym. I've outgrown the space I'm in, and Kylie
and I decided that instead of finding a new place to lease, it
would be a good investment to buy a building. It took a while to
find the right location, but the one we found is perfect.

"Are you serious?" she asks. "This is going to happen?"

I smile. "Yep, it's going to happen. We got a great deal on it
too. It's a pretty big cash outlay, but long term, this is going to be
huge for us."

"Wow," she says. "It's kind of scary, but exciting."

I kiss her forehead. "It is. But don't let it stress you out. We
have a solid plan. We just need to stick to it."

Kylie takes a deep breath and lays her head on my shoulder.
I have another surprise for her. I was planning to wait until after
Selene's wedding to tell her. But I feel like she's going to be
anxious about the business stuff, so maybe now is a good time.

"I have another surprise for you, baby girl."

"Uh oh," she says. "You didn't buy a new house too, did you?"

I laugh. "No. But I did buy some plane tickets."

"Plane tickets? Are we going somewhere?"

"We are."

She glances up at me. "Are you going to tell me where?"

"You need to guess."

"Um..." She caresses my chest while she thinks. I love the
way her hands feel on me. "Honestly, I have no idea."

"I'm taking you back to London."

"What? Are you fucking with me?"

I shift so I can look at her. "Nope. We're going to do London
right this time. I booked it for a few months from now, so we can
both arrange with our clients to be gone."

"Wow, that's amazing," she says. "But ... are you sure we
should do this now?"

"Of course," I say. "This is the perfect time. Once I move my gym into the new space, things are going to get a lot busier. Besides, I want to do this with you."

"But it's so expensive."

"It's fine." I kiss her again. "I'll dip into my inheritance for this if I need to." My parents left Selene and me a considerable amount of money when they died. We both used it to pay for college, and I took out more to buy my condo, as well as open my gym.

Generally, I don't spend what's left of it unless I have to. That money feels sacred to me, because it was theirs. But I won't hesitate to use it for this.

"Oh, Brax," Kylie says.

"This means a lot to me," I say. "I've wanted to go back to London with you since we were there last time. I want to take you to all the places you want to see so we can experience them together, like we should have before."

"Why are you so amazing?" she asks.

I rub my nose against hers and kiss her lightly on the mouth. "Did you need to talk to me about something?"

"Oh," she says, looking away. "I guess I don't remember now."

"Was it something to do with Selene?" I ask. "Is she okay? You didn't tell me why you're back early."

"Selene's fine," she says. "We had fun, but we didn't have anything planned for tomorrow, so we decided we'd rather come home."

"I can't argue with that," I say. "I'm glad you're home."

5

KYLIE

*B*rax and I let ourselves into Selene and Ronan's house. Selene texted me earlier and said she could use help with some wedding stuff. I'm more than happy to help; I just wish I wasn't so tired. It's barely after six, and I feel like I can't keep my eyes open.

Selene is sitting at the dining table with a sprawl of candles, ribbon, and glass vases. "Hey, you guys." She meets my eyes and raises her eyebrows.

I give her a quick head shake and she looks a little confused.

Please don't say anything, Selene. Not yet.

Braxton surveys the table. "This looks like a nightmare. What the fuck are you doing?"

Selene groans. "I thought it would be a good idea to make my own centerpieces for the reception. Pinterest is the devil."

I take a seat next to her. "I'll help. Just tell me how they're supposed to look."

Selene points to a finished one off to the side. "They look simple, but this ribbon is a pain in the ass."

Ronan comes downstairs. He's as tall as Braxton, with dark

hair and a chiseled Disney-prince jaw. He nods to Brax and comes over to kiss Selene.

"This looks like something I should run from," he says.

"I'll go get takeout," Braxton says. He looks at Ronan. "Want to come?"

"Yes," Ronan says. "Definitely."

The guys head out. I try get the layers of ribbon to cooperate, but Selene is right. This is a pain in the ass.

"Why didn't you have the florist do these?" I ask.

Selene rolls her eyes. "Because the internet makes things look so easy. I might just call them in the morning and add centerpieces to our order."

"That's probably a good idea."

She puts her strand of ribbon down. "So, what's up? Did you talk to Brax yet?"

"No. I was going to on Saturday, but we got distracted."

"Distracted? God, Ky, no wonder you're pregnant," she says. "I'm surprised it took this long."

I toss a piece of ribbon at her. "It wasn't that."

She arches an eyebrow at me.

"Okay, it started with that, but I wanted him to be in a good mood. Afterward, he told me the building owners accepted his offer. So this business expansion is really happening."

"Yeah, he told me about that yesterday," she says. "Congratulations."

"Thanks," I say. "But it's kind of scary, you know? And then he told me he booked us a trip to London."

"Oh my god," she says. "That's awesome."

"Yeah, it is. But ... I don't know if we should be doing all this right now. It's so much, and it reminded me how unplanned this pregnancy is. *If* I'm really pregnant, which I still don't know for sure."

"What do you mean, you don't know for sure? The tests were positive."

"Yeah, but I haven't been to the doctor yet," I say. "I don't want to drop this in his lap before I'm completely sure."

"Kylie," she says, a note of sternness in her voice. "Do you really think both those pregnancy tests were wrong?"

I chew on my lower lip. "Maybe."

"Do you have any more?" she asks. "You should take another one."

"Yeah, I have a box in my purse from this weekend."

"Go take it," she says.

"Why?"

"I think you need to see it a few more times before this really sinks in, babe," she says.

I sigh. "Fine, but I'm still not telling Brax until after I see my doctor."

"Fair enough, but you need to talk to him soon," she says. "I'm terrible at lying to him, and if he starts to suspect something is going on, he's going to see right through me. I won't tell, but this is getting really hard to keep in."

I look at her in alarm. "You didn't tell Ronan, did you?"

"No, of course not," she says. "I haven't told anyone. But it's killing me to have such a big secret. You need to tell Brax. Soon."

"I know, I will."

"Good," she says. "Now go pee on that stick and tell me what it says."

I take the test and wait in the bathroom while it sits. I admit, I met Braxton half-naked when I got home on Saturday to put him in a good mood and soften the blow. But then he told me about buying the building, and the trip to London, and I couldn't bring myself to tell him. It all felt like so much.

Going to the doctor first isn't just me procrastinating, however. It makes sense. I should be sure. I glance over at the test. Nothing is showing in the result window yet. I tap my foot and look up at the ceiling while I wait.

What do I want it to say? Do I want it to be negative? I'm not sure how I feel about this anymore. I've had moments when I think I could actually get excited about this. Other times, I'm so overwhelmed I want to crawl in bed and stay there for a week.

I pick up the test and force myself to look. Yep. *Pregnant.*

I'm running out of ways to convince myself this isn't happening.

6

BRAXTON

I get home from work and brush the water off my hair. It's raining like crazy, and I wonder if Selene's freaking out about the weather. Their wedding is at a winery over on the east side, so hopefully things clear up this weekend. You never know around here, even in the summer.

I hear what sounds like Kylie's phone on speaker. I think she's listening to her voicemail, so I stay quiet while I take off my coat.

"This is to confirm your appointment with Dr. Shepherd, tomorrow at nine a.m."

I hesitate near the door. Doctor? That's weird. Why would Ky need to go to the doctor tomorrow?

I head into the kitchen and she smiles at me, then taps her phone a few times and sets it down.

"Hey, love. You're home early. How was your day?" She grabs something out of a grocery bag and puts it in a cupboard.

"Not bad," I say.

She keeps putting groceries away. "Do you have to go in to the gym tomorrow?"

"Yeah, I have clients until early afternoon."

"Okay," she says. "I have a few errands to run in the morning, and then we have the rehearsal tomorrow night."

Errands to run? Should it bother me that she's not telling me about seeing her doctor? It's not like she has to tell me everything she does. But there's something about this that's worrying me. "You okay, baby girl?"

She meets my eyes and smiles again. "Yeah, I'm fine. Why?"

"You sure?"

"Why, do I look bad or something?"

I come around the counter and slide my hands around her waist. "No, of course not. I'm just wondering."

"I'm okay. Just tired, I guess. It's been a busy week."

I put my hand on her cheek and kiss her forehead.

"Oh, I picked up the tuxes earlier," she says. "Would you mind taking Ronan's over to their place? But hurry. We're supposed to bring dinner over to my dad tonight."

"Yeah, of course," I say. "I'll go do that now."

I glance at her again, but she just smiles and keeps putting things away in the kitchen. She seems fine, so I grab Ronan's tux and head for the door.

I let myself into Selene and Ronan's house, hoisting Ronan's tux over my shoulder. "Hey, you guys home?"

"Yeah," Ronan says from somewhere inside.

I bring the tux in and lay it over the back of a dining chair. Ronan's in the kitchen, standing with his arms crossed, staring at something on the counter.

"Hey man, what's up? Is Selene home?"

"No, she's out." His eyes are locked on something in front of him.

"You okay?"

Ronan looks up. "I think Selene might be pregnant."

His words hit me square in the chest. For a second, I'm ready to launch myself across the counter and grab him by the throat.

That fucker got my sister pregnant? But I calm myself before I move. *He's marrying her, dumbass.*

"Holy shit," I say. "What makes you think so?"

He holds up a box of home pregnancy tests. "I found this in the garbage—outside, in the big one, like she took it out there so I wouldn't see it."

"Okay, don't panic," I say. "Maybe she was just checking, and it was negative. It's not like she'd keep something like that from you."

He pulls a test out of the box. It looks just like the picture on the outside. When he turns it, I see in plain letters the word *Pregnant.*

"Oh, shit," I say.

"Yeah." He puts the test back in the box.

"Wow," I say. "I guess, congratulations?"

Ronan rubs his chin. I've never seen this look on his face before. He's really shaken up. "Why wouldn't she tell me?" he asks.

Asking me why women do things is like asking a fish why a bird flies. "I don't know. Maybe she wanted to wait until after the wedding."

"That actually makes sense," he says. "I'm worried about her, though."

This is precisely why I'm glad Ronan is marrying my sister. He gets it. He wants to keep her safe and happy, the way I always tried to do when we were growing up. I feel like I can pass the responsibility on to him. I'll always be protective of her—she's my twin—but I can let my guard down a little. I know Ronan will take care of her.

"Have you guys talked about kids?" I ask.

"Not really," he says. "I guess maybe we should have, but it just hasn't come up."

"So..." This is treading into weird guy-conversation territory, but he's about to become my brother-in-law, so what the hell. "Do you want kids?"

"If you'd asked me that a couple of hours ago—before I saw this," he says, gesturing at the box, "I would have said no. I didn't think I wanted kids. But holy shit, Brax. If this is real, I think I can get on board with it."

I grin at him. "That's freaking you out, isn't it?" Maybe I shouldn't be amused, but Ronan is so fucking collected all the time. It's kind of funny to see him rattled.

"You have no idea." He goes to the fridge, brings out two beers, and hands one to me. "What about you? You and Kylie want kids?"

I take a seat on the barstool and open the bottle. "Yeah, we do. Now that I'm expanding my gym, I guess we'll wait a while. But I can definitely picture a couple little Taylor babies running around."

Ronan laughs a little. "Life is fucking weird, sometimes, isn't it? I'm getting married in two days. A year and a half ago, that wasn't even on my radar. And here I am, thinking about the fact that I might be a father, and I'm actually okay with it."

"Fucking weird is right," I say. "I'd pretty much resigned myself to believing nothing would ever happen between me and Ky. And then, there she was, wearing a wedding dress for me. It wasn't just weird; it was unreal."

"You realize we're a lot luckier than we deserve, don't you?" Ronan asks.

"Every fucking day, man. Every fucking day." I take a long pull from my beer. "But what's up with our girls not telling us what's going on?"

"Why, is something up with Kylie?"

"Maybe," I say. "I overheard her get a message from her doctor's office about an appointment tomorrow. But then she didn't say anything. In fact, she told me she has errands to run in the morning."

"Is she sick?" Ronan asks.

A thread of fear uncurls itself in my chest. Holy shit, *is* Kylie sick? Is something wrong and she doesn't want to tell me before Selene's wedding? "Fuck, man, I don't know. She seems okay. But why would she be going to the doctor and hiding it?"

"No idea," he says. "But I wouldn't worry too much about her. I bet it's nothing. Don't they need to get their birth control refilled or something? Maybe it's just that. Although apparently that isn't always enough." He gestures to the box.

"You guys will be fine," I say. "Just tell her you found the box and ask her what's going on. I bet she's just overwhelmed with the wedding and everything."

"Yeah, you're probably right," he says. "And hey, don't tell Kylie yet. If Selene is pregnant, I know she'll want to tell Ky herself. She'll probably be upset that you know before she has a chance to tell you."

"No problem." I take another drink and stand. "I guess I should get back. I think we're bringing dinner over to Henry tonight, so I should go see what's up with that."

"Sounds good. We'll see you tomorrow for the rehearsal." He pauses. "And thanks."

"Anytime, man."

I head outside and up the street toward my place. My head is spinning a little. Is my sister really going to have a baby? I wonder if Kylie knows already. She probably does, but I won't ask, just in case Selene hasn't talked to her yet.

Uncle Braxton sounds kind of awesome. But my happiness for Selene is tinged with worry for Kylie. I hope nothing is wrong with my girl. The idea that it could be serious is almost too much for me to contemplate.

7

KYLIE

I sip my cup of coffee and stare out at the rain through the café window. Seeing the doctor shook me up more than I thought it would. After all, I've taken at least five pregnancy tests at this point, and they all said the same thing. Why was it surprising when my doctor smiled and congratulated me on my pregnancy?

I have a feeling Braxton knows something is up. All through dinner with my dad last night, he kept giving me weird looks. I wonder if Selene said something that made him wary. I know she didn't tell him what's going on, but she might have let something slip that got him concerned. I almost told him the truth last night, but I decided to stick with my resolve to see the doctor first.

Now that I've seen the doctor, I need to find time to tell him. But he's working until late this afternoon, and we have the wedding rehearsal tonight. Then the wedding tomorrow.

The more I think about it, the more I'd like to do something special to tell him. Rather than just blurt out, "I'm pregnant!" I'd really like to surprise him.

I bring up Pinterest on my phone and search for pregnancy

announcement ideas. The first thirty or so pictures look way too complicated for my capabilities. I'm artistic, but I'm not very crafty, and I don't have a lot of time to work with. But I get a few ideas, and I think I can do something fun for him. I'll wait until Sunday, after the wedding. I figure we should concentrate on one life-changing event at a time.

My eyes scan all the splashes of baby blue, soft pink, and pale yellow. I see little ducks and teddy bears, blankets and bottles. Looking at pregnancy announcements leads me down a rabbit hole of baby stuff. Showers, parties, decorated nurseries. Everything is so fucking *cute*. Yeah, it's overwhelming, and I think it might take the next eight or so months for it to sink in that this is happening. But I can't keep the smile off my face as I browse through pictures of tiny footprints, polka-dotted crib sheets, and some stunningly beautiful maternity photo shoots.

I get to a photo of a father holding a newborn baby on his chest, and the tears that have been threatening finally fall. I can see it so clearly: Braxton holding our tiny newborn against his bare skin, his thick tattooed arms, roped with muscle, contrasting with the baby's soft skin.

I think about how much he loves me. How deep his feelings run, and how they haven't faltered for a single second since that night in London when he put his ring on my finger. He makes me feel like he's laying down at my feet to worship me. It's not just that he loved me in secret for so long. It's that the love he feels for me is so real, and so pure—and so much—that it never runs out. It never wavers.

That's how Brax is going to love our child. He's going to take one look at this baby and he's going to fall for him or her like he fell for me. And just the thought of it—the thought of seeing him melt for our baby—makes me love him so much I break down sobbing in the middle of the coffee shop.

I didn't think I could love him any more. He's been in my

heart for as long as I can remember, and since we've been together that love has done nothing but grow. And yet now, staring at this photo of a man with a tiny infant, I feel my heart swell, like it could burst in my chest.

This is so true, and so real, and so right. I wipe the tears, not caring whether the other people in the café are staring at me. My god, he's going to be such a good father. I desperately hope his parents can see him now, because they are going to be so proud.

It takes me another ten minutes to get my shit together. I tearfully browse through more baby stuff, letting the reality sink in. I wonder if I'm so emotional because this is such a big deal, or because of the pregnancy itself. That's a thing, right? Feeling like you're drowning in feelings you can barely contain?

I head home and take a long shower to settle myself down. The hot water helps. Usually I'd down a shot when I feel this keyed up, but that's not an option.

Before Brax gets home, I design a card to tell him the news. I keep the look simple, with a pinstripe border that turns into a tiny heart in one corner. I decide to get a little saucy, and put *To My Hot DILF* on the front. On the inside, I write *you + me = three.*

It's nothing elaborate, but I think he'll like finding out this way.

I can't wait to see the look on his face.

By the time Brax gets home from work, and it's time to get dressed for the rehearsal, I'm back to my normal self. I put on a fluttery yellow dress that makes my boobs look fantastic (and are they maybe a little bigger?), and help Braxton with the buttons on his shirt. It's not that he can't button them himself—but fuck, he looks so hot when he dresses up, I'll use any excuse to touch him. It takes quite a bit of willpower not to *un*button that shirt and rip it off him. But we can't be late.

The rain has finally stopped, but we still rehearse the ceremony inside. If the sun comes out tomorrow, the staff will move things outdoors. It will be a simple wedding; watching Selene and Ronan stand facing each other, hand in hand, almost makes me start sobbing again. I manage to hold it in check, although a few tears leak from the corners of my eyes.

I'm going to be an absolute wreck tomorrow when they do the real thing.

Afterward, we all meet up at a nearby Italian restaurant for dinner. I'm so tired I don't even want to sit through the meal, but I figure I just need to do my best to pretend I'm fine.

Braxton pulls out my chair at the long table and I take a seat. Something in this place smells odd, and it's making my tummy do strange swirly things.

I lean in so I can speak quietly to Brax. "Do you smell that?"

He sniffs. "I don't know. What am I smelling?"

I breathe in again. Yep, something smells awful. "You can't smell that? Seriously?"

"No." His brow furrows and he puts his hand on my thigh. "Are you sure you're okay?"

"Yeah, I'm fine. I just don't know what smells weird."

The people at the table start to chat, and a waiter comes out to pour wine. I try to decline, but Braxton moves my wineglass closer so he can pour. Uh oh. What am I going to do about this? If I don't drink it, I'll have to explain why. Can I maybe take a few sips? Or is the tiniest amount of alcohol going to poison my child? Fuck.

Ronan's parents and brother are sitting down the table from me, and I'm having a hard time reconciling that these rather soft-spoken people are his family. I suppose I expected his father to be more like him. They look alike—the resemblance between Ronan, his brother Damon, and their father is striking. But where Ronan's face is always full of intensity and drive, his dad and brother both seem very laid back.

His mother is absolutely the sweetest; I found myself hugging her at the rehearsal and almost asking her to adopt me. Brax and I are both short on mothers, so I guess I have a soft spot for nice mothers-in-law. And it's obvious they love Selene, which endears them to me instantly.

My dad is at the end of the table, and although he's in his wheelchair, he's been doing better lately. He grasps his glass of wine and holds it up, and that simple action almost makes me cry. He's having a good day, and I desperately hope it continues through the weekend. He's walking Selene up the aisle tomorrow, although unlike at my wedding, I don't think he'll get up and actually walk. She's been trying to talk him out of it, knowing how much it cost him to do so at my wedding.

"I'd like to propose a toast," Dad says, his clear voice carrying over the din of conversation. We all raise our glasses. "Selene, it has been a privilege to watch you grow up into the wonderful woman you are today. Nothing gives me more joy than seeing my family grow. And on this, the eve of your wedding, I want to tell you both how happy I am for you. To Selene and Ronan."

Everyone lifts their glasses and echoes his toast. "To Selene and Ronan!"

I mutter something incoherent because I can't quite form words, then bite my lip to keep from crying. I give my dad a weak smile and take a sip of my wine. My eyes widen as I realize what I just did. Oh, god. What do I do now? I can't spit it out. I swallow and put the glass down, hoping no one saw my face.

One sip is okay, right? The baby is so tiny now. I don't want to hurt him. Or her. Holy shit, it's going to be a *him*, or a *her*. A real person. But what else would it be? I'm not having a fucking puppy.

I really need to pull myself together.

The waiter brings out the food. It's all served family-style, on large platters in the center of the table. Normally I love Italian food, but I eye the selection warily. The chicken is a definite no-go. I almost can't look at it without gagging. The fettuccine looks like I can probably handle it, and I might be able to stomach a meatball with marinara sauce. The rest looks like it's going to send me running for the bathroom, which would make it very hard to keep my secret from Braxton for another day and a half.

I make it through the meal, and I'm pretty sure I'm not rousing any suspicion. I leave the rest of my wine, but no one mentions it. I almost break down in tears again when someone suggests going out for more drinks—I'm so tired, I can barely keep my eyes open—but Selene and Ronan both decline, and even Brax says he's ready to go home. We say goodbye to everyone outside, and get in Braxton's car.

He turns the key in the ignition, but puts a hand on my thigh and looks at me for a long moment.

"What?" I ask.

"Are you sure you're feeling okay?"

"Yeah." *Uh oh.* He can tell something is going on. "I'm just tired. I'm excited for the wedding, but I'll be kind of glad when it's over."

He leans in and kisses me softly. "All right. If you're sure."

I almost say it, right here. My heart beats wildly, and pings of nervousness tingle my skin. But I want to surprise him on Sunday, when we can focus on this. Focus on *us.* "I'm sure. I think I just need a good night's sleep."

Brax holds my hand on the drive home, his fingers twined with mine. I cast glances at him from the corner of my eye, and it's all I can do not to melt into a puddle of insane laughter and tears right here in the car.

God, I love him so much.

8

KYLIE

*S*aturday dawns clear and beautiful, and by late afternoon the sun bathes the grounds of the winery in a pleasant warmth. Selene and Ronan's ceremony is held outside, and I almost manage to hold myself together. Fortunately, we took most of the pictures beforehand, so I'm not too worried about ruining my makeup. But as I watch Selene walk up the aisle, her hand resting lightly on my dad's arm, I don't even try to hold back the tears.

She's positively stunning in a strapless ivory gown. It hugs her curves and flares slightly at the bottom, for an unbelievable silhouette. She's always gorgeous, but today she looks radiant. Her dark hair is up, showing her slender neck and shoulders, and of course her boobs look fantastic. I helped her pick the dress—and I must say, I did an excellent job.

The ceremony is simple, and sweet. Their vows are beautiful, and bring a renewed set of tears streaming down my face. Braxton looks on from the other side, watching his sister with so much pride in his face. I think getting married before her was a little hard for him—at least, he knew it was hard for her, and he felt bad about that. Watching Selene marry Ronan feels like coming full circle, completing our family in a way that makes everything we've all been through the last couple of years worth it.

So worth it.

As Ronan kisses his wife for the first time, Braxton meets my eyes and gives me a wink. All I can do is smile through the tears.

Afterward, we make our way into the winery for the reception. The banquet hall is decorated beautifully with lots of twinkling lights and floral centerpieces on the tables. Soft music plays in the background, and Braxton and I walk around and chat with people for a while.

I get tired pretty quickly, but I float on the happiness for my best friend long enough to get through dinner. The food is delicious, and I go ahead and take a few sips of wine. I Googled it last night, so I know I can have a tiny bit and nothing bad will happen, and this way I won't rouse suspicion. We are at a winery, after all.

Selene and Ronan aren't really traditionalists, so they don't do a lot of the customary wedding reception things. A few people do stand and offer toasts to the new couple, including Braxton (which makes me cry all over again). There's cake, but they don't pose for pictures and cut it. And after dessert, people have cocktails and mingle.

There's an area sectioned off for dancing, and people meander over while a slow song is playing. I notice Ronan's parents dancing together, as well as some of our friends.

Braxton takes my hand. "Dance with me?"

I smile and stand, but a wave of dizziness passes over me. I clutch at him to keep from losing my balance.

"Are you okay?" he asks.

"Yeah," I say, although I hold his arms tight to keep from falling over. "Sorry, I just got a little dizzy for a second."

He looks at me with his brow furrowed. Without saying anything else, he gently takes my elbow and leads me out into the lobby, where he stops and looks at me. "Kylie, what the fuck is going on?"

"What are you talking about?"

"Something is up with you," he says.

"I'm fine." I put a hand on his arm. "Really."

"I know you went to the doctor," he says. "What aren't you telling me?"

My mouth hangs open for a moment. Shit. What do I say? Do I make something up? Why else would I have gone to the doctor? Do I tell him I wasn't feeling well? That's bullshit, and he'll know it. I've been telling him I'm *fine* all week. Damn it, I thought I could hold out for one more night. I have the card I made for him in my bag. I was going to give it to him in the morning.

"Ky, seriously, you're freaking me the fuck out," he says. "Are you sick? Is something wrong?"

It hits me, as I look into his eyes, that he's scared. He thinks something bad is happening—that something's wrong with me. I don't know how he found out about my appointment, but I bet that's why he's been asking me if I'm okay a million times a day. It's been worrying him.

"Oh god, Brax, no," I say. Screw the card. I didn't mean to upset him. I take his hands, and suddenly I can't stop smiling.

His brow is furrowed, his eyes intense, and I know he must think I'm crazy right now.

"Baby, I'm fine. I'm not sick at all."

"Are you sure?" He puts one hand alongside my face, the other around my waist, drawing me closer. "Why did you need to see a doctor, then? And why didn't you tell me?"

My whole body is pinging with adrenaline, every nerve

sparking. This is it. This moment. This is going to change every-thing. "I'm pregnant."

His hand on my waist tightens until he's gripping the back of my dress in his fist, and he pulls me closer. His chest rises and falls quickly, and his eyes never leave mine.

"What did you say?" he whispers.

I'm not sure if I can say it out loud again. Swirls of excite-ment and fear pour through me, and I start to tremble in his arms.

My voice almost won't work. "I'm pregnant. I went to the doctor to be sure."

His arms rope around me and he pulls me close, burying his face in my neck, his breath hot against my skin. He holds me tight, but there's a gentleness to it. He's so tender, like he's already making room for this new thing in our lives. I cling to him, wrapping my arms around his neck, and close my eyes. I suppose there are people walking by, but I don't care about them. This is our moment.

He pulls away, just enough that he can look at me. "Did you just say you're pregnant?"

I nod.

He swallows hard. "A baby?"

"Yes."

His lips brush against mine, almost a kiss, as he speaks. "Our baby."

I smile and he takes my mouth in a deep kiss, his arms still pressing me against him.

"I'm sorry I didn't tell you sooner," I say. "I made you a card, and I was going to give it to you tomorrow. I wanted to see my doctor to be sure, and then there was all the wedding stuff. I'm so sorry I made you worry."

He leans his forehead down to mine. "It's okay. I'm just glad you're all right." His pulls away a little and his brow furrows. "You are okay, aren't you?"

I nod. "So far, so good. I'm so tired, though."

He kisses my forehead, then my cheeks.

"You're not freaked out?" I ask. "Or upset?"

"Why would I be either of those things?" he asks.

"Well, this is a surprise," I say. "It's not like we planned it."

He kisses my forehead again. "It's the best surprise I've ever had."

We stand there for long moments, resting in each other's arms. I'm filled with warmth. It radiates from my chest through my whole body.

He pulls away and wipes his thumb beneath my eyes.

"Happy tears," I say.

He nods. "I know."

He slides his hand down my neck, brushes between my breasts, and touches my belly. A wide smile crosses his face as he splays his hand, palm down, just below my belly button. "My sweet baby girl, having my baby."

I giggle and bite my lip.

"I guess we should go back in," he says.

"Yeah, we should."

Braxton keeps his arm tight around me as we walk back into the reception. Some people are still at their tables, eating cake and drinking wine. Others are on the dance floor, swaying back and forth to a slow song.

Selene and Ronan are together, talking to a few people near the bar. Selene looks over as soon as we walk in. I see her eyes lock with her brother's, and a huge grin spreads over Braxton's face. She doesn't even say anything to the people she's talking to, just strides over to us, her hand covering her mouth.

She lands in Braxton's arms, and he hugs her so tight he picks her up. My lower lip trembles and tears start to leak out of the corners of my eyes. Again. Brax and Selene stay there for a long moment, holding each other.

Then Ronan walks over, his eyebrows raised, a small smile playing across his face.

Selene pulls away and wipes the tears from her cheeks. "Oh my god, Brax."

"I feel like I missed something," Ronan says. "Is everything okay?"

Selene looks at me and raises her eyebrows. I glance at Braxton. Who wants to say it?

Braxton takes my hand and pulls me closer to him. "We're going to have a baby."

Ronan's mouth opens and his eyes register surprise. "Kylie? *You're* pregnant?"

I nod and swipe my fingers beneath my eyes. "Yes. Selene, I'm so sorry. I didn't want to steal your thunder. I was going to tell him tomorrow, but—"

She shakes her head. "No, I'm so glad you did. Brax, I knew. I knew last weekend and it's been killing me."

Brax hasn't once stopped smiling. Is it possible to say a guy is glowing? That's such a girl thing, but I'm not even kidding; he totally is.

"Wait," Ronan says, holding up a hand. "Kylie's the one who's pregnant? I thought..."

"You thought what?" Selene asks.

"I thought *you* were pregnant," he says.

"Yeah, I did too," Braxton says.

"Why?" Selene asks with a laugh.

"I found a box of pregnancy tests in the garbage," Ronan says. "I figured you were waiting to tell me, so I didn't ask you about it."

I laugh. "No, that was me. I took one at your house before I went to the doctor."

Ronan looks bewildered. "Wow, I really had the wrong impression." He turns to Selene. "So you're not pregnant?"

Selene shakes her head. "No, but I have to be honest, I thought I could be. This whole thing started last weekend. I was late so I took a test to find out, and I made Kylie take one, too. But hers was the one that was positive."

"I suppose considering we've been married for about an hour, this is good news." Ronan turns to Selene and slips a hand around her waist. "But I have to admit I'm a little disappointed."

Selene's lips part. "You are?"

Ronan smiles. "Yeah. It hit me when I saw that test that I'd love to have a baby with you."

"Are you serious?" she asks.

"Absolutely," he says. "Maybe we should talk about it a bit first, but at some point, yes. I think we should have a baby."

He gathers her in his arms and kisses her. Any hope I had of not being a sobbing mess is long gone. I wipe my cheeks, but the tears don't stop.

Braxton lifts my hand and brings it to his lips. "You're so tired. Are you ready to go?"

I take a deep breath. I don't want to bail on Selene's reception, but I'm pretty sure if I sit, I'm either going to put my head down and sob, or pass out. "Yes. I'm exhausted."

Selene reaches out and squeezes my hand. "Go get some rest, babe."

I squeeze her back. "Love you."

"Love you, too."

We gather up our things and say goodbye to people. Braxton puts his arm around me and leads me toward the lobby.

"So," he says, "we can still have sex while you're pregnant, right?"

I laugh. "Of course that's your first question."

He leans away so he can look at me and raises his eyebrows. "But can we?"

"Yes, we definitely can."

He laughs and hugs me tighter. "I'm just teasing. Let's get you to the hotel so we can get in bed. I'm going to cuddle the fuck out of you tonight."

And that sounds absolutely perfect to me.

EPILOGUE: BRAXTON

I look up at the clock, bleary-eyed. Two o'clock. Is that a.m. or p.m.? There's light coming in through the cracks in the blinds. That must mean it's afternoon. It's been a little hard to keep track. To say the last twenty-four hours or so have been a whirlwind would be the understatement of the century.

Kylie is fast asleep in the hospital bed. That fucking woman —I already knew she was amazing, but after what I witnessed a few hours ago I will forever be in awe of her. She was so damn strong. Whoever claimed women are the *weaker sex* didn't know what the fuck they were talking about—and obviously never witnessed a woman give birth.

Yesterday—was it really only yesterday?—we were on the couch, and Kylie couldn't seem to get comfortable. I got her some extra pillows and rubbed her feet while she dozed off. I sat there, watching her for a while. Her eyes were closed, her face still, her hands on the swell of her belly. I was mesmerized. Pregnancy did nothing but make Kylie more beautiful. Her body changed, but it was so sensual. I still loved every inch of her.

Being pregnant wasn't always easy on her. I did what I could to help, but at the end of the day, there's only so much a guy can do. I was always on hand for back rubs, and foot rubs, and bringing home her favorite foods.

And sex when she wanted it. Holy shit, there was about a four month stretch where she could not get enough. It was fucking awesome. It got a little awkward as her belly grew, but all it took was a little creativity. I'm great at being creative.

As I sat there on the couch, caressing her skin, she shifted her hips and her forehead tightened. She held her belly, opened her eyes, and simply said, "Uh oh."

It wasn't a race to the hospital, like you see in the movies. But she definitely started having contractions, and we knew it was close. We hung out at home for a while, until they started to get more intense. She called her doctor's office, and they told her it was time to come in.

I don't think I've ever been so scared in my entire life.

She held my hand in a tight grip on the way to the hospital. I walked her inside and they put her in a wheelchair. For a second, I thought they were going to take her away from me, and I almost lost my shit. But the nurse said, "Come on back, Dad," and I followed.

Hearing those words *really* almost made me lose my shit.

The next ten hours were the most exhausting, incredible, and awe-inspiring hours of my life. Kylie was a fucking rock star. They told us ahead of time that a C-section was likely, but if the conditions were right they'd let Kylie try to give birth naturally. She really hoped it would work out that way.

We got very lucky. It took time for her body to be ready, but when the time came, the babies were in the right position and everything went perfectly.

That's right. *Babies.* We just had twins.

We got that piece of news when she was about four months

along. She was shocked. Somehow, I wasn't. Of course we'd have twins. A boy and a girl, just like me and Selene.

The door opens and a nurse comes in, wheeling a bassinet. I sit up, moving the beige hospital blanket to the side.

She gives me a warm smile and speaks in a soft whisper. "How's Mom doing?"

I glance over at Kylie. She's still sound asleep. She needs it, after everything she's been through. "She's good. Been sleeping for a while."

"Good," the nurse whispers. "We should let her rest."

I stand and stare at the two newborn babies, wrapped in white blankets, little knit hats covering their heads. My heart rate kicks up, and a deep feeling of wonder runs through me. *Our babies.* Kylie's and mine.

"They're doing very well," the nurse says.

They took the babies to the nursery for a while so Kylie and I could get some sleep. I didn't want to let them go, but the nurse had me walk back with them so I could see where they'd be, and she promised to bring them back soon. It was hard, even though I knew she was right. Kylie, in particular, needed rest.

"Can I hold them again?" I ask.

The nurse smiles. "Of course you can. Actually, that will be good for them. They're maintaining their body temperature pretty well, but they could use some skin to skin contact. Here, take off your shirt and have a seat. I'll hand them to you. It's easier that way with two."

I strip off my t-shirt and toss it aside while the nurse picks up my little boy and unwraps him so he's in nothing but a diaper. He squirms and lets out a little grunt. I settle back in the reclining chair and the nurse hands him to me, placing him tummy down on my chest with his head near my shoulder.

"There's one," she says.

She picks up my daughter, and my throat feels tight. She

unwraps her and helps place her tiny form on the other side of my chest. Then she takes a warm blanket and lays it over all three of us.

"There," she says. "Perfect."

I tuck these tiny, perfect little people in the crooks of my arms and look down at them. They both squirm around a bit, but it only takes a couple minutes for them to relax. Their cheeks squish against my chest, and their eyes are closed. Their skin is so soft against mine.

The nurse gives me one last smile, and leaves. Alone in this dim, quiet room, with my wife sleeping nearby, and two babies on my chest, it hits me: I'm a dad.

This is real.

I didn't think I could love anyone as much as I love Kylie. I've loved her so deep, and for so long, it seemed impossible that anything could be bigger than that. But I look down at these two tiny sleeping babies, their warm bodies cradled against my chest, and my eyes burn with the tears of loving them. I love them *fierce*. In the space of the few hours since they were born, they took my heart and opened it up, lodging themselves deep inside.

I press my lips to my son's head. *My son.* Kylie already says he looks like me. He's so small, so innocent. The weight of responsibility for teaching him to be a man is heavy. But I actually think I might be strong enough.

I turn and kiss my daughter's head. I have a *daughter*. This precious little princess is mine. Mine to protect and cherish. I get to show her what it is to be loved.

It makes me wonder if my dad had a moment like this. Did he hold me and Selene when we were hours old, staring at us in awe? Did he worry about whether he'd be a good father? I wish he was here, so I could ask him. I wish they could both be here, to meet their grandchildren.

Kylie stirs and opens her eyes. "Hey."

"Hi," I whisper. I don't want to wake them.

She scoots closer to the edge of the bed and reaches out to caress our baby girl's head. I see the way I feel about them reflected in Kylie's eyes, and my throat feels tight again.

"I don't think I've ever seen anything more amazing than this," she says.

"Them?"

"You, holding them," she says. It looks like she wants to say more, but she just smiles and a few tears trail down her cheeks.

I turn my head and stare at her. "I don't think I've ever loved you more than I do right now."

She slips a hand beneath the blanket and rests it on my arm. "I love you too. So much."

There's a soft knock on the door, and Selene pokes her head inside. "Can we come in?"

"Yeah," Kylie says.

Selene and Ronan come in and shut the door with a soft click. Ronan stands near the foot of the bed, and Selene walks around to where I'm reclining. Her hand covers her mouth, and tears are already springing to her eyes.

"Oh, Brax." She leans over so she can see the babies. "They're so beautiful."

My chest swells with pride. Fuck yeah, my babies are beautiful.

She sits on the edge of the bed and rubs Kylie's leg. "How are you feeling?"

"Exhausted," Kylie says. "But okay, considering."

"We won't stay long," she says. "But I had to see them. I can't even believe this. I'm so happy for you guys."

"Thanks, sis," I say.

Ronan steps forward and hands Kylie a small gift bag. "Here, we brought a present for the babies."

Kylie takes the tissue paper off the top and pulls out two little onesies, one pink, one blue. She unfolds them and lays them in her lap.

I do a double take. "Wait, what do those say?"

Kylie gasps. "*I love my cousin*? Oh, my god, Selene, are you...?"

Selene is absolutely beaming, and Ronan looks at her with an expression I'm pretty familiar with. I've been wearing the same one for the last nine months.

"Yes. I'm pregnant," Selene says.

Kylie starts to squeal, then claps her hand over her mouth. She sits up to hug Selene, and they hold each other for a long moment. With two babies on my chest I can't really move, but I give Ronan a nod and turn back to my sister. She's all lit up, her smile wide. I don't know if I've ever seen her this happy.

"Congratulations, you guys," I say. "You're in for a hell of a ride, but I can tell you firsthand, it's worth it."

Selene wipes the tears from her eyes. "Thanks, Brax. I'm really excited. But enough about us. Have you named them yet?"

"Not yet," I say. "But I'm thinking Clark Kent and Lois Lane."

"Good choices," Ronan says.

Kylie laughs. "Um, no."

"Come on, it's perfect," I say.

"Our wonder twins are not going to be named Lois and Clark," Kylie says.

"You guys will figure it out," Selene says. "But we should go. I can't even fathom how exhausted you are, Ky."

I look over at my wife. "She was incredible."

Selene smiles and kisses us both, then softly kisses each baby's forehead. "Love you guys. Let us know when you're going home, and we'll come help."

"Okay," Kylie says. "Oh my god, Selene, I'm so happy for you."

"Thanks, babe."

After another round of hugs from my sister, she and Ronan leave. I had a feeling Selene might be pregnant. When I saw her a few days ago, something seemed different. I couldn't put my finger on it at the time, but now it makes so much sense.

"Can you believe it?" Kylie asks. "All these babies."

"Your dad is going to be ecstatic."

"He really is," she says.

I adjust myself in the chair a little, careful not to move too much. If I wake the babies, I'll have to hand at least one of them over to Kylie. I'm enjoying holding them so much, I don't want to give them up yet.

"You know, we do need to decide on names," Kylie says. "Because we're not naming them Clark Kent and Lois Lane."

"Well, now that we've met them, what are you thinking?"

"Middle names are easy," she says.

"Are they?"

"Of course," she says. "Dean and Rose."

I swallow hard against the lump in my throat. Dean and Rose were my parents' names. "Yeah, that's perfect, isn't it? And I already know our little boy's first name."

"You do? What is it?"

"Henry, after your dad."

Kylie smiles, and fresh tears fill her eyes. "Oh my god, Brax."

"But what about this little lady?" I kiss our daughter's head again. "What's her name?"

"Well, I know we had a list, but I have another idea," she says. "What about London? It's sweet, and such a special place to us."

"London Rose," I say, listening to the sound of it as I gaze at my little girl. "I think it's perfect."

"Henry Dean and London Rose," Kylie says with a hitch in her voice. She covers her mouth and sniffs.

"You okay, baby girl?"

She nods. "Yeah. I feel like my heart is so full I'm going to burst. You gave me these beautiful babies, and I love them so much, and I love *you* so much." She pauses and takes a trembling breath. "Is this real?"

I glance down at my two beautiful babies, sleeping on my chest, then at my wife, whom I love more than I could possibly put into words.

My precious family.

I grin at Kylie. "It's all real, baby girl. Always."

∿

AFTERWORD

Dear reader,

This was a really fun book to write. It took a different direction than I originally anticipated, but I'm happy I went with my instincts instead of trying to force it into the mold I had in mind at first.

We first meet Selene in ALWAYS HAVE, the story of her twin brother, Braxton, and their best friend, Kylie. Poor Selene gets a little bit of a bad rap in that book, considering she causes some trouble for Brax and Ky. I know more than a few readers were peeved at her over the events in that book, and hopefully by the end, they were able to forgive her. But I'm not going to lie—I was legitimately worried when I wrote this that no one would want to read it because they were still mad at Selene.

This book gave me the chance to explore her as a character in a way I didn't in ALWAYS HAVE. I spent a lot of time thinking about what Selene would be like. She's a woman who lost her parents as a child, and that would certainly have an influence on the person she becomes. She also has an overprotective brother with a big personality.

Her social life is very tied to her brother, which means in

some ways, she lives in his shadow. Because of that, her professional life is where she really blossomed as an individual. It's the sphere where she gets to be truly herself. Where she can excel without leaning on her twin, or having him constantly shadowing her. So, it's no surprise that she's done well professionally, and earned a reputation for being competent and hard working.

But her social life still comes into play. Selene has a weakness for the wrong men. When it comes to the types of relationships my characters have, I always want to know *why*. Why would Selene be attracted to men who ultimately screw her over? Part of it is probably the loss of her parents and the hole they left in her life. But a lot of it is Braxton. In many ways, Braxton took over as the man in Selene's life in the absence of their father. And Selene is drawn to men who are a lot like her brother. The problem is, Braxton was a bad boy on the outside, but a good man underneath. That's something of a rarity. Selene keeps dating bad boys who are straight up assholes, without the redeeming good man qualities. Unfortunately, she hasn't found one who is different.

When I was considering what sort of man to pair Selene with, my first thought was that maybe this is a story about finally falling for the "good guy." That she'd meet a nice guy type, and perhaps the struggle would be him convincing her that she doesn't need a bad boy to be happy.

But ... wouldn't it be even more fun if Selene met another bad boy? Another man who is everything she *doesn't* need in her life? Except what if he's EXACTLY what she needs in her life? And he needs her just as much?

That sounded awesome. And thus, Ronan Maddox.

I need to know the "whys" behind my heroes too, and I spent a lot of time contemplating why Ronan would be the way he is. I like it when a character's backstory, flaws, and inner demons all make sense, and those things are what get in their way when it comes to their new relationship. Ronan experienced a traumatic event in college, losing his girlfriend in a tragic car accident. He survives, but he's changed. He feels no fear.

So, he lives for the adrenaline highs, whether it's from extreme sports, taking business risks, or fucking women who are hard to get. It's his way of coping with what happened to him. Healthy? Probably not entirely. But he feels like it's worked for him this long. Why change things now?

(Oh, Ronan. I'll give you a reason.)

He and Selene collide when he buys the company she works for. It felt very natural to set this book in an office—centering their story around where they work. It's the place where Selene is truly Selene, not Braxton's twin sister. And their story could unfold as she and Ronan are thrown into working together.

My favorite part of writing this book was the dialogue. Their banter throughout the book was pure fun for me. They were so evenly matched when it came to their verbal sparring. Ronan held nothing back, but Selene was right there, ready to hit every curve ball out of the park.

Most of them, anyway.

And yeah, I know we get really pissed at Ronan in this book. This is one where you're reading along and the hero just fucks everything up so royally, you kind of want to punch him in the face. I know. I get it. But I think he does a pretty good job of making up for it in the end. He needed to realize what he really had—that Selene is the perfect woman for him, and he's just as perfect for her. I think we can cut him a little slack. He's a guy who doesn't normally feel fear, so when panic took him, he was ill-equipped to cope with it.

Thanks for reading!

CK

ALSO BY CLAIRE KINGSLEY

For a full and up-to-date listing of Claire Kingsley books visit www. clairekingsleybooks.com/books/

For comprehensive reading order, visit www.clairekingsleybooks. com/reading-order/

∼

The Haven Brothers

Small-town romantic suspense with CK's signature endearing characters and heartwarming happily ever afters. Can be read as stand-alones.

Obsession Falls (Josiah and Audrey)

Storms and Secrets (Zachary and Marigold)

The rest of the Haven brothers will be getting their own happily ever afters!

∼

How the Grump Saved Christmas (Elias and Isabelle)

A stand-alone, small-town Christmas romance.

∼

The Bailey Brothers

Steamy, small-town family series with a dash of suspense. Five unruly brothers. Epic pranks. A quirky, feuding town. Big HEAs. Best read in order.

Protecting You (Asher and Grace part 1)

Fighting for Us (Asher and Grace part 2)

Unraveling Him (Evan and Fiona)

Rushing In (Gavin and Skylar)

Chasing Her Fire (Logan and Cara)

Rewriting the Stars (Levi and Annika)

The Miles Family

Sexy, sweet, funny, and heartfelt family series with a dash of suspense.
Messy family. Epic bromance. Super romantic. Best read in order.

Broken Miles (Roland and Zoe)

Forbidden Miles (Brynn and Chase)

Reckless Miles (Cooper and Amelia)

Hidden Miles (Leo and Hannah)

Gaining Miles: A Miles Family Novella (Ben and Shannon)

Dirty Martini Running Club

Sexy, fun, feel-good romantic comedies with huge... hearts. Can be
read as stand-alones.

Everly Dalton's Dating Disasters (Prequel with Everly, Hazel, and Nora)

Faking Ms. Right (Everly and Shepherd)

Falling for My Enemy (Hazel and Corban)

Marrying Mr. Wrong (Sophie and Cox)

Flirting with Forever (Nora and Dex)

Bluewater Billionaires

Hot romantic comedies. Lady billionaire BFFs and the badass heroes who love them. Can be read as stand-alones.

The Mogul and the Muscle (Cameron and Jude)

The Price of Scandal, Wild Open Hearts, and Crazy for Loving You

More Bluewater Billionaire shared-world romantic comedies by Lucy Score, Kathryn Nolan, and Pippa Grant

Bootleg Springs

by Claire Kingsley and Lucy Score

Hot and hilarious small-town romcom series with a dash of mystery and suspense. Best read in order.

Whiskey Chaser (Scarlett and Devlin)

Sidecar Crush (Jameson and Leah Mae)

Moonshine Kiss (Bowie and Cassidy)

Bourbon Bliss (June and George)

Gin Fling (Jonah and Shelby)

Highball Rush (Gibson and I can't tell you)

Book Boyfriends

Hot romcoms that will make you laugh and make you swoon. Can be read as stand-alones.

Book Boyfriend (Alex and Mia)

Cocky Roommate (Weston and Kendra)

Hot Single Dad (Caleb and Linnea)

Finding Ivy (William and Ivy)

A unique contemporary romance with a hint of mystery. Stand-alone.

His Heart (Sebastian and Brooke)

A poignant and emotionally intense story about grief, loss, and the transcendent power of love. Stand-alone.

The Always Series

Smoking hot, dirty talking bad boys with some angsty intensity. Can be read as stand-alones.

Always Have (Braxton and Kylie)

Always Will (Selene and Ronan)

Always Ever After (Braxton and Kylie)

The Jetty Beach Series

Sexy small-town romance series with swoony heroes, romantic HEAs, and lots of big feels. Can be read as stand-alones.

Behind His Eyes (Ryan and Nicole)

One Crazy Week (Melissa and Jackson)

Messy Perfect Love (Cody and Clover)

Operation Get Her Back (Hunter and Emma)

Weekend Fling (Finn and Juliet)

Good Girl Next Door (Lucas and Becca)

The Path to You (Gabriel and Sadie)

ABOUT THE AUTHOR

Claire Kingsley is a #1 Amazon bestselling author of sexy, heartfelt contemporary romance and romantic comedies. She writes sassy, quirky heroines, swoony heroes who love their women hard, panty-melting sexytimes, romantic happily ever afters, and all the big feels.

She can't imagine life without coffee, her Kindle, and the sexy heroes who inhabit her imagination. She lives in the inland Pacific Northwest with her three kids.

www.clairekingsleybooks.com

Made in the USA
Coppell, TX
05 June 2024